A Book Of

QUANTUM MECHANICS

T.Y.B.Sc. Physics : PH - 342 : Semester-IV
As Per New Revised Syllabus With Effect from June 2015

Dr. S. D. AGHAV
M.Sc., M.Phil., Ph.D.
Vice Principal,
Baburaoji Gholap College,
Sangavi, **PUNE**.

Dr. P. S. TAMBADE
M.Sc., Ph.D.
Prof. Ramkrishna More,
Arts, Commerce & Science College,
Akurdi Pradhikaran, **PUNE**.

B. M. LAWARE
M.Sc., M. Phil.
Head, Department of Physics,
Prof. Ramkrishna More,
Arts, Commerce & Science College,
Akurdi Pradhikaran, **PUNE**.

V. K. DHAS
M. Sc., M. Phil.
Ex. Head, Department of Physics,
New Arts, Commerce and Science College,
AHMEDNAGAR.

NIRALI PRAKASHAN
ADVANCEMENT OF KNOWLEDGE

N1864

T.Y.B.Sc. : QUANTUM MECHANICS (S-IV)   **ISBN 978-93-5164-921-2**

First Edition   :   December 2015

©   **:   Authors**

Published By :
NIRALI PRAKASHAN

Abhyudaya Pragati, 1312, Shivaji Nagar,
Off J.M. Road, PUNE – 411005
Tel - (020) 25512336/37/39, Fax - (020) 25511379
Email : niralipune@pragationline.com

☞ **DISTRIBUTION CENTRES**

PUNE

Nirali Prakashan   :   19, Budhwar Peth, Jogeshwari Mandir Lane, Pune 411002, Maharashtra
Tel : (020) 2445 2044, 66022708, Fax : (020) 2445 1538
Email : bookorder@pragationline.com, niralilocal@pragationline.com

Nirali Prakashan   :   S. No. 28/27, Dhyari, Near Pari Company, Pune 411041
Tel : (020) 24690204 Fax : (020) 24690316
Email : dhyari@pragationline.com, bookorder@pragationline.com

MUMBAI

Nirali Prakashan   :   385, S.V.P. Road, Rasdhara Co-op. Hsg. Society Ltd.,
Girgaum, Mumbai 400004, Maharashtra
Tel : (022) 2385 6339 / 2386 9976, Fax : (022) 2386 9976
Email : niralimumbai@pragationline.com

☞ **DISTRIBUTION BRANCHES**

JALGAON

Nirali Prakashan   :   34, V. V. Golani Market, Navi Peth, Jalgaon 425001,
Maharashtra, Tel : (0257) 222 0395, Mob : 94234 91860

KOLHAPUR

Nirali Prakashan   :   New Mahadvar Road, Kedar Plaza, 1st Floor Opp. IDBI Bank
Kolhapur 416 012, Maharashtra. Mob : 9850046155

NAGPUR

Pratibha Book Distributors   :   Above Maratha Mandir, Shop No. 3, First Floor,
Rani Jhanshi Square, Sitabuldi, Nagpur 440012, Maharashtra
Tel : (0712) 254 7129

DELHI

Nirali Prakashan   :   4593/21, Basement, Aggarwal Lane 15, Ansari Road, Daryaganj
Near Times of India Building, New Delhi 110002
Mob : 08505972553

BENGALURU

Pragati Book House   :   House No. 1, Sanjeevappa Lane, Avenue Road Cross,
Opp. Rice Church, Bengaluru – 560002.
Tel : (080) 64513344, 64513355,Mob : 9880582331, 9845021552
Email:bharatsavla@yahoo.com

CHENNAI

Pragati Books   :   9/1, Montieth Road, Behind Taas Mahal, Egmore,
Chennai 600008 Tamil Nadu, Tel : (044) 6518 3535,
Mob : 94440 01782 / 98450 21552 / 98805 82331,
Email : bharatsavla@yahoo.com

niralipune@pragationline.com | www.pragationline.com
Also find us on 🇫 www.facebook.com/niralibooks

Preface ...

The present book entitled **"Quantum Mechanics"** is written as per new revised syllabus prescribed for the IV Semester of T.Y.B.Sc. (Physics) from June 2015. As per syllabus every topic is discussed in detail with examples. At the end of each topic, there are number of solved problems for understanding of the subject. There are also some unsolved problems at the end of each topic.

An attempt has been made to present the subject matter in a simple and lucid manner. Efforts have been made to explain the basic terms and mathematical treatment in a simple way.

All precautions have been taken to avoid mistakes and misprint in the book. However, it is possible that some mistakes and misprints might have passed unnoticed. Such mistakes and misprint, is brought to our notice will be thankfully acknowledged.

We are thankful to Shri Jignesh Furia and staff of Nirali publication for publishing the book in attractive look. We have a pleasure to thank Mr. Santosh Bare for the bulk of typing and Mr. Kiran Velankar for proof reading. We are indebted to Mrs. Anjali Muley for line drawings, to Ravi Walodare for designing cover page and all staff in the distribution of books network.

We are also thankful to all the Marketing Staff especially Mr. Nilesh Deshmukh and others for co-ordinating the matter well in time.

Suggestions to improve the quality of the book will be gladly accepted.

DECEMBER 2015   **AUTHORS**

PUNE

Syllabus ...

1. Origin of Quantum Mechanics   (10 L)

1. Historical Background

    (a) Review of Black body radiation.

    (b) Review of photoelectric effects.

2. Matter waves-De Broglie hypothesis, Davisson and Germer experiment.

3. Wave particle duality.

4. Wave function of a particle having definite momentum.

5. Concept of wave packet, phase velocity, group velocity and relation between them.

6. Heisenberg's uncertainty principle with thought experiment.

    – Electron diffraction experiment, Different forms of uncertainty.

2. The Schrödinger's Equation   (15 L)

1. Physical interpretation of wave function

2. Schrödinger's time dependent equation

3. Schrödinger's time independent equation (Steady-state equation)

4. Requirements of wave function

5. Probability current density, Equation of continuity and its physical significance

6. Definition of an operator in Quantum Mechanics

    – Eigen function and Eigen values

7. Expectation value – Ehrenfest's theorem

3. Applications of Schrödinger's Steady State Equation   (12 L)

1. Free particle.

2. Particle in infinitely deep potential well (one-dimension).

3. Particle in three dimension rigid box

4. Step potential

5. Potential barrier. (Qualitative discussion). Barrier penetration and tunneling effect.

6. Harmonic oscillator (one-dimension), Correspondence principle.

4. Spherically Symmetric Potentials   (06 L)

1. Schrödinger's equation in spherical polar co-ordinate system.
2. Rigid rotator (free axis).
3. Hydrogen atom : Qualitative discussion on the radial and angular parts of the bound state energy, energy state functions. Quantum numbers n, l, m_l, m_s – Degeneracy.

5. Operators in Quantum Mechanics   (05 L)

1. Hermitian operator.
2. Position, momentum operator, angular momentum operator and total energy operator (Hamiltonian).
3. Commutator brackets - Simultaneous eigen functions.
4. Commutator algebra.
5. Commutator brackets using position, momentum and angular momentum operator.
6. Raising and lowering angular momentum operator.
7. Concept of parity, parity operator and its eigen values.

❑❑❑

Reference Books :

1. **Quantum Mechanics of Atoms, Molecules, Solids, Nuclei and Particles**
   – By R. Eisberg and R. Resnik Published by Wiley.
2. **Quantum Mechanics**
   – B. H. Brandsen and C. J. Joachain – Pearson Education.
3. **Concepts of Modern Physics**
   – By A. Beiser Published by Mc. Grawthill Chapter 2, 3, 5, 6.
4. **Introduction to Quantum Mechanics**
   – By D. Griffiths Published by Prentice Hall.
5. **Quantum Mechanics**
   – By Ghatak and Lokanathan Published by Mc. Millan.
6. **Quantum Mechanics**
   – By L. I. Schiff.
7. **Quantum Mechanics**
   – By Powell and Crasemann, Addison – Wesley Publication Co.
8. **Quantum Mechanics an Accessible Introduction**
   – Robert Scherrer Pearson – Addison Wesley

Contents ...

❑❑❑

Chapter **1**...
Origin of Quantum Mechanics

> *Not only is the Universe stranger than we think, it is stranger than we can think.*
> *– Werner Heisenberg*

Werner Heisenberg
(1901-1976)

Heisenberg was a German theoretical physicist and one of the pioneers of quantum mechanics. He published his uncertainty principle upon which he build his philosophy. He was awarded Nobel Prize in physics in 1932. He also made important contribution in theories of hydrodynamics, the atomic nucleus and subatomic particles, ferromagnetism and cosmic rays.

Introduction

- Classical Mechanics explained successfully the motion of all objects which are directly observable or observable with the help of instruments. When the objects like electrons are not observable by these instruments, classical concepts cannot be applied, i.e. the classical idea doesn't hold in the region of atomic dimension.

- By the end of 19th century, many of the experimental results could not be explained on the basis of contemporary classical theories. For example, Rayleigh - Jeans law and Wien's law of black body radiations could not confirm the experimental energy distribution of radiations. Rayleigh-Jeans law agreed only for long wavelengths but failed for short wavelengths while Wien's law agreed quite well with experimental results for small wavelengths, but failed for large wavelengths.

(1.1)

- Max Planck in 1901 introduced a quantum concept and it eventually led to the conclusion that radiation is not emitted in continuous manner but in discrete packets of energy, each equal to energy $h\nu$, where ν is the frequency and h is a constant called Planck's constant. These packets are called photons or quanta. Using this concept, Planck was able to obtain correct energy distribution of black body radiations. Later Einstein used this concept to explain the specific heat of solids at low temperature and also for the explanation of photoelectric effect. This theory is called Quantum Theory.

1.1 Historical Background

- Let us take brief view of some theories that led to the foundation of quantum mechanics.

(a) Review of Black body radiations:

- A body having a surface which can absorb the entire radiations incident on it is called a perfectly black body. Its coefficient of absorption is one and its coefficient of emission is also one. A black body not only completely absorb all radiations falling on it but conversely behaves as a perfectly radiator when heated. A black body emits radiations when it is in thermal contact with surroundings. The radiations contain all the wavelengths ranging from 0 to ∞. Kirchhoff showed that the distribution of black body radiations is independent of nature of the black body (*i.e.* materials of the wall of the black body) and depends only on the temperature T. The energy density E_λ against the wavelength for different temperatures is shown in Fig. 1.1.

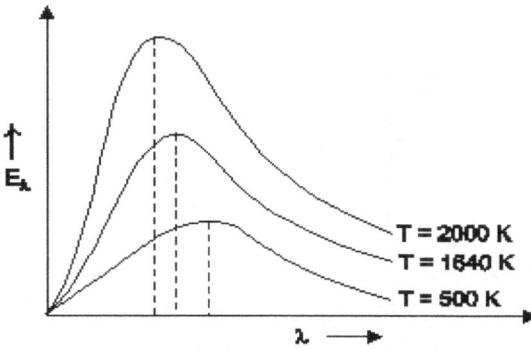

Fig. 1.1 : Black body distribution law

- Using the idea of pressure exerted by radiations on the walls of the black body, Stefan and Boltzmann (1884) showed that the total energy density was proportional to the fourth power of absolute temperature of the body *i.e.* $E \propto T^4$. Stefan's law of black body radiations is given by

$$E = \sigma T^4$$

where σ is Stefan's constant and its value is 5.67×10^{-8} W/m^2 K^4.

- The law is experimentally verified and found satisfactory. However, this law does not tell anything about the individual wavelengths.

  Wien in 1893 established *displacement laws,* which are

  (1) λT = constant and (2) ET^{-5} = constant.

  where λ is the wavelength corresponding to the temperature T and emissivity E of the black body.

- Combining these laws and using Maxwell distribution, Wien obtained the following law :

$$E_\lambda \, d\lambda \; = \; \frac{A}{\lambda^5} \, e^{-B/\lambda T} \, d\lambda \qquad\qquad \text{... (1.1)}$$

  where A and B are constants. It was observed that this law is valid only for the short wavelength region.

- In 1900, Rayleigh and Jeans approached the energy distribution problem differently. They obtained the following law :

$$E_\lambda \, d\lambda \; = \; \frac{8\pi kT}{\lambda^4} \, d\lambda \qquad\qquad \text{... (1.2)}$$

  where k is Boltzmann constant. This formula is in agreement with the experimental results in the long wavelength region but failed totally in the short wavelength region.

- Thus, all attempts to obtain a single formula which can be valid over entire range of the wavelengths using classical ideas about radiation failed miserably.

- **Planck** (1901) proposed a new formula for black body radiations. According to him each oscillator in the black body surface will not emit energy continuously but in the discrete packets of energies

$$E = 0, \, \varepsilon, \, 2\varepsilon, \, 3\varepsilon, \, 4\varepsilon, \, ...$$

- With $\varepsilon = h\nu$, h is called Planck's constant having value 6.625×10^{-34} J-sec. This is called quantization of energy. With this idea, Planck successfully explained the black body radiations. He obtained formula for energy density as

$$E_\lambda \, d\lambda \; = \; \frac{8\pi \, h \, c}{\lambda^5} \frac{1}{(e^{hc/\lambda kT} - 1)} \, d\lambda \qquad\qquad \text{... (1.3)}$$

- This is *Planck's radiation formula*. This is in exact agreement with the experimental results.

- It is observed that for small wavelengths, Planck's law reduces to Wien's formula and for longer wavelengths it reduces to Rayleigh and Jeans formula.

(b) Review of Photoelectric effect :

- It was observed by Lenard that when ultraviolet light was incident upon a metal surface like aluminium, electrons are ejected from the surface. **The ejection of electrons from the metal surface when light is incident on it is called photoelectric effect**. The ejected electrons are called photoelectrons.

  It was observed experimentally that

  (1) When the frequency of incident radiation was changed, the energy of photoelectrons was also changed.

  (2) The energy of photoelectrons is independent of intensity of incident radiations.

  (3) Electrons were not emitted from the metal surface when frequency of incident radiation is less than certain frequency. This frequency below which there is no emission of electrons is called threshold frequency.

- These three major features of the photoelectric effect could not be explained on the basis of classical wave theory of radiations. According to classical wave theory of light:

  (i) one could expect that as the intensity of the incident radiations is increased, the energy of the photoelectrons would increase and not their number.

  (ii) the photoelectric effect should occur for any frequency provided that the light of sufficient intensity falls on the surface to eject electrons.

  (iii) if light of feeble intensity falls on the metal surface, there will be large time required to absorb sufficient light to eject electrons *i.e.* there should be time lag in the ejection of electrons. However, it is observed that the photoelectric effect is instantaneous and no time lag is observed.

- In order to provide satisfactory explanation for Lenard's experimental observations, Einstein in 1905 proposed a new revolutionary theory. According to him, the light (electromagnetic radiation) that is incident upon the metal surface consists of bundles (called quanta) of energy which later came to be called *photons*. He assumed that energy constant E of the bundle or photons is related to its frequency v by the relation

$$E = hv$$

  where h is Planck's constant.

- When such a photon is incident on the surface, all of its energy is absorbed by the electron. Part of the energy is used to eject the electron and remaining is given as kinetic energy to the electron. Kinetic energy of the ejected electron is given as

$$\text{K.E.} = hv - W = \frac{1}{2} mv^2 \qquad \qquad ... (1.4)$$

  where W is called the work function and it is the energy required to remove the electron from the metal surface.

- Theoretical prediction based on the Einstein's photon hypothesis satisfied all the experimental results.

- In 1921, Einstein received the Nobel Prize for predicting theoretically the law of photoelectric effect.

Problem 1.1 : *Radiation of wavelength 300 nm falls on a metal surface for which the work function is 4.00 eV. What potential is needed to stop the most energetic photoelectrons ?*

Solution : The energy of photon is

$$E = h\nu = hc/\lambda$$

$$= \frac{(6.64 \times 10^{-34} \text{ Js}) (3 \times 10^8 \text{ m/s})}{(3 \times 10^{-7} \text{ m})} = \frac{6.64 \times 10^{-19} \text{ J}}{(1.6 \times 10^{-19}) \text{ J/eV}} = 4.15 \text{ eV}$$

Maximum K.E. = E – W = 4.15 – 4.00 = **0.15 eV**   **... Ans.**

So the potential difference is 0.15 volts.

1.2 Matter Waves

- It is evident from physical phenomenon that the electromagnetic radiation must be considered as particles (or corpuscles). The phenomena of photoelectric effect, Compton effect etc. are explained by using particle nature of light.

- The phenomena like interference, diffraction, polarization etc, can be explained only on the basis of wave nature of light. Electromagnetic radiation, therefore must be considered as wave in some process and as particle or photon in other.

(A) de Broglie Hypothesis :

- In 1924, Louis de Broglie put forward the suggestion that *matter, like radiation, has dual nature,* i.e. matter which is made up of discrete particles, atoms, protons, electrons etc., might exhibit wave like properties under appropriate conditions. His argument was: if electromagnetic radiation can act like a wave sometimes and like particle at other times, then things like electrons, protons etc. should also exhibit wave properties when are in motion.

- He made following arguments :
  1. Nature loves symmetry.
  2. Therefore, the two fundamental entities matter and energy must be mutually symmetrical as regards their properties.
  3. Since radiant energy earlier believed to have wave nature, exhibited particle nature, the material particle in motion must have wave nature.

  The waves associated with a moving particle are called *matter waves.*

- Louis de Broglie suggested that certain basic physical concepts should apply to both the fundamental entities viz. waves and particles.

  The energy of photon of frequency ν is given as

$$E = h\nu \qquad \qquad ... (1.5)$$

- The rest mass of photon is zero. If m is mass of photon in motion and c is its speed then according to theory of relativity, the energy is given by

$$E = mc^2 \qquad \qquad ... (1.6)$$

Since energy and matter are mutually symmetrical, from equations (1.5) and (1.6), we get

$$h\nu = mc^2 \qquad \qquad ... (1.7)$$

The photon travels with speed c in free space, therefore, its momentum will be

$$p = mc$$

$$\therefore \quad p = \frac{mc^2}{c} = \frac{E}{c}$$

As $E = h\nu$,

$$p = \frac{h\nu}{c}$$

Since $c = \nu\lambda$, where λ is wavelength, we get

$$p = \frac{h}{\lambda} \qquad \qquad ... (1.8)$$

$$\therefore \quad \lambda = \frac{h}{p} \qquad \qquad ... (1.9)$$

- Equation (1.9) can be applied to moving particle also. If the particle of mass m moves with speed v, then its momentum is $p = mv$. Therefore, wavelength associated with moving particle is

$$\lambda = \frac{h}{mv} \qquad \qquad ... (1.10)$$

- The wavelength of moving particle given by equation (1.10) is *called de Broglie wavelength.*
- The velocity of de Broglie waves (matter waves) associated with a moving particle is not necessarily the velocity of the particle.
- Let u be the velocity of matter waves associated with moving particle. Then,

$$u = \nu\lambda \qquad \qquad ... (1.11)$$

where ν is the frequency of waves. Using equation (1.10) in equation (1.11), we get

$$u = \nu\frac{h}{mv} = \frac{h\nu}{mv}$$

But $E = h\nu$ and $E = mc^2$, therefore,

$$u = \frac{mc^2}{mv}$$

$$\therefore \quad u = \frac{c^2}{v} \qquad \qquad ... (1.12)$$

- Thus, two different velocities are associated with a moving particle – one refers to the mechanical motion of the particle (v) and the other refers to the velocity of the associated matter wave (u). These two are connected by the equation (1.12). Now the particle velocity v < c, hence the velocity of propagation of the matter wave u > c. Thus, the de Broglie waves are different from the electromagnetic waves which travel with a constant speed.

Note : The relativistic energy of a particle is given as

$$E = \sqrt{p^2c^2 + m_o^2c^4}$$

where m_o is the rest mass of particle, p momentum of particle and c the speed of light.

Problem 1.2 : *Calculate the wavelength associated with a particle moving of mass 2 gm with velocity of 3312.5 m/sec.*

Solution : Here m = 2 gm = 2×10^{-3} kg and v = 3312.5 m/sec.

Therefore, momentum $\qquad p = mv = 2 \times 10^{-3} \times 3312.5$

$$= 6625 \times 10^{-3} \text{ kg-m/sec} = 6.625 \text{ kg-m/sec}$$

The wavelength, $\qquad \lambda = \dfrac{h}{p} = \dfrac{6.625 \times 10^{-34}}{6.625} = \mathbf{10^{-34} \ m} \qquad$ **... Ans.**

This associated wavelength is too small as compared to the dimensions of particle. It has, therefore, no significance for macroscopic particles. However, the de Broglie wavelength has great significance for microscopic particles.

Problem 1.3 : *Calculate the de Broglie wavelength of an electron moving with speed $1/10^{th}$ of the velocity of light.*

Solution : Mass of electron m = 9.1×10^{-31} kg.

Velocity of electron v = $1/10^{th}$ of c = $\dfrac{1}{10} \times 3 \times 10^8$ m/s = 3×10^7 m/s.

Planck's constant h = 6.625×10^{-34} J-sec.

Momentum of electron, $p = mv = 9.1 \times 10^{-31} \times 3 \times 10^7 = 2.73 \times 10^{-23}$ kg-m/sec

The wavelength $\qquad \lambda = \dfrac{h}{p} = \dfrac{6.625 \times 10^{-34}}{2.73 \times 10^{-23}} = 2.43 \times 10^{-11}$ m

$$= 0.234 \times 10^{-10} \text{ m} = \mathbf{0.234 \ A°} \qquad \textbf{... Ans.}$$

Problem 1.4 : *Obtain an expression for the de Broglie wavelength associated with an electron accelerated through V volts. Also find wavelength for 100 V and 54 volt.*

Solution : The kinetic energy acquired by the electron accelerated through V volts is

$$\frac{1}{2} mv^2 = eV, \qquad \text{where e is charge on electron.}$$

$\therefore \qquad mv^2 = 2eV$ and $\qquad m^2v^2 = 2meV$

$\therefore \qquad mv = \sqrt{2meV}$ or

$$p = \sqrt{2meV}$$

Therefore, wavelength associated with electron $\lambda = \dfrac{h}{p} = \dfrac{h}{\sqrt{2meV}}$

We have, h = 6.625×10^{-34} J-sec., m = 9.1×10^{-31} kg, and e = 1.6×10^{-19} C

Using all these values, we get

$$\lambda = \frac{12.27 \times 10^{-10}}{\sqrt{V}} \text{ m}$$

$\therefore \qquad \lambda = \dfrac{12.27}{\sqrt{V}} \text{ A°} \qquad\qquad$ ... (1.13)

If V = 100 volt, $\qquad \lambda = \dfrac{12.27}{\sqrt{100}}$ A° = **1.227 A°**   **... Ans.**

If V = 54 volt, $\qquad \lambda = \dfrac{12.27}{\sqrt{54}}$ A° = **1.67 A°**   **... Ans.**

Problem 1.5 : *Find the de Broglie wavelength of neutron whose energy is 1 eV.*

Given : Mass of neutron = 1.676×10^{-27} kg.

Solution : Kinetic energy of neutron = 1 eV

$$= 1 \times 1.6 \times 10^{-19} \text{ J}$$

$\therefore \qquad \dfrac{1}{2}mv^2 = 1.6 \times 10^{-19}$ J

$\therefore \qquad v^2 = \dfrac{2 \times 1.6 \times 10^{-19}}{m} = \dfrac{2 \times 1.6 \times 10^{-19}}{1.676 \times 10^{-27}} = 1.9093 \times 10^8$

$\therefore \qquad v = 1.38 \times 10^4$ m/sec

The de Broglie wavelength is given by

$$\lambda = \dfrac{h}{mv}$$

$\therefore \qquad \lambda = \dfrac{6.625 \times 10^{-34}}{1.676 \times 10^{-27} \times 1.38 \times 10^4}$

$$= 2.864 \times 10^{-11} \text{ m} = \textbf{0.286 A°} \qquad \textbf{... Ans.}$$

Problem 1.6 : *What is the energy of gamma radiation having a wavelength 1 A°.*

Solution : Momentum is given by $\quad p = \dfrac{h}{\lambda} = \dfrac{6.625 \times 10^{-34}}{1 \times 10^{-10}}$

$$= 6.625 \times 10^{-24} \text{ J.s/m}$$

Energy of gamma photon $\qquad E = p \times c$

$$= 6.625 \times 10^{-24} \times 3 \times 10^8 = 19.875 \times 10^{-16} \text{ J}$$

Energy of gamma photon in eV $= \dfrac{19.875 \times 10^{-16}}{1.6 \times 10^{-19}}$

$$= \textbf{1.24} \times \textbf{10}^4 \textbf{ eV} \qquad \textbf{... Ans.}$$

(B) Experimental evidence of de Broglie Theory :

- Different scientists performed different experiments to establish the existence of matter waves. Direct evidence of the existence of de Broglie waves is furnished by experiments on diffraction of electrons. We will consider here one such an experiment.

    Davisson and Germer's Experiments : In 1927 two American physicists, Davisson and Germer showed experimentally the electron waves predicted by de Broglie

    Experimental arrangement : The experimental arrangement is shown in Fig. 1.2.

- Electrons are produced by the filament, which are heated by low-tension battery (L.T.). These electrons are accelerated by a potential difference applied between F and grid G by means of high-tension battery (H.T.). These electrons pass through a series of apertures and emerge out in the form of collimated beam, all having the same velocity. The total assembly is called electron gun. These mono-energetic electrons fall on the target N, a single crystal of nickel. [The nickel crystal belongs to the face centered cubic type and it is so cut to present a smooth reflecting surface parallel to the lattice plane (1 1 1)].

- The electrons are scattered by crystal in all directions. These scattered electrons can be collected by Faraday cylinder C known as collector. The collector current was amplified and measured with a sensitive galvanometer G'. The collector can be moved along a graduated circular scale S to receive electrons at various angles between 20° and 90°. The collector consists of a double walled metallic cylinder having an entrance aperture. The two walls are insulated from each other. A retarding potential is applied between inner and outer walls of the collector such that only fast moving electrons having the minimum velocity as the velocity of emission from gun can enter the inner cylinder of the collector. The whole apparatus is enclosed, highly evacuated and degassed.

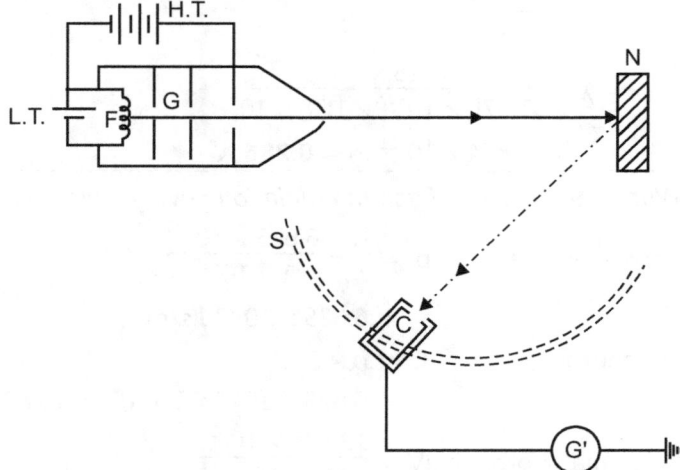

Fig. 1.2 : Schematic diagram of Davisson and Germer apparatus

Experimental Procedure : Normal incidence : The beam of electrons from electron gun falls normally on the surface of the crystal. The atomic planes of the crystal act like a plane grating. The electrons are diffracted in all directions. The diffracted electrons are collected by the collector moving through different angles on the scale S. For different angles the deflection in galvanometer is measured. The galvanometer deflection is plotted against the angle between the incident beam direction and the beam entering the collector (*colatitude*). The observations are repeated for different accelerating voltages and a number of curves are drawn which is shown in Fig. 1.3.

- It is observed that a bump (spur) begins to appear in the curve for 44 volts. This bump moves upward as the voltage increases and attains maximum at 54 volts at an angle of 50°. With further increase in the accelerating voltage, the bump decreases in length and finally disappears at 68 V.

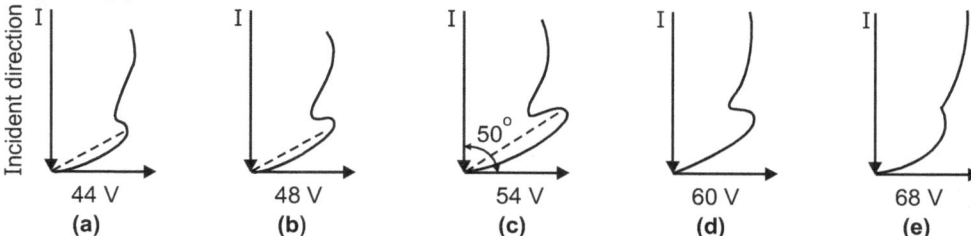

| 44 V | 48 V | 54 V | 60 V | 68 V |
| (a) | (b) | (c) | (d) | (e) |

Fig. 1.3 : Polar diagrams of current : Variation of intensity I w.r.t. θ at various potentials

- The occurrence of maximum bump at 54 volts can be taken as the proof of the existence of electron wave. At this voltage and 50° angle, the constructive interference of the electron waves, scattered in this direction, from the regularly spaced atomic planes takes place.

- According to de Broglie theory, the wavelength of electrons accelerated through potential V is given by

$$\lambda = \frac{12.27}{\sqrt{V}} \; A°$$

Therefore, for V = 54 V, we get

$$\lambda = \frac{12.27}{\sqrt{54}} \; A° = 1.67 \; A° \qquad \text{... (1.14)}$$

- For the nickel crystal, for the (1 1 1) reflecting plane, the separation between atomic planes is d = 2.15 A°. Applying law of reflection grating,

$$n\lambda = d \sin \theta \qquad \text{... (1.15)}$$

n = 1 for first order and θ = 50°.

∴ $\qquad\qquad\qquad \lambda = 2.15 \sin 50°$

∴ $\qquad\qquad\qquad \lambda = 1.65 \; A°$

- Thus, the experimental value is in close agreement with the theoretical value. This shows that electron behaves like a wave.

- Thus, the Davisson and Germer's experiment confirmed the wave nature of moving electron.

1.3 Wave Particle Duality

- The nature of light is mysterious since the days of Newton. Newton assumed light to consist of tiny particles called corpuscles and these corpuscles are emitted by the luminous bodies. Using this theory he could explain the phenomenon of reflection and refraction. But this theory failed to explain the phenomenon of interference of light.

Huygen, Young, Fresnel, therefore, proposed wave theory of light. According to wave theory, light propagates in the form of waves in a hypothetical medium called ether and it is supposed to be present everywhere i.e. in vacuum also. The wave theory could explain not only phenomenon of reflection and refraction but also the polarization and diffraction of light. In 1900, Maxwell showed that light waves are electromagnetic in nature and for their propagation no medium is necessary. Later, Hertz produced electromagnetic waves in laboratory and the wave nature of light was accepted by the world.

- In 1887, Hallwachs discovered the phenomenon of photoelectric effect, but he could not explain it on the basis of wave theory of light. In order to explain the phenomenon of photoelectric effect. Einstein took into account particle nature of light. He assumed the light energy to consist of packets of energy $h\nu$, where ν is the frequency of light. These packets are called photon or quanta. In 1923, Compton used particle nature of electromagnetic radiations to explain scattering of X rays by electron. This effect is called Compton effect.

- The question thus arises, what is true nature of light? Electromagnetic radiation has to be considered waves in some processes and as particles in some other processes. Both the natures are not observed in one process simultaneously. The processes in which path travelled by light is considered, the wave nature of light is applied. e.g. interference, diffraction. The processes in which there is interaction of light with material particles, the particle nature of light is applied. e.g. photoelectric effect, Compton scattering. Thus a dual nature (wave and particle) came to be associated with light.

1.4 Wave Function of Particle having Finite Momentum

- In classical physics, the motion of a body is governed by the Newton's laws of motion. The position, momentum, angular momentum etc. can be measured precisely at an instant of time. But in quantum mechanics the precise simultaneous measurement of the dynamical variables is discarded and we talk in terms of probability.

- The moving particle has wave nature and the motion of a particle is guided by the wave group. The mathematical function which describes wave group is the wave function ψ (x, y, z, t). As the particle moves under the action of external forces, the wave function changes with time. The motion of a particle is described by the wave function ψ. Wave function in quantum mechanics illustrates the quantum states of an isolated system of one or more particles. There is one wave function containing containing all the information about entire system, not a separate wave function for each particle in the system. It's interpretation is in terms of probability amplitude. Quantities associated with measurement such as average momentum can be derived from wave function. It is a central entity in quantum mechanics. It is denoted by Greek letters ψ (psi).

- The state of a particle is completely described by its wave function, ψ (x, t), where x is the position and t is the time. This is a complex valued function of two real variables x and t.

- If interpreted as a probability amplitude, the square modulus of the wave function, the positive real number $|\psi(x, t)|^2 = \upsilon(x, t) \times \psi(x, t) = \rho(x, t)$ is interpreted as the probability density that the particle is at x.

- Wave function can be added together and multiplied by complex number to form new wave function, hence they are elements of vector space. This is the superposition in quantum mechanics.

- Classically momentum is given by

$$p = mv$$

where m is the mass and v is the velocity of moving particle

and kinetic energy

$$E = \frac{1}{2} mv^2$$

$$E = p^2/2m \qquad \qquad \text{... (1.16)}$$

- In physics, free particle is the particle which is not bound by any force or not in the region where potential energy varies. In classical physics, this means that particle is in field free space. In quantum mechanics, it means in the region of uniform potential, usually set to zero in the region of interest since potential can be arbitrarily set to zero at any point in space.

Quantum mechanically,

$$\text{Total energy } E = h\nu = \frac{h}{2\pi} \cdot 2\pi\nu = \frac{h}{2\pi} \omega = \hbar\omega \qquad \qquad \text{... (1.17 a)}$$

$$\text{where } \hbar = \frac{h}{2\pi}$$

and

$$p = mv = \frac{h}{\lambda}$$

$$= \frac{h}{2\pi} \cdot \frac{2\pi}{\lambda}$$

$$p = \hbar k \text{ and } k = p/\hbar \qquad \qquad \text{... (1.17 b)}$$

The general equation of wave motion is

$$y = Ae^{i(kx - \omega t)}$$

Using equation (1.17 a) and (1.17 b), we get

$$\psi = A e^{i\left(\frac{p}{\hbar}x - \frac{E}{\hbar}t\right)}$$

or

$$\psi = Ae^{\frac{i}{\hbar}(px - Et)} \qquad \qquad \text{... (1.18)}$$

Equation (1.18) represent wave function of a particle having momentum p.

1.5 Concept of Wave Packet, Phase Velocity, Group Velocity and Relation between them

- Matter has dual nature, it behaves like a particle and sometimes as a wave. The amplitude of de Broglie wave corresponding to the moving particle will represent the probability with which the particle be found at a particular place at a particular time. de Broglie wave associated with particle is a pilot wave which controls the motion of particle in space. Therefore it is necessary that the amplitude of the de Broglie wave must be modulated in such a way that it is non-zero only over the finite region of space in the vicinity of the particle at an instant. According to de Broglie's view, each particle of matter in motion may be regarded as consisting of a group of waves or wave packet.

- A **wave packet** is a group of waves, each having slightly different wavelength and velocity. This is also called **wave group**. Their phases and amplitudes are such that they interfere constructively over a small region; over which the particle is located and outside the region they interfere destructively. As time passes, the wave group must surely move along the direction of motion of particle with the same velocity as the particle. Such a wave packet is shown in Fig. 1.4 below.

Fig. 1.4 : Wave group

- To understand the nature of the wave packet or wave group and how the amplitude is modulated, let us assume that a moving particle is associated with a number of plane waves having slightly different wavelengths and velocities and propagating along positive x-direction. For mathematical simplicity, consider two such waves. They are represented as

$$\left. \begin{array}{l} \psi_1 = A \sin(\omega t - kx) \\ \psi_2 = A \sin\{(\omega + d\omega)t - (k + dk)x\} \end{array} \right\} \quad \dots (1.19)$$

and

where $\omega = 2\pi v$ and $k = \dfrac{2\pi}{\lambda}$ (propagation constant) and wave velocity or phase velocity

$$v_p = \frac{\omega}{k}$$

- **Phase velocity** is the velocity with which the wave propagates.

- According to the principle of superposition, the resultant displacement is given by

$$\psi = \psi_1 + \psi_2$$

$$\psi = A[\sin(\omega t - kx) + \sin\{(\omega + d\omega)t - (k + dk)x\}]$$

$$\therefore \qquad \psi = 2A \cos\left(\frac{d\omega}{2}t - \frac{dk}{2}x\right) \sin\left\{\left(\omega + \frac{d\omega}{2}\right)t - \left(k + \frac{dk}{2}\right)x\right\} \quad \dots (1.20)$$

dω and dk are very small. Therefore, above equation can be written as

$$\psi = 2A \cos\left(\frac{d\omega}{2}t - \frac{dk}{2}x\right)\sin(\omega t - kx) \qquad \dots (1.21)$$

$$= B \sin(\omega t - kx)$$

- Thus, the above equation represents a wave travelling with wave or phase velocity $v_p = \dfrac{\omega}{k}$ whose amplitude is

$$B = 2A \cos\left(\frac{d\omega}{2}t - \frac{dk}{2}x\right) \qquad \dots (1.22)$$

The amplitude B represents another wave travelling with velocity v_g called group velocity and it is given by

$$v_g = \frac{\text{Coefficient of } t}{\text{Coefficient of } x} = \frac{d\omega/2}{dk/2} = \frac{d\omega}{dk}$$

$\therefore$ **Group velocity** $v_g = \dfrac{d\omega}{dk}$ $\dots (1.23)$

- Depending upon how the phase velocity varies with ω and k in a particular situation the group velocity may be less or more than the phase velocities of the member waves of a wave group.

Since $\omega = 2\pi v$ and $k = \dfrac{2\pi}{\lambda}$, equation (1.23) can also be written as

$$v_g = \frac{d\omega}{dk} = \frac{2\pi\, dv}{-\frac{2\pi}{\lambda^2}\, d\lambda} = -\lambda^2 \frac{dv}{d\lambda} \qquad \dots (1.24)$$

The two waves with resultant wave group are shown in Fig. 1.5.

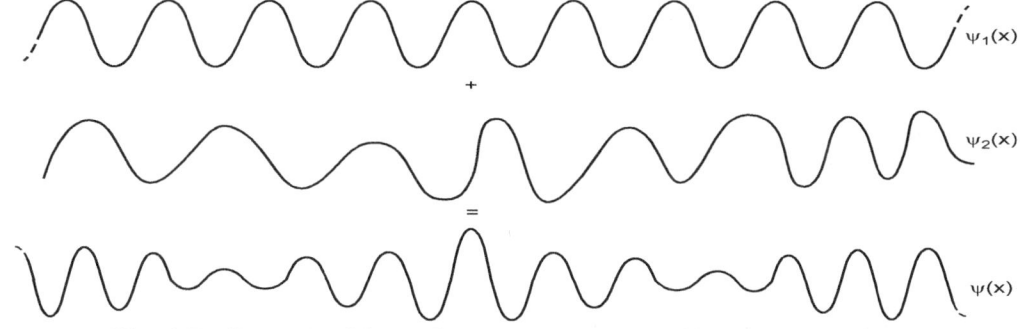

Fig. 1.5 : Superposition of two waves with different frequencies

Since $v_p = \dfrac{\omega}{k}$, we can write $\omega = kv_p$. Using in equation (1.23), we get

$$v_g = \frac{d\,(kv_p)}{dk}$$

$\therefore$ $$v_g = v_p + k\frac{dv_p}{dk} \qquad \dots (1.25)$$

- Equation (1.25) represents the relation between group velocity v_g, phase or wave velocity v_p and propagation constant k.

Since $k = \dfrac{2\pi}{\lambda}$ $\therefore$ dk $= -\dfrac{2\pi}{\lambda^2}\,d\lambda$.

Using in equation (1.25), we get

$$v_g = v_p - \lambda\,\frac{dv_p}{d\lambda} \qquad\qquad \text{... (1.26)}$$

- Equation (1.26) represents the relation between group velocity v_g, phase or wave velocity u and wavelength λ.

To show that the particle velocity (v) is the same as the group velocity (v_g) :

If E and V are the total energy and potential energy of a particle, then its kinetic energy is given by

$$\frac{1}{2}mv^2 = E - V \qquad\qquad \text{... (1.27)}$$

where v being the velocity of a particle.

But the total energy $E = h\nu = \hbar\omega$ where $\hbar = \dfrac{h}{2\pi}$

and $\qquad\qquad\qquad p = \hbar k$

With these values, equation (1.27) can be written as

$$\frac{1}{2}\cdot\frac{\hbar^2 k^2}{m} = \hbar\omega - V$$

$\therefore \qquad\qquad\qquad \omega = \dfrac{1}{2}\cdot\dfrac{\hbar k^2}{m} - \dfrac{V}{\hbar}$

Differentiating with respect to k, we get

$$\frac{d\omega}{dk} = \frac{\hbar k}{m}$$

But $v_g = \dfrac{d\omega}{dk}$ and $p = mv = \hbar k$. Therefore,

$$v_g = \frac{mv}{m} = v$$

$\therefore \qquad\qquad\qquad v_g = v. \qquad\qquad\qquad \text{...(1.28)}$

Thus, we see that velocity of particle is equal to the group velocity or the velocity of wave packet. Hence, we conclude that the wave group propagates with the particle.

Problem 1.7 : *The velocity of ocean waves is given by* $\sqrt{\dfrac{g\lambda}{2\pi}}$. *Find the group velocity.*

Solution : The group velocity v_g is given by

$$v_g = v_p - \lambda\,\frac{dv_p}{d\lambda}$$

The velocity of ocean waves is $v_p = \sqrt{\dfrac{g\lambda}{2\pi}}$

$\therefore$ $\qquad v_g = \sqrt{\dfrac{g\lambda}{2\pi}} - \lambda\sqrt{\dfrac{g}{2\pi}} \times \dfrac{1}{2}\lambda^{-1/2}$

$\therefore$ $\qquad v_g = \dfrac{1}{2}\sqrt{\dfrac{g\lambda}{2\pi}}$

$\therefore$ $\qquad \mathbf{v_g = \dfrac{1}{2}\,v_p}$ $\qquad\qquad$ ... **Ans.**

i.e., the group velocity is half the phase or wave velocity.

Problem 1.8 : *The velocity of waves through the medium of refractive index n is $\sqrt{n/k}$. Find the group velocity in the medium.*

Solution : The velocity of wave or phase velocity $v_p = \sqrt{\dfrac{n}{k}}$

But refractive index $n = \dfrac{c}{v_p}$, where c is velocity of waves in vacuum.

$\therefore$ $\qquad v_p = \sqrt{\dfrac{c}{k\,v_p}}$

or $\qquad v_p{}^2 = \dfrac{c}{k\,v_p}$

$\therefore$ $\qquad v_p{}^3 = \dfrac{c}{k}$

or $\qquad v_p = \left(\dfrac{c}{k}\right)^{1/3}$

The relation between the group velocity and the phase velocity is given as

$$v_g = v_p + k\dfrac{dv_p}{dk}$$

$$v_g = v_p + k\dfrac{d}{dk}\left(\dfrac{c}{k}\right)^{1/3} = v_p + kc^{1/3}\dfrac{d\,(k^{-1/3})}{dk}$$

$$= v_p - \dfrac{1}{3}kc^{1/3} \times k^{-4/3} = v_p - \dfrac{1}{3}\left(\dfrac{c}{k}\right)^{1/3}$$

$\therefore$ $\qquad \mathbf{v_g = v_p - \dfrac{1}{3}\,v_p = \dfrac{2}{3}\,v_p}$ $\qquad\qquad$ ... **Ans.**

Problem 1.9 : *Show that the phase velocity of the de Broglie wave of a particle of rest mass m_o and wavelength λ is given by*

$$v_p = c\sqrt{1 + \left(\dfrac{m_o c\lambda}{h}\right)^2} \quad \text{where c is the velocity of light.}$$

Solution : The phase velocity is given by $v_p = \dfrac{\omega}{k} = \dfrac{2\pi v}{2\pi/\lambda} = v\lambda$

We have energy $\qquad\qquad\qquad E = hv$

The relativistic energy is given by

$$E = \sqrt{p^2c^2 + m_o^2c^4}$$

$$\therefore\qquad E = pc\sqrt{1 + \dfrac{m_o^2c^4}{p^2c^2}}$$

$$= pc\sqrt{1 + \dfrac{m_o^2c^2}{p^2}}$$

Since $p = \dfrac{h}{\lambda}$, we get $\qquad E = \dfrac{h}{\lambda}c\sqrt{1 + \left(\dfrac{m_oc\lambda}{h}\right)^2}$

$$\therefore\qquad \dfrac{E\lambda}{h} = c\sqrt{1 + \left(\dfrac{m_oc\lambda}{h}\right)^2}$$

or $\qquad\qquad \dfrac{hv\lambda}{h} = c\sqrt{1 + \left(\dfrac{m_oc\lambda}{h}\right)^2}$

$$\therefore\qquad v\lambda = c\sqrt{1 + \left(\dfrac{m_oc\lambda}{h}\right)^2}$$

or $\qquad\qquad \mathbf{v_p = c\sqrt{1 + \left(\dfrac{m_oc\lambda}{h}\right)^2}}$

Problem 1.10 : *Velocity of ripple waves is equal to* $\sqrt{\dfrac{2\pi T}{\rho\lambda}}$ *where T is surface tension, λ is the wavelength and ρ is the density of liquid. Find the group velocity.*

Solution : We have $\qquad\qquad v_p = \sqrt{\dfrac{2\pi T}{\rho\lambda}}$

$$\therefore\qquad \dfrac{dv_p}{d\lambda} = -\dfrac{1}{2\lambda}\sqrt{\dfrac{2\pi T}{\rho\lambda}} = -\dfrac{1}{2\lambda}v_p$$

$$\therefore\qquad \lambda\dfrac{dv_p}{d\lambda} = -\dfrac{1}{2}v_p$$

Now, $\qquad\qquad v_g = v_p - \lambda\dfrac{dv_p}{d\lambda}$

$$\therefore\qquad v_g = v_p - \left(-\dfrac{1}{2}v_p\right)$$

$$\therefore\qquad \mathbf{v_g = \dfrac{3}{2}v_p} \qquad\qquad\qquad\qquad \textbf{... Ans.}$$

1.6 Heisenberg's Uncertainty Principle

- In Classical Physics, the dynamical variables like position, components of linear momenta, components of angular momenta etc. are assumed to be measured with precise accuracy at a given instant of time *i.e.* the basic laws in physics (such as Newton's laws) have deterministic nature. The probability considerations are not foreign in classical physics but in it the statistical probability theory, which is used as a practical device in the study of complicated systems.

- According to Bohr and Heisenberg, the probabilistic nature is fundamental one in quantum physics and the deterministic nature is discarded. A careful analysis of motion of microphysical system shows that there is a fundamental limit to the accuracy to which variables like position, momentum, angular momentum etc. are measured.

- We have seen that the moving material particle has dual nature i.e., it behaves like a particle in some processes and wave in some processes. At any instant the particle should have definite position and a definite momentum. To study the motion of a particle, its position and momentum must be simultaneously measured. Werner Heisenberg in 1927 proposed a very far reaching principle called *uncertainty principle*. According to this principle, if we measure accurately the position of particle its momentum become uncertain and vice versa. The moving particle is considered to have wave packet. The particle may be anywhere in the wave packet and if the packet is small i.e. wave group is narrow, its position can be found more accurately. But when the wave packet is small the wavelength spread is more i.e. wavelength and consequently the momentum of the particle becomes uncertain. On the other hand, if the wave packet is long the momentum of the particle becomes more certain but the position becomes uncertain.

- Heisenberg's uncertainty principle states that *it is impossible to determine precisely and simultaneously the momentum and position of the particle.* The short wave group is shown in Fig. 1.6 (a) and long wave group is shown in Fig. 1.6 (b).

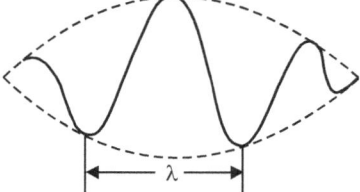 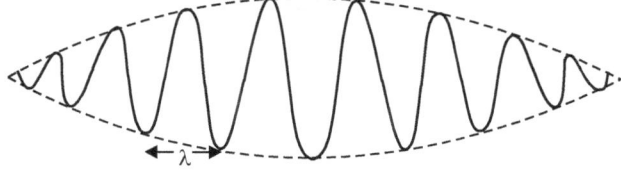

(a) Short wave group   **(b) Long wave group**

Fig. 1.6

- In mathematical form the uncertainty principle is given as : If Δx is the uncertainty in the measurement of position and Δp_x is the uncertainty in the measurement of momentum, then the product of two uncertainties is approximately of the order of Planck's constant. It is given as

$$\Delta x \cdot \Delta p_x \approx \hbar \qquad \qquad \text{... (1.29)}$$

- If Δx is small, Δp_x will be large and *vice versa*. It means that if one quantity is measured accurately, the other quantity becomes less accurate. More precise relation of uncertainty principle is

$$\Delta x \cdot \Delta p_x \geq \frac{\hbar}{2}$$

where momentum p_x is known to within accuracy of Δp_x and the position x at the same time to within accuracy Δx. Here $\hbar$ (read as h-bar) is taken as $h/2\pi$, the quantity appears often in quantum mechanics as basic unit of angular momentum.

- There are corresponding relations for another components of linear momentum and are given as

$$\Delta y \cdot \Delta p_y \geq \frac{\hbar}{2}$$

and $$\Delta z \cdot \Delta p_z \geq \frac{\hbar}{2} \qquad \qquad \dots (1.30)$$

- This is law of nature and not due to any defects in the measuring instrument and principle says that even with ideal instruments we can in principle will never do better than $\Delta x \cdot \Delta p_x \geq \hbar/2$.

- Heisenberg's principle of uncertainty can be illustrated in a number of ways. Let us consider such illustrations.

1. γ-ray microscope :

- We shall consider here the famous argument by Bohr with the so called 'γ-ray microscope'. This is *thought experiment* and cannot be performed experimentally.

- The experimental arrangement is shown in Fig. 1.7 (a).

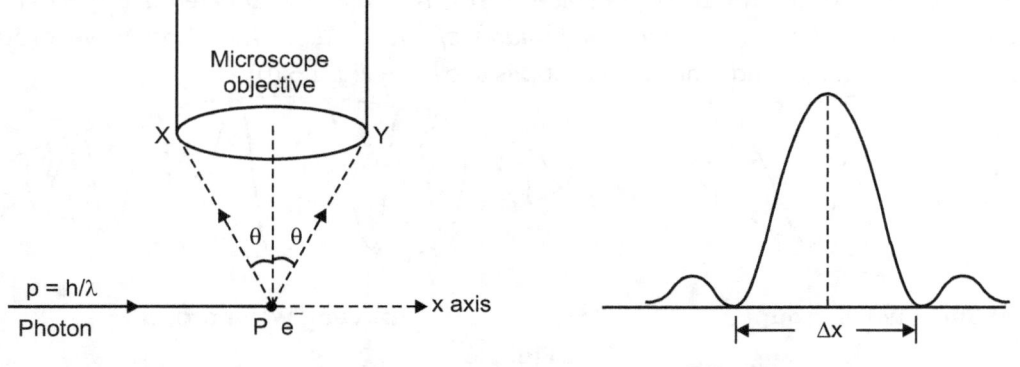

(a) Experimental arrangement   **(b) Diffraction pattern**

Fig. 1.7 : Measurement of position with γ ray microscope

- Suppose we try to measure the position and linear momentum of an electron using an imaginary microscope of high resolution. The electron can be observed when at least one photon scattered from electron enters in the aperture of the microscope. The resolving power of the microscope is given by the relation,

$$\Delta x = \frac{\lambda}{2 \sin \theta} \qquad \text{... (1.31)}$$

where Δx is the smallest distance between two points which can be just resolved by the microscope, λ is the wavelength of light used for illumination and θ is the semi-vertical angle of the cone of rays entering in the objective of the microscope as shown in Fig. 1.7 (a). The corresponding diffraction pattern is shown in Fig. 1.7 (b). To increase the resolving power i.e. to make the uncertainty in position Δx small from equation (1.31), we see that λ must be made small, because $\sin \theta$ could not be increased above unity. Therefore, the radiations of smaller wavelength i.e. γ radiations are employed, to illuminate the electron at P. Such γ-ray microscope cannot be devised but is just a *thought experiment*. But in its consideration, no physical laws are violated.

- The incoming photon (γ-ray) along x-direction will interact with the electron and scattered in all directions. In order to see the electron, the scattered photon should enter the microscope within the angle 2θ. The momentum imparted by the photon to the electron will be of the order of h/λ.

- The component of momentum of scattered photon along PX is $\sim -\frac{h}{\lambda} \sin \theta$.

- The component of momentum of scattered photon along PY is $\sim \frac{h}{\lambda} \sin \theta$.

- The momentum imparted by the photon to the electron is therefore anything between the above two limits. Hence uncertainty in the momentum measurement in the x-direction is

$$\Delta p = \frac{h}{\lambda} \sin \theta - \left(-\frac{h}{\lambda} \sin \theta \right) = \frac{2h}{\lambda} \sin \theta \qquad \text{... (1.32)}$$

$$\therefore \qquad \Delta x \cdot \Delta p = \frac{\lambda}{2 \sin \theta} \times \frac{2h}{\lambda} \sin \theta = h$$

i.e. $\qquad \Delta x \cdot \Delta p = h$

A more sophisticated approach will show that $\Delta x \cdot \Delta p \geq \hbar$.

2. Electron diffraction experiment:

- Consider a beam of electrons falling on a narrow slit of width 'd' as shown in Fig. 1.8. The beam spreads out after passing through the slit due to diffraction and the diffraction pattern is observed on the photographic plate P kept at a distance from the slit. Every electron registered on the photographic plate must have passed through the slit, but cannot specify its exact location in the slit as the electron crosses it. Hence the uncertainty in specifying the position of electron is equal to the slit width i.e. $\Delta x = d$.

From the wave theory of light, we know that for diffraction

$$2d \sin \theta = \lambda$$

For first order, $$\Delta x = \frac{\lambda}{2 \sin \theta}$$ ...(1.33)

where λ be the wavelength and θ be the angle of diffraction for first order.

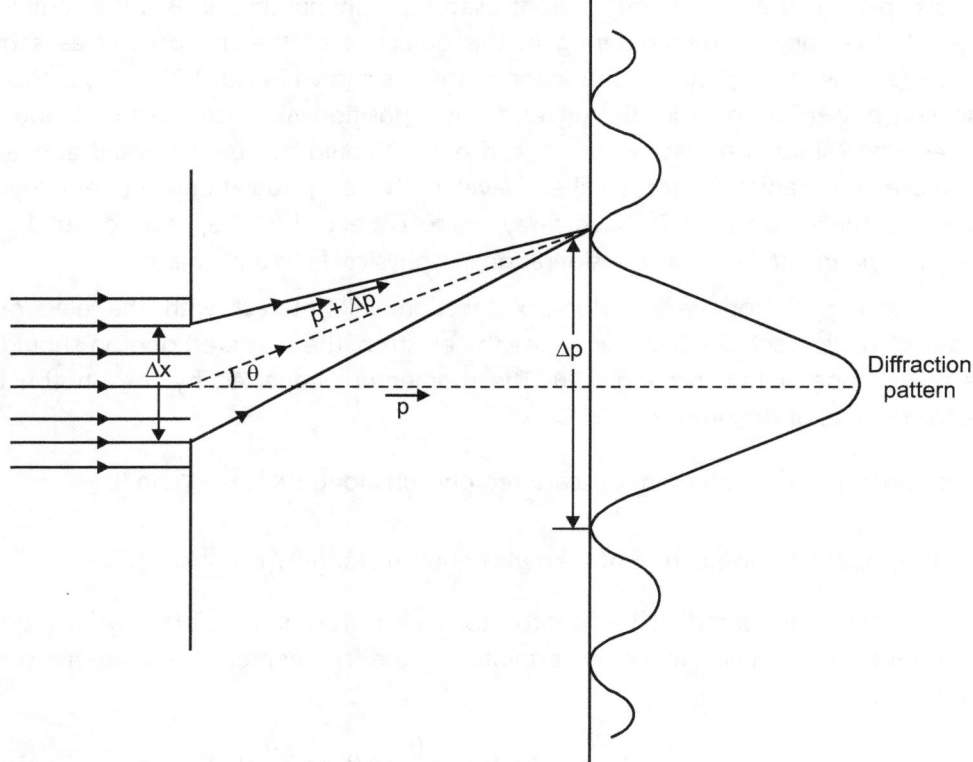

Fig. 1.8 : Electron diffraction experiment

- Let p be the momentum of electron along the incident direction. When the electron is deflected at the slit, it acquires an additional momentum $p \sin \theta$ in the direction perpendicular to the original direction. As the electron may be anywhere within the pattern from angle $- \theta$ to $+ \theta$, the component of momentum of the electron may have any value between $- p \sin \theta$ to $p \sin \theta$. Therefore uncertainty in the component of momentum is

$$\Delta p = p \sin \theta - (- p \sin \theta) = 2p \sin \theta.$$

From de Broglie hypothesis, $$p = \frac{h}{\lambda}$$

$\therefore$ $$\Delta p = \frac{2h}{\lambda} \sin \theta$$ ... (1.34)

From equations (1.33) and (1.34), we get

$$\Delta x \cdot \Delta p = \frac{\lambda}{2 \sin \theta} \times \frac{2h}{\lambda} \sin \theta$$

$\therefore \qquad\qquad \Delta x \cdot \Delta p \sim h$

This is the uncertainty relation.

1.7 Different Forms of Uncertainty Relation

1. Time energy uncertainty relation :

The kinetic energy of the particle

$$E = \frac{1}{2} m v^2 = \frac{p^2}{2m}$$

The uncertainty in E is ΔE and it is given by

$$\Delta E = \frac{p}{m} \Delta p = v \cdot \Delta p \qquad\qquad \text{(since } p = mv\text{)}$$

If v is taken as the recoil velocity of the particle due to incident light, the uncertainty in the position is related to the uncertainty of the time of observation.

$$\Delta x = v \Delta t$$

$\therefore \qquad\qquad \Delta E \, \Delta t = v \Delta p \times \dfrac{\Delta x}{v} = \Delta p \times \Delta x$

$\therefore \qquad\qquad \Delta E \cdot \Delta t = \hbar/2 \qquad\qquad\qquad …(1.35)$

The physical interpretation of energy-time uncertainty relation is quite different from that of position momentum uncertainty relation. If ΔE is the maximum uncertainty in the determination of energy of system in a particular state, then according to relation (1.35), the minimum time interval for which time remain in state is given by

$$\Delta t = \hbar/2\Delta E$$

If a system remains in a particular state for a maximum time interval, Δt, then the minimum uncertainty in the energy of system in that state is given by

$$\Delta E = \hbar/2\Delta t$$

2. Angular momentum-angular displacement uncertainty relation :

Consider a particle of mass m moving with speed v in a circle of radius r.

The angular momentum at an instant is given by

$$L = mvr = pr$$

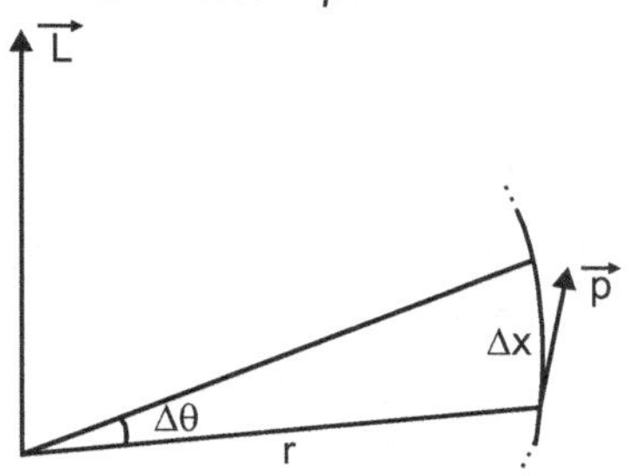

Fig. 1.9

If the particle is displaced through angular displacement $\Delta\theta$, the distance travelled by the particle along the circular arc is s = r $\Delta\theta$.

This will be the uncertainty in its position.

$\therefore$ $\Delta x = r\, \Delta\theta$

If uncertainty in the momentum is Δp, then the uncertainty in the angular momentum is $\Delta L = r\, \Delta p$.

Hence $\Delta p = \dfrac{\Delta L}{r}$

$\therefore$ $\Delta p\, \Delta x = \dfrac{\Delta L}{r}\, r\, \Delta\theta = \Delta L\, \Delta\theta$

But $\Delta p\, \Delta x \geq \hbar/2$

$\therefore$ $\Delta L\, \Delta\theta \geq \hbar/2$ ... (1.36)

This is the required result.

Applications of uncertainty principle :

1.   To calculate the binding energy of hydrogen atom and radius of Bohr orbit.

2.   Explanation of stability of atoms.

3.   To calculate strength of nuclear force.

4.   Non-existence of electron in nucleus. (Refer Problem 1.14)

Problem 1.11 : *What is the smallest possible uncertainty in the position of an electron moving with velocity 10^6 m/sec ?*

Solution : Let Δx be the minimum uncertainty in the determination of position of the electron, then according to uncertainty principle,

$$\Delta x \cdot \Delta p = \hbar/2 \quad \text{where } \hbar = \frac{h}{2\pi} = 1.055 \times 10^{-34} \text{ J-sec.}$$

Taking the maximum uncertainty in the momentum $\Delta p = p = mv$

Mass of electron $m = 9.1 \times 10^{-31}$ kg. and velocity v = 10^6 m/sec

$\therefore$ $\Delta p = 9.1 \times 10^{-31} \times 10^6$ kg-m/s = 9.1×10^{-25} kg-m/s

$\therefore$ $\Delta x = \dfrac{\hbar}{2\Delta p}$

                         $= \dfrac{1.055 \times 10^{-34}}{2 \times 9.1 \times 10^{-25}} = 0.5795 \times 10^{-10}$ m = 0.5795 A°.

$\therefore$ $\Delta x = \textbf{0.5795 A°}$ **... Ans.**

Problem 1.12 : *An electron has speed of 6000 m/s with an accuracy of 0.05%. Calculate the uncertainty with which the position of electron can be located.*

Solution : Mass of the electron $m = 9.1 \times 10^{-31}$ kg.

           Velocity of the electron v = 6000 m/s.

The momentum of the electron $p = mv = 9.1 \times 10^{-31} \times 6000 = 54.6 \times 10^{-28}$ kg-m/s

Uncertainty in momentum $\qquad \Delta p = 0.05\%$ of $p = \dfrac{0.05}{100} \times 54.6 \times 10^{-28}$

$$= 5 \times 54.6 \times 10^{-32}\,\text{kg-m/s}$$

$\therefore \qquad\qquad \Delta p = 2.83 \times 10^{-29}\,\text{kg-m/sec}$

Uncertainty in position is given by $\Delta x = \dfrac{\hbar}{2\Delta p} = \dfrac{1.055 \times 10^{-34}}{2 \times 2.83 \times 10^{-29}} = 0.189 \times 10^{-5}\,\text{m}$

$\therefore \qquad\qquad\qquad \mathbf{\Delta x = 1.89 \times 10^{-6}\,m} \qquad\qquad\qquad$ **... Ans.**

Problem 1.13 : *Show that for a free particle the uncertainty relation can also be written as*

$$\Delta\lambda\, \Delta x \geq \lambda^2/4\pi$$

where Δx is uncertainty in the position and $\Delta\lambda$ is the simultaneous uncertainty in the wavelength.

Solution : We have uncertainty relation

$$\Delta x \cdot \Delta p \geq \frac{\hbar}{2} \qquad\qquad\qquad \text{... (i)}$$

According to de Broglie hypothesis,

$$p = \frac{h}{\lambda}$$

On differentiation, we get $\qquad dp = -\dfrac{h}{\lambda^2}\, d\lambda$

Magnitude of above equation can be written as

$$\Delta p = \frac{h}{\lambda^2}\, \Delta\lambda \qquad\qquad\qquad \text{...(ii)}$$

Using equation (ii) in equation (i), we get

$$\Delta x \frac{h}{\lambda^2}\, \Delta\lambda \geq \frac{\hbar}{2}$$

$\therefore \qquad\qquad\qquad \Delta x\, \Delta\lambda \geq \dfrac{\hbar}{2}\, \dfrac{\lambda^2}{h}$

or $\qquad\qquad\qquad \Delta x\, \Delta\lambda \geq \dfrac{h}{4\pi}\, \dfrac{\lambda^2}{h}$

$\therefore \qquad\qquad\qquad \Delta x\, \Delta\lambda \geq \dfrac{\lambda^2}{4\pi}$

Problem 1.14 : *A typical atomic nucleus has diameter 0.5×10^{-14} m. Using uncertainty principle show that an electron cannot exist inside the nucleus.*

Solution : The diameter of the nucleus is $d = 2 \times 0.5 \times 10^{-14}$ m. So for an electron to be confined within the nucleus, the uncertainty in position must not exceed d.

$\therefore \qquad\qquad\qquad \Delta x = 1 \times 10^{-14}\,\text{m}$

We have uncertainty relation $\Delta x \cdot \Delta p \geq \dfrac{\hbar}{2}$

$\therefore \qquad\qquad \Delta p = \dfrac{\hbar}{2\Delta x}$

$$= \dfrac{1.055 \times 10^{-34}}{2 \times 10^{-14}}$$

$$= 0.5275 \times 10^{-20} \text{ kg m/s.}$$

If this is uncertainty in the momentum of electron in the nucleus, the momentum itself must be at least comparable to in magnitude i.e. $p \sim \Delta p$. The velocity of electron with this momentum is nearly equal to velocity of light and hence the kinetic energy will be

$$E = mc^2 = mc \times c = p \times c = \Delta p \times c$$

$$= 0.5275 \times 10^{-20} \times 3 \times 10^8$$

$\therefore \qquad\qquad E = 1.5825 \times 10^{-12} \text{ J}$

$\therefore \qquad\qquad E = \dfrac{1.5825 \times 10^{-12}}{1.6 \times 10^{-19}} \text{ eV}$

$$= 0.9890 \times 10^7 \text{ eV}$$

$$= 9.89 \times 10^6 \text{ eV} = 9.89 \text{ MeV}$$

or $\qquad\qquad\qquad\qquad$ **E ≈ 10 MeV** $\qquad\qquad\qquad\qquad\qquad$ **... Ans.**

This shows that if the electron exists in the nucleus, its energy must be at least 10 MeV. Experiments showed that the electron in an atom never has more than a small fraction of this energy. Thus, the electron cannot be present in the nucleus.

Problem 1.15 : *An electron of energy 200 eV is passed through a circular hole of radius equal to 2×10^{-4} cm. What is the uncertainty introduced in the angle of emergence?*

Given mass of electron = 0.9×10^{-27} gm and $\hbar = 10^{-27}$ erg sec

Solution : We know that $\qquad p \approx (2mE)^{1/2}$

$$\approx [2 \times 0.9 \times 10^{-27} \times 200 \times 1.6 \times 10^{-12}]^{1/2}$$

$$\approx 7.6 \times 10^{-19} \text{ g cm/sec}$$

Now $\qquad\qquad\qquad \Delta p \approx \hbar/\Delta x \cdot$

$$\approx \dfrac{10^{-27}}{4 \times 10^{-4}} = 2.5 \times 10^{-24} \text{ g cm/sec}$$

$$\theta = \dfrac{\Delta p}{p} \approx \dfrac{2.5 \times 10^{-24}}{7.6 \times 10^{-19}}$$

$$\approx \textbf{0.33} \times 10^{-5} \textbf{ radians} \qquad\qquad\qquad\qquad \textbf{... Ans.}$$

Summary

1. Classical theory fails to explain energy distribution in the spectrum of a black body. It also fails to explain photoelectric effect.

2. Electromagnetic radiation has to be considered waves in some processes and as particles in some other processes. This is dual nature of electromagnetic radiation.

3. Louis de Broglie put forward the suggestion that *like radiation, matter has dual nature,* i.e. matter which is made up of discrete particles, atoms, protons, electrons etc., might exhibit wavelike properties under appropriate conditions.

    de Broglie wavelength $= \lambda = \dfrac{h}{p}$

4. Energy $E = h\nu = \dfrac{h}{2\pi} \cdot 2\pi\nu = \dfrac{h}{2\pi}\,\omega = \hbar\omega$

5. Momentum $p = mv = \dfrac{h}{\lambda} = \dfrac{h}{2\pi} \cdot \dfrac{2\pi}{\lambda} = \hbar k$

6. A wave packet is a group of waves, each having slightly different wavelength and velocity. This is also called wave group.

7. Phase velocity is the velocity with which the wave propagates $v_p = \dfrac{\omega}{k}$.

8. Group velocity, $v_g = \dfrac{d\omega}{dk}$ ... (1.20)

9. Heisenberg's uncertainty principle states that it is impossible to determine precisely and simultaneously the momentum and position of the particle. According to uncertainty principle, if we measure accurately the position of particle, its momentum becomes uncertain and vice versa.

    $$\Delta x \cdot \Delta p_x \approx \hbar$$

    If Δx is small, Δp_x will be large and *vice versa*. More precise relation of uncertainty principle is

    $$\Delta x \cdot \Delta p_x \geq \dfrac{\hbar}{2}$$

10. Time energy uncertainty relation is $\Delta E . \Delta t \approx h$

11. Angular momentum-angular displacement uncertainty relation is $\Delta L\ \Delta\theta \geq \hbar/2$.

Exercises

(A) Short Answer Type Questions :

1. State two phenomena where classical physics fails to explain the phenomena.

2. What is the wave particle duality ?

3. What is de Broglie wavelength ?

4. What is the wave packet ?

5. Define phase velocity and group velocity.

6. State uncertainty principle.

(B) Long Answer Type Questions :

1. Give an informative account of dual nature of matter and radiation.

2. What are matter waves ? Obtain an expression for their wavelength.

3. Write short notes on wave velocity and group velocity.

4. Obtain the expression for group velocity.

5. Show that the group velocity is equal to the particle velocity.

6. Write a note on de Broglie hypothesis.

7. Write a note on uncertainty principle. Give different forms of uncertainty relations.

8. Show that $\Delta L\,\Delta\theta \geq \hbar/2$ and $\Delta E\,\Delta t \geq \hbar/2$.

9. Discuss the γ ray microscope to illustrate uncertainty relation.

10. Discuss the electron diffraction experiment to illustrate uncertainty relation.

11. Show that $v_g = v_p + k\dfrac{dv_p}{dk}$.

12. Show that $v_g = v_p - \lambda\dfrac{dv_p}{d\lambda}$.

13. What is uncertainty principle? Write different forms of uncertainty principle.

(C) Unsolved Problems :

1. What is the energy of gamma photon having wavelength 1 A°, given that :
    $h = 6.62 \times 10^{-34}$ J-sec   **(Ans.** 1.24×10^4 eV)

2. Photon of energy 10 eV falls on molybdenum whose work function is 4.15 eV. Find the stopping potential.   **(Ans.** 5.85 volt)

3. Calculate the de Broglie wavelength of an electron travelling with velocity 3/5 c, where c is the speed of light.
    (Hint : $m = m_o /(1 - v^2/c^2)^{1/2}$, where m_o is the mass of electron)   **(Ans.** 0.0323 A°)

4. What is the de Broglie wave of neutron whose energy is 5M eV ? **(Ans.** 2.23×10^{-3} A°)

5. Find the de Broglie wavelength of 50 eV electron.   **(Ans.** 1.54 A°)

6. Show that the de Broglie wavelength of a particle of charge, rest mass m_o, moving with relativistic speed is given by

    $$\lambda = \frac{h}{\sqrt{2m_o eV}} \sqrt{1 + \frac{eV}{2m_o c^2}}$$

    (Hint : Use relativistic energy $E = \sqrt{p^2 c^2 + m_0^2 c^4}$ and $p = h/\lambda$)

7. What is the energy uncertainty of states with life time of 2.8×10^{-10} sec. ?

    (**Ans.** 1.178 MeV)

8. A particle moving with its kinetic energy equal to its 50 eV has wavelength 2.8 A°. If the kinetic energy is doubled, what would be its wavelength ?   (**Ans.** 1.97 A°)

9. The average life time for which electron stays in a given excited state before it jumps to lower energy state is about 10^{-8} seconds. What is the uncertainty in the frequency of emitted spectral lines ? Use $\tau = 1/\upsilon$.   (**Ans.** 10^8 Hz)

10. If the average period that elapses between the excitation of an atom and time it radiates the energy is 10^{-8} sec. Calculate uncertainty in the energy of emitted photon. Use $\Delta E . \Delta t = h$.   (**Ans.** 4.14×10^{-7} eV)

11. Calculate the uncertainty in the position of an electron of mass 9×10^{-31} kg with uncertainty in speed of 3×10^9 cm/sec.   (**Ans.** 2.2×10^{-9} m)

12. Electron has a speed of 2×10^4 cm/sec accurate to 0.01%. With what fundamental accuracy can we locate the position of this electron? Use $\Delta x \cdot \Delta p_x \approx \hbar$.

    (**Ans.** 3.66×10^{-2} m)

13. A nucleus has a radius of 4 Fermis. Use the uncertainty principle to estimate the kinetic energy for a neutron localized inside the nucleus. Do the same for an electron.

    [**Use** : $E = p^2/2m$ where $p = \Delta x \cdot \Delta p \approx \hbar$ or $p\, r \approx \hbar$ (**Ans.** 1.3 MeV)

    ❏❏❏

Chapter 2...
Schrödinger's Equation

> *The task is......not so much to see what no one has yet seen; but to think what nobody has yet thought, about that which every body sees.*
>
> *– Erwin Schrödinger*

Erwin Schrödinger
(1887-1961)

Erwin Schrödinger, was a Nobel prize (1933) winning Austrian physicist who developed number of fundamental results in the field of quantum theory, which formed the basis of wave mechanics. He formulated the wave equation and revelled identity of his development of formalism and matrix mechanism. He proposed original interpretation of the physical meaning of wave function.

Introduction

- Scientists attempted to build up a mathematical formulation for wave function, $\psi(x, y, z, t)$. In 1926, Erwin Schrödinger developed an equation in terms of $\psi(x, y, z, t)$. The equation is now called Schrödinger's equation. In subsequent sections, we will see the solutions of quantum mechanical problems that can be solved by using this equation.

2.1 Physical Interpretation of Wave Function

- We know that the moving particle has a wave nature. The mathematical function which describes motion is the wave function $\psi(x, y, z, t)$. The wave function actually contains all the information which the uncertainty principle allows us to know about the associated particle. But the wave function ψ itself has no physical interpretation, as it may be positive, negative or complex.

- The basic connection between the properties of the particle and its associated wave function is expressed in terms of the **probability density**. The square of absolute magnitude of wave function $|\psi|^2$ (called probability density) evaluated at a particular place at a particular instant of time is proportional to the probability of finding the particle there at that time. As the wave functions are usually complex with real and imaginary parts, the probability density $|\psi|^2$ is taken as the product $\psi\psi^*$, where ψ^* is a complex conjugate of ψ. This interpretation was given by Max Born in 1926. According to Born's postulate,

"If, at an instant t, a measurement is made to locate a particle having the wave function $\psi(x, t)$, then the probability P(x, t) of finding the particle in a range x and x + dx will be equal to $\psi(x, t)\psi^*(x, t) dx$".

- In general the probability of finding the particle in volume element dV is

$$P (r,t) dV = |\psi (r,t)|^2 dV$$

The function $\psi (r,t)$ is called probability amplitude.

- Since $|\psi|^2$ or $\psi\psi^*$ represents the probability density, the integral of $|\psi|^2$ over all space representing the total probability must be finite because the particle is present somewhere. Because of the way of definition of ψ, $|\psi|^2$ cannot be negative or complex. Since the particle under consideration will always be found somewhere, total probability always equal to unity *i.e.*

$$\int |\psi|^2 dV = 1 \quad \text{or} \quad \int \psi\psi^* dV = 1$$

- The integral in the above equation is carried out over the entire space. The above condition on ψ is called the *normalisation condition*. The wave function that satisfies the above condition is called normalised wave function.

- If the wave function is not normalised, in order to normalise the wave function it is multiplied by some arbitrary constant and then the above integral is evaluated over the entire space. The normalisation procedure is as follows :

If ψ is not normalised, multiply it by some constant A. Then evaluate the integral and equate it to unity and calculate the constant A called normalisation constant i.e.

$$\int A\psi(A\psi)^* dV = 1$$

or $$AA^* \int \psi\psi^* dV = 1$$

As A is real constant, we get

$$|A|^2 \int \psi\psi^* dV = 1$$

This gives normalisation constant as

$$|A|^2 = \frac{1}{\int \psi\psi^* dV}$$

The normalisation constant can be taken as positive square root of above result.

2.2 Schrödinger's Time Dependent Equation

We will start with a equation

The general equation of a wave propagating along +x axis is given by

$$y = Ae^{i(kx - \omega t)}$$

- In quantum mechanics the wave function ψ corresponds to a variable y of general wave motion. However, ψ itself is not a measurable quantity, and may, therefore, be complex. For this reason, we assume that ψ for a particle moving freely along +x axis is specified by

$$\psi = Ae^{i(kx - \omega t)} \qquad ...(2.1)$$

- The de Broglie - Einstein postulates are

$$\lambda = \frac{h}{p} \quad \text{and} \quad E = h\nu$$

We can write above equations as

$$p = \frac{h}{\lambda} = \frac{h}{2\pi}\frac{2\pi}{\lambda} = \hbar k \qquad (\because k = 2\pi/\lambda)$$

and

$$E = h\nu = \frac{h}{2\pi} 2\pi\nu = \hbar\omega \qquad (\because \omega = 2\pi\nu)$$

Therefore,

$$k = \frac{p}{\hbar} \text{ and } \omega = \frac{E}{\hbar}$$

Using these in equation (2.1), we get

$$\psi = A\, e^{i\left(\frac{p}{\hbar}x - \frac{E}{\hbar}t\right)}$$

or

$$\psi = Ae^{\frac{i}{\hbar}(px - Et)} \qquad ... (2.2)$$

- Equation (2.2) represents the wave equivalent of a free particle of total energy E and momentum p moving in the +x direction. Equation (2.2) is correct only for the particles moving freely. But we are interested in situations where the motion of particle is constrained by some restrictions. We can now obtain differential equation for ψ, which can be solved in specific situation.

- Differentiating equation (2.2) with respect to x, we get

$$\frac{\partial \psi}{\partial x} = \frac{ip}{\hbar} Ae^{\frac{i}{\hbar}(px - Et)} \qquad ... (2.3)$$

- Again differentiating above equation with respect to x, we get

$$\frac{\partial^2 \psi}{\partial x^2} = -\frac{p^2}{\hbar^2} Ae^{\frac{i}{\hbar}(px - Et)}$$

$$\therefore \qquad \frac{\partial^2 \psi}{\partial x^2} = -\frac{p^2}{\hbar^2} \psi \qquad \qquad ... (2.4)$$

which gives

$$p^2 \psi = -\hbar^2 \frac{\partial^2 \psi}{\partial x^2} \qquad \qquad ...(2.5)$$

Differentiating equation (2.2) with respect to t, we get

$$\frac{\partial \psi}{\partial t} = -\frac{iE}{\hbar} Ae^{\frac{i}{\hbar}(px - Et)}$$

or

$$\frac{\partial \psi}{\partial t} = -\frac{iE}{\hbar} \psi$$

Above equation can be written as

$$-\frac{\hbar}{i} \frac{\partial \psi}{\partial t} = E\psi$$

or

$$E\psi = i\hbar \frac{\partial \psi}{\partial t} \qquad \qquad ...(2.6)$$

- When speed of particle is small compared to the velocity of light, the total energy E of a particle is the sum of kinetic energy $p^2/2m$ and potential energy $V(x)$.

$$E = \frac{p^2}{2m} + V \qquad \qquad ... (2.7)$$

Multiplying equation (2.7) on both sides by ψ, we get

$$E\psi = \frac{p^2 \psi}{2m} + V\psi \qquad \qquad ...(2.8)$$

Substituting $p^2 \psi$ and $E\psi$ from equations (2.5) and (2.6) in equation (2.8), we get

$$i\hbar \frac{\partial \psi}{\partial t} = -\frac{\hbar^2}{2m} \frac{\partial^2 \psi}{\partial x^2} + V\psi \qquad \qquad ...(2.9)$$

- Equation (2.9) was first obtained by Schrödinger in 1926 and called Schrödinger's wave equation. This is **Schrödinger's time dependent equation**. Equation (2.9) is one-dimensional equation, since it is for motion along x direction.

In two dimensions, the equation (2.9) can be written as

$$i\hbar \frac{\partial \psi}{\partial t} = -\frac{\hbar^2}{2m} \left(\frac{\partial^2 \psi}{\partial x^2} + \frac{\partial^2 \psi}{\partial y^2} \right) + V\psi \qquad \qquad ...(2.10)$$

where $\psi = \psi(x, y, t)$

- In three dimensions, the equation (2.9) can be written as

$$i\hbar \frac{\partial \psi}{\partial t} = -\frac{\hbar^2}{2m}\left(\frac{\partial^2 \psi}{\partial x^2} + \frac{\partial^2 \psi}{\partial y^2} + \frac{\partial^2 \psi}{\partial z^2}\right) + V\psi$$

or

$$i\hbar \frac{\partial \psi}{\partial t} = -\frac{\hbar^2}{2m}\nabla^2\psi + V\psi \qquad \qquad ...(2.11)$$

where

$$\psi = \psi(x, y, z, t)$$

and

$$\nabla^2\psi = \frac{\partial^2 \psi}{\partial x^2} + \frac{\partial^2 \psi}{\partial y^2} + \frac{\partial^2 \psi}{\partial z^2} \qquad \qquad ...(2.12)$$

2.3 Schrödinger's Time Independent Equation (Steady-State Equation)

- In number of situations the potential energy of a particle is independent of the time explicitly and depends on the position only. In such situation, Schrödinger's equation is simplified by removing all time dependent part.

  We have one-dimensional Schrödinger's equation (Equation 2.9)

$$i\hbar \frac{\partial \psi}{\partial t} = -\frac{\hbar^2}{2m}\frac{\partial^2 \psi}{\partial x^2} + V\psi$$

  where $\psi = \psi(x, t)$

- This equation can be solved by separation of variables method.

  Let

$$\psi(x, t) = \psi(x)\, \phi(t) \qquad \qquad ...(2.13)$$

- Using equation (2.13) in equation (2.9), we get

$$i\hbar \frac{\partial \psi\phi}{\partial t} = -\frac{\hbar^2}{2m}\frac{\partial^2 \psi\phi}{\partial x^2} + V\psi\phi$$

$$\therefore \qquad i\hbar\psi \frac{\partial \phi}{\partial t} = -\frac{\hbar^2}{2m}\phi\frac{\partial^2 \psi}{\partial x^2} + V\psi\phi$$

  Dividing above equation throughout by $\psi\phi$, we get

$$i\hbar \frac{1}{\phi}\frac{\partial \phi}{\partial t} = -\frac{\hbar^2}{2m}\frac{1}{\psi}\frac{\partial^2 \psi}{\partial x^2} + V \qquad \qquad ...(2.14)$$

- The right side of above equation is a function of x only and the left side is a function of t only. This is only possible when both sides are equal to some constant, say E.

- Therefore, we denote this constant as energy E because first term on RHS is kinetic energy and second term is potential energy. Therefore,

$$-\frac{\hbar^2}{2m}\frac{1}{\psi}\frac{\partial^2 \psi}{\partial x^2} + V = E \qquad \qquad ...(2.15)$$

and

$$i\hbar \frac{1}{\phi}\frac{\partial \phi}{\partial t} = E \qquad \qquad ...(2.16)$$

- From equations (2.15) and (2.16) it is observed that the constant E has dimensions of energy.

  Equation (2.15) can be written as

$$\frac{d^2\psi}{dx^2} + \frac{2m}{\hbar^2}(E - V)\psi = 0 \qquad \qquad ...(2.17)$$

- Equation (2.17) is called the **time-independent Schrödinger's equation**, because the time variable does not enter the equation.

- The solution $\psi(x)$ of equation (2.17) determines the space dependence of the solutions $\psi(x, t)$ to the Schrödinger's equation. In all cases the time-independent Schrödinger equation may not contain the imaginary number i, and, therefore, its solutions $\psi(x)$ not necessarily be complex.

- Since the differential equation does not involve time variable t, the solution ψ also does not depend upon time t. Hence the equation is called **steady-state equation**.

  In three dimensions, Schrödinger's time independent equation is

$$\frac{\partial^2\psi}{\partial x^2} + \frac{\partial^2\psi}{\partial y^2} + \frac{\partial^2\psi}{\partial z^2} + \frac{2m}{\hbar^2}(E - V)\psi = 0$$

or $\qquad \qquad \nabla^2\psi + \frac{2m}{\hbar^2}(E - V)\psi = 0 \qquad \qquad ...(2.18)$

where $\quad \psi = \psi(x, y, z) \quad$ and $\quad \nabla^2\psi = \frac{\partial^2\psi}{\partial x^2} + \frac{\partial^2\psi}{\partial y^2} + \frac{\partial^2\psi}{\partial z^2}$

Solution of time part equation :

Equation (2.16) can be written as

$$\frac{1}{\phi}\frac{\partial\phi}{\partial t} = \frac{1}{i\hbar}E$$

or $\qquad \qquad \frac{1}{\phi}\frac{d\phi}{dt} = -\frac{i}{\hbar}E$

$\therefore \qquad \qquad \frac{d\phi}{\phi} = -\frac{i}{\hbar}Edt$

On integration, we get $\qquad ln(\phi) = -\frac{i}{\hbar}Et$

$\therefore \qquad \qquad \phi = e^{-\frac{iE}{\hbar}t}$

Thus, we can write $\qquad \psi(x, t) = \psi(x)\, e^{-\frac{iE}{\hbar}t} \qquad \qquad ...(2.19)$

The functions $\psi(x)$ are called **eigen functions**.

- In three dimensions, the wave function is given by

$$\psi(x, y, z, t) = \psi(x, y, z)\, e^{-\frac{iE}{\hbar}t}$$

- The student should keep clearly in mind the difference between Schrödinger's equation and time-independent Schrödinger's equation, and also the difference between eigen function $\psi(x)$ and the wave function $\psi(x, t)$. Wave function is always represented by a capital letter ψ, and the eigen function by small letter ψ. Eigen function $\psi(x)$ is a solution of time-independent Schrödinger's equation, while $\psi(x, t)$ is a solution of Schrödinger's equation itself and is given by equation (2.19).

2.4 Requirements of Wave Function

- To be an acceptable solution of Schrödinger's time-independent equation, the wave function $\psi(x)$ and its first order derivative $d\psi/dx$ should satisfy certain requirements. These requirements are :

    1. $\psi(x)$ must be continuous everywhere. i.e. at each and every point on space.
    2. $\psi(x)$ must be finite everywhere.
    3. $\psi(x)$ must be single valued everywhere.
    4. Similarly, the first order derivative must be continuous, finite and single valued everywhere.

- In order to ensure that the wave function must be mathematically 'well behaved' above requirements are imposed on the wave function. Fig. 2.1 illustrates the meaning of the properties of wave functions. If $\psi(x)$ and $d\psi/dx$ are not finite and single valued, then the wave function $\psi(x, t) = \psi(x)\ e^{-iEt/\hbar}$ and its derivative $\dfrac{d\psi\,(x,\,t)}{dx} = e^{-iEt/\hbar}\ \dfrac{d\psi\,(x)}{dx}$ will not be continuous and single valued. The general formula of calculation of expectation values of x and p contain either $\psi\,(x,\,t)$ or $\dfrac{d\psi\,(x,\,t)}{dx}$. Therefore, in any of these cases we might not obtain finite and definite values of the measurable quantity. This is completely unacceptable because the measurable quantities like $<x>$ and $<p>$ do not behave in unreasonable way.

- In order that $d\psi/dx$ be finite, the wave function must be continuous. If the wave function $\psi(x)$ is discontinuous, the first order derivative $d\psi/dx$ will be infinite at the discontinuity and the second order derivative will also be infinite. We have Schrödinger's time-independent equation

$$\frac{d^2\psi}{dx^2} + \frac{2m}{\hbar^2}\,(E - V)\,\psi = 0$$

- For finite values of E, V and $\psi\,(x)$, the second order derivative $\dfrac{d^2\psi}{dx^2}$ must be finite. This requires that $d\psi/dx$ must be finite and hence the wave function should be continuous.

- Thus it is necessary that the wave function must be mathematically 'well behaved' and satisfies the above requirements. In Fig. 2.1 the wave functions in (a), (b), (c) and (d) are not acceptable. The wave function in (e) is well behaved and hence acceptable.

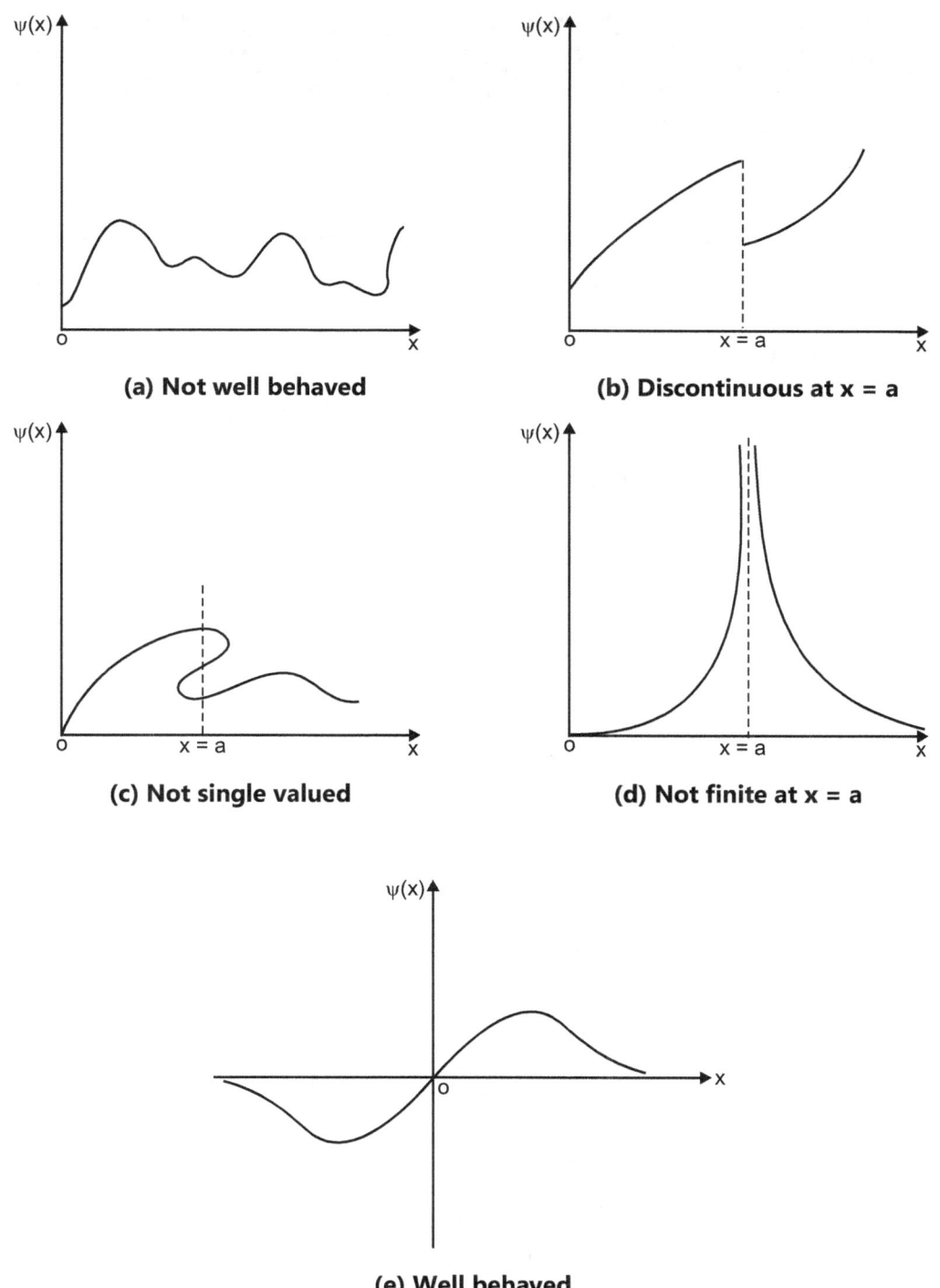

(a) Not well behaved

(b) Discontinuous at x = a

(c) Not single valued

(d) Not finite at x = a

(e) Well behaved

Fig. 2.1 : Different types of wave functions

2.5 Probability Current Density, Equation of Continuity and its Physical Significances

- Physical interpretation of wave function says that it is a measure of probability of finding a particle in a certain region of space.

- The probability density is given as $\rho = \psi\psi^*$, where ψ^* is complex conjugate of ψ. Since the particle is certainly to be found somewhere in space the total probability must be equal to unity $i.e.$ $\int_\tau \psi\psi^* d\tau = 1$, where $d\tau$ is volume element. In other words, the wave function must be normalised to unity.

- Now this statement must be true for all the time, since the particle will be certainly found somewhere in a whole region of space.

- Therefore, total probability must be conserved $i.e.$ $\psi\psi^*$ must be independent of time. This gives

$$\frac{\partial}{\partial t}\left(\int \psi\psi^* d\tau\right) = 0$$

or

$$\int \frac{\partial}{\partial t}(\psi\psi^*)d\tau = 0 \qquad \qquad ...(2.20)$$

We can write,

$$\frac{\partial}{\partial t}\left(\int \psi\psi^* d\tau\right) = \int \frac{\partial}{\partial t}(\psi\psi^*)d\tau$$

or

$$\int \frac{\partial}{\partial t}(\psi\psi^*)d\tau = \int\left[\psi^*\frac{\partial\psi}{\partial t} + \psi\frac{\partial\psi^*}{\partial t}\right]d\tau \qquad \qquad ...(2.21)$$

- We have Schrödinger's time dependent equation

$$i\hbar\frac{\partial\psi}{\partial t} = -\frac{\hbar^2}{2m}\nabla^2\psi + V\psi \qquad \qquad ...(2.22)$$

$$\therefore \qquad \frac{\partial\psi}{\partial t} = \frac{1}{i\hbar}\left(-\frac{\hbar^2}{2m}\nabla^2\psi + V\psi\right)$$

Complex conjugate of equation (2.22) is

$$-i\hbar\frac{\partial\psi^*}{\partial t} = -\frac{\hbar^2}{2m}\nabla^2\psi^* + V\psi^* \qquad \qquad ...(2.23)$$

$$\therefore \qquad \frac{\partial\psi^*}{\partial t} = -\frac{1}{i\hbar}\left(-\frac{\hbar^2}{2m}\nabla^2\psi^* + V\psi^*\right)$$

Using $\dfrac{\partial \psi^*}{\partial t}$ and $\dfrac{\partial \psi}{\partial t}$ in equation (2.21), we get

$$\int \frac{\partial}{\partial t}(\psi\psi^*)\,d\tau = \int \left[\psi^* \frac{\partial \psi}{\partial t} + \psi \frac{\partial \psi^*}{\partial t}\right] d\tau \quad \text{becomes}$$

$$= \int \left[\psi^* \frac{1}{i\hbar}\left(-\frac{\hbar^2}{2m}\nabla^2\psi + V\psi\right) - \psi \frac{1}{i\hbar}\left(-\frac{\hbar^2}{2m}\nabla^2\psi^* + V\psi^*\right)\right] d\tau$$

$$= \frac{1}{i\hbar}\int \left[\psi^*\left(-\frac{\hbar^2}{2m}\nabla^2\psi + V\psi\right) - \psi\left(-\frac{\hbar^2}{2m}\nabla^2\psi^* + V\psi^*\right)\right] d\tau$$

$$= \frac{1}{i\hbar}\int \left[-\frac{\hbar^2}{2m}[\psi^*\nabla^2\psi - \psi\nabla^2\psi^*] + V\psi\psi^* - V\psi^*\psi\right] d\tau$$

Since　　$V\psi^*\psi = V\psi\psi^*$, we get

$$\int \frac{\partial}{\partial t}(\psi\psi^*)\,d\tau = \frac{1}{i\hbar}\int \left[-\frac{\hbar^2}{2m}[\psi^*\nabla^2\psi - \psi\nabla^2\psi^*]\right] d\tau$$

$$\int \frac{\partial}{\partial t}(\psi\psi^*)\,d\tau = -\frac{\hbar}{2mi}\int_\tau [\psi^*\nabla^2\psi - \psi\nabla^2\psi^*]\,d\tau \qquad \text{...(2.24)}$$

Using Green's theorem, the volume integral can be converted into surface integral. Therefore,

$$\int_\tau [\psi^*\nabla^2\psi - \psi\nabla^2\psi^*]\,d\tau = \int_S [\psi^*\nabla\psi - \psi\nabla\psi^*]\cdot\overrightarrow{dS}$$

With this equation (2.24) becomes

$$\int \frac{\partial}{\partial t}(\psi\psi^*)\,d\tau = -\frac{\hbar}{2mi}\int_S [\psi^*\nabla\psi - \psi\nabla\psi^*]\cdot\overrightarrow{dS}$$

or

$$\int \frac{\partial}{\partial t}(\psi\psi^*)\,d\tau = -\int_S \frac{\hbar}{2mi}[\psi^*\nabla\psi - \psi\nabla\psi^*]\cdot\overrightarrow{dS}$$

Let

$$\overrightarrow{J} = \frac{\hbar}{2mi}[\psi^*\nabla\psi - \psi\nabla\psi^*] \qquad \text{...(2.25)}$$

$\therefore$

$$\frac{\partial}{\partial t}\left(\int \psi\psi^*\,d\tau\right) = -\int_S \overrightarrow{J}\cdot\overrightarrow{dS}$$

$\therefore$

$$\int \frac{\partial \rho}{\partial t}\,d\tau = -\int_S \overrightarrow{J}\cdot\overrightarrow{dS} \qquad \text{...(2.26)}$$

According to Gauss divergence theorem, $\int_S \vec{J} \cdot \vec{dS} = \int_\tau \nabla \cdot \vec{J} \, d\tau$

Using in equation (2.26), we get

$$\int \frac{\partial \rho}{\partial t} \, d\tau = - \int_\tau \nabla \cdot \vec{J} \, d\tau$$

$\therefore$

$$\int_\tau \left(\nabla \cdot \vec{J} + \frac{\partial \rho}{\partial t} \right) d\tau = 0$$

This is true for any arbitrary volume, therefore,

$$\nabla \cdot \vec{J} + \frac{\partial \rho}{\partial t} = 0 \qquad \qquad ...(2.27)$$

- Equation (2.27) is called *equation of continuity*. This is same as the equation of continuity in fluid mechanics. We have

$$\vec{J} = \frac{\hbar}{2mi} \, [\psi^* \nabla \psi - \psi \nabla \psi^*]$$

$\vec{J}$ **is called probability current densit**y.

It can also be written as

$$\vec{J} = \text{Re} \left[\psi^* \frac{\hbar}{im} \nabla \psi \right]$$

Here Re stands for real part of the quantity inside the bracket.

Physical significance of equation of continuity

(i) Equation (2.26) may be written as

$$\nabla \cdot \vec{J} = - \frac{\partial \rho}{\partial t}$$

- If $\frac{\partial \rho}{\partial t}$ is positive, $\nabla \cdot \vec{J}$ is negative, then there is net inward flow of the probability current and there is increase in total probability inside a given region. If there is increase in probabilty density in a given volume, there is decrease in density somewhere else.

- If $\frac{\partial \rho}{\partial t}$ is negative, $\nabla \cdot \vec{J}$ is positive, then there is net outward flow of the probability current and there is decrease in total probability in a given region. If there is decrease in probability density in a given volume, there is increase in density somewhere else.

- If for any states ρ is independent of time, then $\frac{\partial \rho}{\partial t} = 0$. Thus, $\nabla \cdot \vec{J} = 0$. These states are called stationary states.

2.6 Definition of an Operator in Quantum Mechanics

- The mathematical operations like differentiation, integration, multiplication, division, addition, subtraction etc. can be represented by certain symbols known as operators.

  In other words, an operator $\hat{O}$ is a mathematical operation which may be applied to function $f(x)$, which changes the function $f(x)$ to another function $g(x)$. This can be represented as

$$\hat{O} f(x) = g(x)$$

For example, $\qquad \dfrac{d}{dx} (4x^2 + 2x) = 8x + 2$

- In operator language $\hat{O} = \dfrac{d}{dx}$ operates on the function $f(x) = 4x^2 + 2x$ and changes the function $f(x)$ to function $g(x) = 8x + 2$.

Operators in Quantum mechanics

The wave function is given as

$$\psi(x,t) = Ae^{\frac{i}{\hbar}(px - Et)}$$

Differentiating equation (2.2) with respect to x, we get

$$\frac{\partial \psi}{\partial x} = \frac{ip}{\hbar} Ae^{\frac{i}{\hbar}(px - Et)}$$

or $\qquad\qquad \dfrac{\partial \psi}{\partial x} = \dfrac{ip}{\hbar} \psi$

$\therefore \qquad\qquad p\psi = \dfrac{\hbar}{i} \dfrac{\partial \psi}{\partial x}$

or $\qquad\qquad p\psi = -i\hbar \dfrac{\partial \psi}{\partial x}$ $\qquad\qquad$ ...(2.28)

Differentiating $\psi(x, t)$ with respect to t, we get

$$\frac{\partial \psi}{\partial t} = -\frac{iE}{\hbar} Ae^{\frac{i}{\hbar}(px - Et)}$$

or $\qquad\qquad \dfrac{\partial \psi}{\partial t} = -\dfrac{iE}{\hbar} \psi$

$\therefore \qquad\qquad -\dfrac{\hbar}{i} \dfrac{\partial \psi}{\partial t} = E\psi$

or $\qquad\qquad E\psi = i\hbar \dfrac{\partial \psi}{\partial t}$ $\qquad\qquad$ ...(2.29)

- Equation (2.28) indicates that there is an association between the dynamical quantity p and the differential operator $-i\hbar \dfrac{\partial}{\partial x}$. That is the effect of multiplying $\psi(x, t)$ by p is same as the operating the differential operator $-i\hbar\dfrac{\partial}{\partial x}$ on $\psi(x, t)$. This differential operator is called *momentum operator*. It can be written as

$$\hat{p} = -i\hbar\dfrac{\partial}{\partial x} \qquad \qquad ...(2.30)$$

As it is related to variable x, therefore, we have

$$\hat{p}_x = -i\hbar\dfrac{\partial}{\partial x}$$

Corresponding components of momentum operators for y and z variables are

$$\hat{p}_y = -i\hbar\dfrac{\partial}{\partial y}$$

and

$$\hat{p}_z = -i\hbar\dfrac{\partial}{\partial z}$$

In three dimensions, the momentum operator is

$$\hat{p} = -i\hbar\nabla$$

- From equation (2.29), a similar association can be found between dynamical variable E and the differential operator $i\hbar\dfrac{\partial}{\partial t}$. Thus,

$$E = i\hbar\dfrac{\partial}{\partial t} \qquad \qquad ...(2.31)$$

We have Schrödinger's time independent equation

$$\nabla^2\psi + \dfrac{2m}{\hbar^2}(E - V)\psi = 0$$

or

$$-\dfrac{\hbar^2}{2m}\nabla^2\psi + V\psi = E\psi$$

or

$$\left[-\dfrac{\hbar^2}{2m}\nabla^2 + V\right]\psi = E\psi \qquad \qquad ...(2.32)$$

or

$$H\psi = E\psi$$

where $H = -\dfrac{\hbar^2}{2m}\nabla^2 + V$ is the differential operator and called as **Hamiltonian operator.**

EIGEN FUNCTION AND EIGEN VALUE

- Let ψ be the well behaved function of the state of the system and an operator $\hat{A}$ operates on this function such that it satisfies the equation

$$\hat{A}\,\psi(x) = a\,\psi(x) \qquad \qquad ...(2.33)$$

where a is a number then we say that a is an eigen value of the operator $\hat{A}$ and the operand $\psi(x)$ is called the eigen function of $\hat{A}$. Eigen is the German word meaning characteristic or proper.

- An operator is a rule which changes a function into another function. For example, when operator $\frac{d}{dx}$ operates on a function i.e.

$$f(x) = x^n$$

$$\frac{df}{dx} = n\,x^{n-1}$$

- Another example is, $\quad \frac{d^2}{dx^2}\,e^{4x} = 16\,e^{4x}$

- We say that $\frac{d^2}{dx^2}$ is the operator operating on function e^{4x} giving result $16e^{4x}$. The operand e^{4x} is called eigen function of operator $\frac{d^2}{dx^2}$ and 16 is the eigen value.

The total energy operator E of equation (2.31) is usually written as

$$E = -\frac{\hbar^2}{2m}\,\nabla^2 + V$$

and is called Hamiltonian operator. If the Hamiltonian operator $H = -\frac{\hbar^2}{2m}\,\nabla^2 + V$ operates on a wave function ψ_n, we get

$$\left[-\frac{\hbar^2}{2m}\,\nabla^2 + V\right]\psi_n = E_n\,\psi_n$$

or $\qquad\qquad\qquad\qquad H\,\psi_n = E_n\,\psi_n$

- The wave function ψ_n is called eigen function and E_n is called energy eigen value of the Hamiltonian operator H for a state of the system.

2.7 Expectation Values

- Consider a wave function $\psi(x, t)$ associated with a particle. In measurement of position of a particle in a system described by wave function, there is certain finite probability that a particle be found at any co-ordinate x within the range x and $x + dx$ as long as the wave function is not zero in this range. Generally wave function is non-zero over the extended range of x-axis. Thus, in general, we are not able to state that x co-ordinate has definite value.

- We, therefore, calculate average position of the particle. If $P(x, t)\,dx = \psi(x, t)\,\psi^*(x, t)\,dx$ be the probability of finding the particle in a range x and $x + dx$. Then the expectation value of x over whole the range is given by

$$<x> = \frac{\int x P(x, t)dx}{\int P(x, t)dx}$$

or $\qquad\qquad\qquad\qquad <x> = \frac{\int \psi^* x \psi\,dx}{\int \psi^* \psi\,dx} \qquad\qquad\qquad ...(2.34)$

- If the wave function is normalised, we have $\int \psi^*\psi dx = 1$ for whole region, then

$$<x> = \int \psi^* x \psi dx \qquad \qquad ...(2.35)$$

- Thus, in general, the expectation value of any dynamical variable f obtained by wave function $\psi(x, t)$ is given as

$$<f> = \frac{\int \psi^* f\, \psi dx}{\int \psi^* \psi dx}$$

For normalised wave function,

$$<f> = \int \psi^* f\, \psi dx$$

- The expectation value of momentum and energy cannot be found in the same way. The expectation value of p and E corresponding operators are used in integrand. Thus,

$$<p> = \int \psi^* \,\hat{p}\, \psi dx = \int \psi^* \left(-i\hbar \frac{\partial}{\partial x} \right) \psi dx$$

$$\therefore \qquad <p> = -i\hbar \int \psi^* \frac{\partial \psi}{\partial x}\, dx \qquad \qquad ...(2.36)$$

Similarly,

$$<E> = \int \psi^* \left(i\hbar \frac{\partial}{\partial t} \right) \psi dx$$

or

$$<E> = i\hbar \int \psi^* \frac{\partial \psi}{\partial t}\, dx \qquad \qquad ...(2.37)$$

- Thus, if the dynamical variable is expressed in terms of its operator, the expectation value is obtained by using the corresponding operator.

2.8 Ehrenfest's Theorem

- We know that a particle's momentum is equal to its mass times group velocity of a wave packet of a particular type that is associated with it. But this type of treatment is not adequate to the general case, in which the shape and size of wave packet changes as the packet moves.

Then the question arises how the $<x>$ and $<p_x>$ behave as wave packet moves, that is, what is $\frac{d<x>}{dt}$? This difficulty was solved by Ehrenfest.

- According to him Newton's laws of motion in classical physics of the form like

$$m\frac{dx}{dt} = p \quad \text{and} \quad \frac{dp}{dt} = -\frac{dV}{dx}$$

are still valid in quantum mechanics provided that we use the expectation values of the dynamical variables. This is Ehrenfest's theorem.

- **In other words, the theorem states that the average motion of wave packet agrees with the motion of the corresponding classical motion of particle.**

  Ehrenfest's theorems are
  1. First theorem :

  $$m\frac{d<x>}{dt} = <p_x>$$

  For all components,

  $$m\frac{d<\vec{r}>}{dt} = <\vec{p}>$$

  2. Second theorem : For conservative force field,

  $$\frac{d<p_x>}{dt} = \left\langle -\frac{dV}{dx}\right\rangle$$

  For all components,

  $$\frac{d<\vec{p}>}{dt} = <-\nabla V>$$

Proof of first theorem :

The expectation value of x is given as

$$<x> = \int \psi^* x \psi d\tau$$

$$\therefore \quad \frac{d<x>}{dt} = \int\left(\frac{d\psi^*}{dt} x \psi + \psi^* x \frac{d\psi}{dt}\right)d\tau \qquad \qquad ...(2.38)$$

We have Schrödinger's time dependent equation

$$i\hbar\frac{\partial \psi}{\partial t} = -\frac{\hbar^2}{2m}\nabla^2\psi + V\psi$$

$$\therefore \quad \frac{\partial \psi}{\partial t} = \frac{1}{i\hbar}\left(-\frac{\hbar^2}{2m}\nabla^2\psi + V\psi\right)$$

Complex conjugate of above equation is

$$\frac{\partial \psi^*}{\partial t} = -\frac{1}{i\hbar}\left(-\frac{\hbar^2}{2m}\nabla^2\psi^* + V\psi^*\right)$$

Using $\dfrac{\partial \psi^*}{\partial t}$ and $\dfrac{\partial \psi}{\partial t}$ in equation (2.38), we get

$$\frac{d<x>}{dt} = \int\left[\left(-\frac{1}{i\hbar}\left(-\frac{\hbar^2}{2m}\nabla^2\psi^* + V\psi^*\right)\right) x \psi + \psi^* x \left(\frac{1}{i\hbar}\left(-\frac{\hbar^2}{2m}\nabla^2\psi^* + V\psi^*\right)\right)\right]d\tau$$

$$= \frac{\hbar}{2mi}\int_\tau\left[(\nabla^2\psi^*) x \psi - \psi^* x (\nabla^2\psi)\right]d\tau$$

$$= \frac{\hbar}{2mi}\left[\int_\tau(\nabla^2\psi^*) x \psi d\tau - \int_\tau \psi^* x (\nabla^2\psi)d\tau\right] \qquad \qquad ...(2.39)$$

Green's second theorem is given as

$$\int_\tau [\psi_1(\nabla^2\psi_2) - \psi_2(\nabla^2\psi_1)]\, d\tau = \int_S [\psi_1\nabla\psi_2 - \psi_2\nabla\psi_1] \cdot \vec{dS}$$

where S is the surface which encloses the volume τ.

Let $\psi_1 = \psi^*$ and $\psi_2 = x\,\psi$

Then using the above theorem, we get

$$\int_\tau [\psi^*\nabla^2(x\psi) - (x\psi)\nabla^2\psi^*]\, d\tau = \int_S [\psi^*\nabla(x\psi) - (x\psi)\nabla\psi^*] \cdot \vec{dS} \qquad ...(2.40)$$

- Since the volume integral is over the entire space, the surface 'S' which encloses the entire volume will be at infinity. But $\psi \to 0$ and $\nabla\psi \to 0$ at infinity. Hence the surface integral in the above case vanishes at infinity. Therefore, from equation (2.40), we get

$$\int_\tau [\psi^*\nabla^2(x\psi) - (x\psi)\nabla^2\psi^*]\, d\tau = 0$$

or $$\int_\tau \psi^*\nabla^2(x\psi)\, d\tau - \int_\tau (x\psi)\nabla^2\psi^*\, d\tau = 0$$

This gives $$\int_\tau (x\psi)\nabla^2\psi^*\, d\tau = \int_\tau \psi^*\nabla^2(x\psi)\, d\tau \qquad ...(2.41)$$

Using equation (2.41) in first term on RHS of equation (2.39), we get

$$\frac{d\langle x\rangle}{dt} = \frac{\hbar}{2mi}\left[\int_\tau \psi^*\nabla^2(x\psi)d\tau - \int_\tau \psi^*\, x\,(\nabla^2\psi)\, d\tau \right]$$

$$\frac{d\langle x\rangle}{dt} = -\frac{i\hbar}{2m}\left[\int_\tau \psi^*\nabla^2(x\psi)d\tau - \int_\tau \psi^*\, x\,(\nabla^2\psi)\, d\tau \right] \qquad ...(2.42)$$

Now consider the term $\nabla^2(x\psi)$.

We have $$\nabla^2(x\psi) = \frac{\partial^2(x\psi)}{\partial x^2} + \frac{\partial^2(x\psi)}{\partial y^2} + \frac{\partial^2(x\psi)}{\partial z^2}$$

$$= \frac{\partial}{\partial x}\frac{\partial(x\psi)}{\partial x} + \frac{\partial^2(x\psi)}{\partial y^2} + \frac{\partial^2(x\psi)}{\partial z^2}$$

$$= \frac{\partial}{\partial x}\left(\psi + x\frac{\partial\psi}{\partial x}\right) + x\frac{\partial^2\psi}{\partial y^2} + x\frac{\partial^2\psi}{\partial z^2}$$

$$= \frac{\partial\psi}{\partial x} + \frac{\partial\psi}{\partial x} + x\frac{\partial^2\psi}{\partial x^2} + x\frac{\partial^2\psi}{\partial y^2} + x\frac{\partial^2\psi}{\partial z^2}$$

$$= 2\frac{\partial\psi}{\partial x} + x\left(\frac{\partial^2\psi}{\partial x^2} + \frac{\partial^2\psi}{\partial y^2} + \frac{\partial^2\psi}{\partial z^2}\right)$$

$$\therefore \qquad \nabla^2(x\psi) = 2\frac{\partial\psi}{\partial x} + x\nabla^2\psi \qquad ...(2.43)$$

Using equation (2.43) in equation (2.42), we get

$$\frac{d<x>}{dt} = -\frac{i\hbar}{2m}\left[\int_\tau \psi^*\left(2\frac{\partial \psi}{\partial x} + x\nabla^2\psi \right)d\tau - \int_\tau \psi^* x (\nabla^2\psi)\, d\tau \right]$$

$$= -\frac{i\hbar}{2m}\left[\int_\tau \psi^*\left(2\frac{\partial \psi}{\partial x} \right) + \int_\tau \psi^* x\nabla^2\psi\, d\tau - \int_\tau \psi^* x (\nabla^2\psi)\, d\tau \right]$$

$$= -\frac{i\hbar}{2m} \int_\tau \psi^*\left(2\frac{\partial \psi}{\partial x} \right)d\tau$$

$$= -\frac{i\hbar}{m} \int_\tau \psi^*\left(\frac{\partial \psi}{\partial x} \right)d\tau$$

$$\therefore \quad \frac{d<x>}{dt} = \frac{1}{m}\left(-i\hbar \int_\tau \psi^*\left(\frac{\partial \psi}{\partial x} \right)d\tau \right)$$

But from equation (2.36), $<p_x> = -i\hbar \int \psi^* \frac{\partial \psi}{\partial x}\, dx$

$$\therefore \qquad \frac{d<x>}{dt} = \frac{<p_x>}{m} \qquad\qquad\qquad ...(2.44)$$

• This is the required result, which gives the validity of the classical connection between position and velocity on the average, even though they both cannot be known exactly simultaneously.

Proof of second theorem :

We have expectation value of momentum

$$<p_x> = -i\hbar \int \psi^* \frac{\partial \psi}{\partial x}\, d\tau$$

Differentiating with respect to t, we get

$$\frac{d<p_x>}{dt} = -i\hbar \frac{\partial}{\partial t} \int \psi^* \frac{\partial \psi}{\partial x}\, d\tau$$

$$= -i\hbar \int \left(\frac{\partial \psi^*}{\partial t}\frac{\partial \psi}{\partial x} + \psi^*\frac{\partial}{\partial t}\frac{\partial \psi}{\partial x} \right)d\tau$$

$$= -i\hbar \int \left(\frac{\partial \psi^*}{\partial t}\frac{\partial \psi}{\partial x} + \psi^*\frac{\partial}{\partial x}\frac{\partial \psi}{\partial t} \right)d\tau$$

$\therefore$

$$\frac{d< p_x>}{dt} = \int_\tau \left[\left(-i\hbar \frac{\partial \psi^*}{\partial t} \right) \frac{\partial \psi}{\partial x} - \psi^* \frac{\partial}{\partial x} \left(i\hbar \frac{\partial \psi}{\partial t} \right) \right] d\tau \qquad ...(2.45)$$

We have Schrödinger's time dependent equation.

$$i\hbar \frac{\partial \psi}{\partial t} = -\frac{\hbar^2}{2m} \nabla^2 \psi + V\psi$$

Complex conjugate of above equation is

$$-i\hbar \frac{\partial \psi^*}{\partial t} = -\frac{\hbar^2}{2m} \nabla^2 \psi^* + V\psi^*$$

Using above two equations in equation (2.44), we get

$$\frac{d< p_x>}{dt} = \int_\tau \left[\left(-\frac{\hbar^2}{2m} \nabla^2 \psi^* + V\psi^* \right) \frac{\partial \psi}{\partial x} - \psi^* \frac{\partial}{\partial x} \left(-\frac{\hbar^2}{2m} \nabla^2 \psi + V\psi \right) \right] d\tau$$

$$= \int_\tau \left[-\frac{\hbar^2}{2m} \nabla^2 \psi^* \frac{\partial \psi}{\partial x} + V\psi^* \frac{\partial \psi}{\partial x} + \frac{\hbar^2}{2m} \psi^* \frac{\partial}{\partial x} (\nabla^2 \psi) - \psi^* \frac{\partial V\psi}{\partial x} \right] d\tau$$

$$= \int_\tau \left[-\frac{\hbar^2}{2m} \nabla^2 \psi^* \frac{\partial \psi}{\partial x} + V\psi^* \frac{\partial \psi}{\partial x} + \frac{\hbar^2}{2m} \psi^* \nabla^2 \left(\frac{\partial \psi}{\partial x} \right) - \psi^* \frac{\partial V\psi}{\partial x} \right] d\tau$$

Rearranging the terms on RHS, we get

$$\frac{d< p_x>}{dt} = \frac{\hbar^2}{2m} \int_\tau \left[\psi^* \nabla^2 \left(\frac{\partial \psi}{\partial x} \right) - \nabla^2 \psi^* \frac{\partial \psi}{\partial x} \right] d\tau + \int_\tau \left[V\psi^* \frac{\partial \psi}{\partial x} - \psi^* \frac{\partial V\psi}{\partial x} \right] d\tau \qquad ...(2.46)$$

Consider the integral of the first term $\int_\tau \left[\psi^* \nabla^2 \left(\frac{\partial \psi}{\partial x} \right) - \nabla^2 \psi^* \frac{\partial \psi}{\partial x} \right] d\tau$. Using Green's

second theorem, we can convert this integral into surface integral i.e.

$$\int_\tau \left[\psi^* \nabla^2 \left(\frac{\partial \psi}{\partial x} \right) - \nabla^2 \psi^* \frac{\partial \psi}{\partial x} \right] d\tau = \int_S \left[\psi^* \nabla \left(\frac{\partial \psi}{\partial x} \right) - \nabla \psi^* \frac{\partial \psi}{\partial x} \right] \cdot \vec{dS} \qquad ... (2.47)$$

But the surface S encloses the entire volume. The surface is at infinity, but at infinity ψ and its first order derivative tends to zero. Therefore, the surface integral is zero. Thus, we get

$$\int_\tau \left[\psi^* \nabla^2 \left(\frac{\partial \psi}{\partial x} \right) - \nabla^2 \psi^* \frac{\partial \psi}{\partial x} \right] d\tau = 0 \qquad ... (2.48)$$

Using equation (2.48) in equation (2.46), we get

$$\frac{d<p_x>}{dt} = \int_\tau \left[V\psi^* \frac{\partial\psi}{\partial x} - \psi^* \frac{\partial V\psi}{\partial x} \right] d\tau$$

$$= \int_\tau \left[V\psi^* \frac{\partial\psi}{\partial x} - \psi^* \frac{\partial V}{\partial x} \psi - \psi^* V \frac{\partial\psi}{\partial x} \right] d\tau$$

$$= \int_\tau \left[-\psi^* \frac{\partial V}{\partial x} \psi \right] d\tau$$

$$\therefore \qquad \frac{d<p_x>}{dt} = \int_\tau \psi^* \left(-\frac{\partial V}{\partial x} \right) \psi d\tau$$

The R.H.S. of the above equation represents the expectation value of $-\dfrac{\partial V}{\partial x}$.

$$\therefore \qquad \frac{d<p_x>}{dt} = \left< -\frac{dV}{dx} \right>$$

This is the required result. Thus there exists a relation among expectation values which is exactly parallel to Newton's second law expressed in terms of potential energy.

Solved Problems

Problem 2.1 : *Find the eigen function and eigen values of operator* $\left(x + \dfrac{d}{dx} \right)$

Solution: The operator satisfies the equation

$$\left(x + \frac{d}{dx} \right) \psi(x) = a \, \psi(x)$$

$$x\psi(x) + \frac{d}{dx} \psi = a \, \psi(x)$$

$$\frac{d}{dx} \psi = (a - x) \, \psi(x)$$

Integrating $\log_e \psi = ax - \dfrac{x^2}{2} + \log_e C$ where C is constant of integration,

Thus $\psi = C \exp (ax - x^2/2)$

This function is finite and continuous for any value of a. Thus eigen values form a continuous spectrum.

Problem 2.2 : *Normalise the wave function*

$$\psi(x) = A \, e^{-x^2/2a^2 + ikx}$$

The range of x is from $-\infty$ *to* $+\infty$.

Solution : If A is the normalisation constant, then $\int \psi\psi^* \, dx = 1$

$\therefore \quad \int\limits_{-\infty}^{\infty} A\, e^{-x^2/2a^2 + ikx} \; A^*\, e^{-x^2/2a^2 - ikx} \, dx = 1$

or $\quad |A|^2 \int\limits_{-\infty}^{\infty} e^{-x^2/a^2} \, dx = 1$

We have the general integral $\int\limits_{-\infty}^{\infty} e^{-\beta x^2} \, dx = \sqrt{\dfrac{\pi}{\beta}}$

$\therefore \qquad\qquad |A|^2 \sqrt{\dfrac{\pi}{1/a^2}} = 1$

$\qquad\qquad\qquad |A|^2\, a\, \sqrt{\pi} = 1$

$\therefore \qquad\qquad\qquad |A| = \dfrac{1}{\sqrt{a}\ \pi^{1/4}}$

$\therefore \qquad\qquad \psi(x) = \dfrac{1}{\sqrt{a}\ \pi^{1/4}}\, e^{-x^2/2a^2 + ikx}$ is the normalised wave function

---

Problem 2.3 : *A wave function of the free particle in the range* $-\infty$ *to* $+\infty$ *is given by*

$$\psi(x) = e^{-\alpha x^2/2}$$

Normalise the wave function and find the expectation value of x and p_x.

Solution : In order to normalise the wave function, multiply R.H.S. by constant A.

$\therefore \qquad\qquad\qquad \psi(x) = A\, e^{-\alpha x^2/2}$

Condition for normalisation is

$$\int |\psi|^2 \, dx = 1 \quad \text{or} \quad \int \psi\psi^* \, dx = 1$$

$\therefore \qquad \int\limits_{-\infty}^{\infty} A\, e^{-\alpha x^2/2} \; A^*\, e^{-\alpha x^2/2} \, dx = 1$

$\therefore \qquad\qquad AA^* \int\limits_{-\infty}^{\infty} e^{-\alpha x^2} \, dx = 1$

or $\qquad |A|^2 \int\limits_{-\infty}^{\infty} e^{-\alpha x^2} \, dx = 1$

We have the general integral $\int\limits_{-\infty}^{\infty} e^{-\beta x^2} dx = \sqrt{\dfrac{\pi}{\beta}}$

$\therefore$　　　　$|A|^2 \sqrt{\dfrac{\pi}{\alpha}} = 1$

$\therefore$　　　　$|A|^2 = \sqrt{\dfrac{\alpha}{\pi}}$

or　　　　$A = \left(\dfrac{\alpha}{\pi}\right)^{1/4}$

$\therefore$　　　　$\psi(x) = \left(\dfrac{\alpha}{\pi}\right)^{1/4} e^{-\alpha x^2/2}$

Expectation value of x is given as

$$<x> = \int\limits_{-\infty}^{\infty} x\,|\psi|^2\, dx \qquad \text{or} \quad <x> = \int\limits_{-\infty}^{\infty} \psi\, x\, \psi^*\, dx$$

$\therefore$ $<x> = \int\limits_{-\infty}^{\infty} x \left(\dfrac{\alpha}{\pi}\right)^{1/4} e^{-\alpha x^2/2} \left(\dfrac{\alpha}{\pi}\right)^{1/4} e^{-\alpha x^2/2}\, dx = \left(\dfrac{\alpha}{\pi}\right)^{1/2} \int\limits_{-\infty}^{\infty} x\, e^{-\alpha x^2}\, dx$

The integral on R.H.S. is odd integral and its value is zero.

$\therefore$　　　　　　　　$<x> = 0$

The expectation value of $<p_x>$ is given as

$$<p_x> = -i\hbar \int\limits_{-\infty}^{\infty} \psi^* \dfrac{\partial \psi}{\partial x}\, dx = -i\hbar \int\limits_{-\infty}^{\infty} \left(\dfrac{\alpha}{\pi}\right)^{1/4} e^{-\alpha x^2/2} \dfrac{\partial}{\partial x}\left(\left(\dfrac{\alpha}{\pi}\right)^{1/4} e^{-\alpha x^2/2}\right) dx$$

$$= -i\hbar \left(\dfrac{\alpha}{\pi}\right)^{1/2} \int\limits_{-\infty}^{\infty} e^{-\alpha x^2/2} \dfrac{\partial}{\partial x}\left(e^{-\alpha x^2/2}\right) dx$$

$$= -i\hbar \left(\dfrac{\alpha}{\pi}\right)^{1/2} \int\limits_{-\infty}^{\infty} e^{-\alpha x^2/2} (-\alpha x) e^{-\alpha x^2/2}\, dx$$

$$= i\hbar\, \alpha \left(\dfrac{\alpha}{\pi}\right)^{1/2} \int\limits_{-\infty}^{\infty} x\, e^{-\alpha x^2}\, dx$$

The integral on R.H.S. is odd integral and its value is zero.

$\therefore$　　　　$<p_x> = 0$

Problem 2.4 : *Normalise the wave function* $\psi(x) = \dfrac{1 + ix}{1 + ix^2}$. *The range of x is from* $-\infty$ *to* $+\infty$.

Solution : Let $\psi(x) = A\,\dfrac{1 + ix}{1 + ix^2}$, where A is the normalisation constant.

$$\therefore \qquad \psi^*\psi = A^*\,\frac{1 - ix}{1 - ix^2}\,A\,\frac{1 + ix}{1 + ix^2} = |A|^2\,\frac{1 + x^2}{1 + x^4}$$

Condition for normalisation is

$$\int |\psi|^2\, dx = 1 \quad \text{or} \quad \int \psi\psi^*\, dx = 1$$

$$\therefore \qquad |A|^2 \int\limits_{-\infty}^{\infty} \frac{1 + x^2}{1 + x^4}\, dx = 1$$

Consider the integral $\displaystyle\int\limits_{-\infty}^{\infty} \frac{1 + x^2}{1 + x^4}\, dx = \int\limits_{-\infty}^{\infty} \frac{1 + 1/x^2}{x^2 + 1/x^2}\, dx$

Let $x - \dfrac{1}{x} = t$

Squaring on both sides, we get

$$x^2 - 2 + \frac{1}{x^2} = t^2$$

$$\therefore \qquad x^2 + \frac{1}{x^2} = t^2 + 2$$

and $\qquad\qquad dt = \left(1 + \dfrac{1}{x^2}\right) dx$

Using these in above integral, we get

$$\int\limits_{-\infty}^{\infty} \frac{1 + x^2}{1 + x^4}\, dx = \int\limits_{-\infty}^{\infty} \frac{1}{t^2 + 2}\, dt$$

Range of t is also from $-\infty$ to ∞ as when $x \to \infty$, $t \to \infty$.

$$\therefore \qquad |A|^2 \int\limits_{-\infty}^{\infty} \frac{1}{t^2 + 2}\, dt = 1$$

$$\therefore \qquad |A|^2 \left[\frac{1}{\sqrt{2}} \tan^{-1}\left(\frac{t}{\sqrt{2}}\right) \right]_{-\infty}^{\infty} = 1$$

$$|A|^2 \frac{1}{\sqrt{2}} \left[\frac{\pi}{2} - \left(-\frac{\pi}{2} \right) \right] = 1$$

$$|A|^2 \frac{\pi}{\sqrt{2}} = 1$$

∴ $$A = \left(\frac{\sqrt{2}}{\pi} \right)^{1/2}$$

∴ $$\psi(x) = \left(\frac{\sqrt{2}}{\pi} \right)^{1/2} \frac{1 + ix}{1 + ix^2}$$

Problem 2.5 : *A wave function of the free particle in the range* $-\infty$ *to* $+\infty$ *is given by*

$$\psi(x) = x\,e^{-\alpha x^2}$$

Normalise the wave function.

Solution : In order to normalise the wave function, multiply the R.H.S. by constant A.

∴ $$\psi(x) = A\,x\,e^{-\alpha x^2}$$

Condition for normalisation is

$$\int |\psi|^2 \, dx = 1 \quad \text{or} \quad \int \psi\psi^* \, dx = 1$$

∴ $$\int_{-\infty}^{\infty} A\,x\,e^{-\alpha x^2}\, A^*\,x\,e^{-\alpha x^2} \, dx = 1$$

∴ $$AA^* \int_{-\infty}^{\infty} x^2\, e^{-2\alpha x^2} \, dx = 1$$

or $$|A|^2 \int_{-\infty}^{\infty} x^2\, e^{-2\alpha x^2} \, dx = 1$$

We have the general integral $$\int_{-\infty}^{\infty} x^2\, e^{-\beta x^2} \, dx = \frac{1}{2\beta}\sqrt{\frac{\pi}{\beta}}$$

Thus, $$\int_{-\infty}^{\infty} x^2\, e^{-\alpha x^2} \, dx = \frac{1}{2(2\alpha)}\sqrt{\frac{\pi}{(2\alpha)}}$$

∴ $$|A|^2 = 1$$

∴ $$|A|^2 = 4\alpha\sqrt{\frac{2\alpha}{\pi}}$$

or $$A = 2\left(\frac{2\alpha^3}{\pi} \right)^{1/4}$$

∴ $$\psi(x) = 2\left(\frac{2\alpha^3}{\pi} \right)^{1/4} x\,e^{-\alpha x^2/2}$$

Problem 2.6 : *Find the expectation value of momentum and position for a particle having wave function*

$$\psi(x,\ t)\ =\ A\ e^{-x^2/2a\ +\ ikx}$$

The range of x is from $-\infty$ to $+\infty$.

Solution : If A is the normalisation constant, then $\int \psi\psi^* \, dx\ =\ 1$

$$\therefore \quad \int_{-\infty}^{\infty} A\ e^{-x^2/2a\ +\ ikx}\ A^*\ e^{-x^2/2a\ -\ ikx}\ dx\ =\ 1$$

or $\qquad |A|^2 \int_{-\infty}^{\infty} e^{-x^2/a}\ dx\ =\ 1 \qquad\qquad\qquad …(i)$

Expectation value of $<x>$ is given as

$$<x>\ =\ \int_{-\infty}^{\infty} \psi\ x\ \psi^*\ dx$$

$$=\ |A|^2 \int_{-\infty}^{\infty} x\ e^{-x^2/a}\ dx$$

But the integral on R.H.S. is an odd integral, therefore, it is zero.

$\therefore \qquad\qquad\qquad\qquad <x>\ =\ 0$

The expectation value of $<p_x>$ is given as

$$<p_x>\ =\ -\ i\hbar\ \int_{-\infty}^{\infty} \psi^*\ \frac{\partial \psi}{\partial x}\ dx$$

$$=\ -\ i\hbar\ \int_{-\infty}^{\infty} A^*\ e^{-x^2/2a\ -\ ikx}\ \frac{\partial}{\partial x}\left(A\ e^{-x^2/2a\ +\ ikx}\right)\ dx$$

$$=\ -\ i\hbar\ |A|^2 \int_{-\infty}^{\infty} e^{-x^2/2a\ -\ ikx}\ \frac{\partial}{\partial x}\left(e^{-x^2/2a\ +\ ikx}\right)\ dx$$

$$=\ -\ i\hbar\ |A|^2 \int_{-\infty}^{\infty} e^{-x^2/2a\ +\ ikx}\left(-\frac{x}{a}\ +\ ik\right) e^{-x^2/2a\ +\ ikx}\ dx$$

$$\therefore \ <p_x> \ = - i\hbar \ |A|^2 \int\limits_{-\infty}^{\infty} \left(e^{-x^2/2a - ikx} \left(-\frac{x}{a}\right) e^{-x^2/2a + ikx} + e^{-x^2/2a - ikx} \ ik \ e^{-x^2/2a + ikx} \right) dx$$

$$= |A|^2 \ \frac{i\hbar}{a} \int\limits_{-\infty}^{\infty} x \, e^{-x^2/a} \ dx + \hbar k \ |A|^2 \int\limits_{-\infty}^{\infty} e^{-x^2/a} \ dx$$

The first integrand on R.H.S. is odd integral and hence zero. In second term using equation (i), we get

$$<p_x> \ = \hbar k$$

Problem 2.7 : *Consider the wave function of a particle*

$$\psi(x) \ = A\left(1 - \frac{x}{a}\right) \text{ for } a/2 < x < a$$

Find the normalisation constant A and also obtain <x>.

Solution : $\qquad |\psi(x)|^2 = |A|^2 \left(1 - \frac{x}{a}\right)^2 = |A^2| \left(1 - \frac{2x}{a} + \frac{x^2}{a^2}\right)$

We have $\qquad\qquad\qquad \int\limits_{a/2}^{a} |\psi(x)|^2 \ dx \ = 1$

$$\therefore \qquad\qquad |A|^2 \int\limits_{a/2}^{a} \left(1 - \frac{2x}{a} + \frac{x^2}{a^2}\right) dx = 1$$

$$|A|^2 \left[x - \frac{x^2}{a} + \frac{x^3}{3a^2} \right]_{a/2}^{a} = 1$$

$$|A|^2 \left[a - \frac{a^2}{a} + \frac{a^3}{3a^2} - \left(\frac{a}{2} - \frac{a^2}{4a} + \frac{a^3}{24a^2}\right) \right] = 1$$

$$|A|^2 \left(\frac{a}{24}\right) = 1$$

$$\therefore \qquad\qquad\qquad |A| \ = \sqrt{\frac{24}{a}}$$

$$\therefore \qquad\qquad\qquad \psi(x) \ = \sqrt{\frac{24}{a}} \left(1 - \frac{x}{a}\right)$$

Expectation value of *x* is given as

$$<x> \ = \int\limits_{a/2}^{a} x \, |\psi(x)|^2 \ dx \ = |A|^2 \int\limits_{a/2}^{a} x \left(1 - \frac{2x}{a} + \frac{x^2}{a^2}\right) dx$$

$$= \frac{24}{a} \int\limits_{a/2}^{a} \left(x - \frac{2x^2}{a} + \frac{x^3}{a^2} \right) dx = \frac{24}{a} \left[\frac{x^2}{2} - \frac{2x^3}{3a} + \frac{x^4}{4a^2} \right]_{a/2}^{a}$$

$$= \frac{24}{a} \left[\frac{a^2}{2} - \frac{2a^3}{3a} + \frac{a^4}{4a^2} - \left(\frac{a^2}{8} - \frac{2a^3}{24a} + \frac{a^4}{64a^2} \right) \right]$$

$$= \frac{24}{a} \left[\frac{a^2}{2} - \frac{2a^3}{3a} + \frac{a^4}{4a^2} - \frac{a^2}{8} + \frac{2a^3}{24a} - \frac{a^4}{64a^2} \right]$$

$$= \frac{24}{a} a^2 \left[\frac{1}{2} - \frac{2}{3} + \frac{1}{4} - \frac{1}{8} + \frac{2}{24} - \frac{1}{64} \right]$$

$$\therefore \qquad <x> = 0.625 \, a$$

Problem 2.8 : *Find the current density if the wave function is* $\psi(x) = Ae^{ikx}$.

Solution : The current density is given as

$$\vec{J} = \frac{\hbar}{2mi} [\psi^* \nabla \psi - \psi \nabla \psi^*]$$

The x component of current density is given as

$$J_x = \frac{\hbar}{2mi} \left[\psi^* \frac{d\psi}{dx} - \psi \frac{d\psi^*}{dx} \right]$$

We have $\psi(x) = Ae^{ikx}$ and $\psi^*(x) = A^*e^{-ikx}$

$$\therefore \qquad J_x = \frac{\hbar}{2mi} \left[A^*e^{-ikx} \frac{dAe^{ikx}}{dx} - Ae^{ikx} \frac{dA^*e^{-ikx}}{dx} \right]$$

$$= \frac{\hbar}{2mi} AA^* \left[e^{-ikx} (ik)e^{ikx} - e^{ikx} (-ik)e^{-ikx} \right]$$

$$= \frac{\hbar}{2mi} AA^* \left[(ik) - (-ik) \right]$$

$$= \frac{\hbar}{2mi} AA^* (2ik)$$

$$= \frac{\hbar k}{m} |A|^2$$

$$\because \qquad \hbar k = p = mv$$

$$\therefore \qquad J_x = \frac{mv}{m} |A|^2 = v |A|^2.$$

Problem 2.9 : *Consider the particle whose wave function is given as*

$$\psi(x) = x \, e^{-\alpha x} \quad , \quad x \geq 0$$
$$= 0 \quad , \quad x < 0$$

(1) *Normalise the wave function.*

(2) *Find* <x>.

(3) *Find the value of x at which the probability is maximum.*

Solution : (1) To normalise the wave function, let us write the wave function as

$$\psi(x) = A\, x\, e^{-\alpha x}$$

where A is the normalisation constant.

The condition for normalisation is given as

$$\int_0^\infty |\psi(x)|^2\, dx = 1$$

$$\therefore \qquad \int_0^\infty |A|^2\, x^2\, e^{-2\alpha x}\, dx = 1$$

$$|A|^2 \int_0^\infty x^2\, e^{-2\alpha x}\, dx = 1$$

We have general integral $\int_0^\infty x^n\, e^{-\beta x}\, dx = \dfrac{n!}{(\beta)^{n+1}}$

Therefore, $\quad \int_0^\infty x^2\, e^{-2\alpha x}\, dx = \dfrac{2!}{(2\alpha)^3} = \dfrac{1}{4\alpha^3}$

Hence $\qquad\qquad\qquad |A|^2 \dfrac{1}{4\alpha^3} = 1$

$$\therefore \qquad\qquad\qquad |A| = (4\alpha^3)^{1/2} = 2\alpha\sqrt{\alpha}$$

$$\therefore \qquad\qquad\qquad \psi(x) = 2\alpha\sqrt{\alpha}\, x\, e^{-\alpha x}$$

(2) Expectation value of x is given as

$$<x> = \int_0^\infty x\, |\psi(x)|^2\, dx = \int_0^\infty 4\alpha^3\, x^3\, e^{-2\alpha x}\, dx$$

$$= 4\alpha^3 \int_0^\infty x^3\, e^{-2\alpha x}\, dx = 4\alpha^3 \dfrac{3!}{(2\alpha)^4} = \dfrac{3!}{4\alpha}$$

$$\therefore \qquad\qquad\qquad <x> = \dfrac{3}{2\alpha}$$

(3) The peak of the probability function P(x) occurs when $\dfrac{dP}{dx} = 0$

$$\psi(x) = 2\alpha\sqrt{\alpha}\, x\, e^{-\alpha x}$$

$$P(x) = |\psi(x)|^2 = 4\alpha^3\, x^2\, e^{-2\alpha}$$

$$\therefore \qquad \dfrac{dP}{dx} = 4\alpha^3\, [2x\, e^{-2\alpha x} - 2\alpha\, x^2\, e^{-2\alpha x}]$$

For peak value of probability,

$$4\alpha^3[\, 2x\, e^{-2\alpha x} - 2\alpha\, x^2\, e^{-2\alpha x}\,] = 0$$

$$\therefore \qquad 2x\, e^{-2\alpha x} - 2\alpha\, x^2\, e^{-2\alpha x} = 0$$

or $$\qquad x - \alpha x^2 = 0 \quad \therefore \quad x = \frac{1}{\alpha}$$

Thus, the probability will have the peak value at $x = \dfrac{1}{\alpha}$.

Problem 2.10 : *The wave function for the ground state of the hydrogen atom is given as*

$$\psi(r) = A\, e^{-r/a_o} \qquad a_o = \text{Bohr's radius}$$

Normalise the wave function and find the expectation value of r.

Solution : The range of r is from 0 to ∞. The normalisation condition is

$$\int\limits_0^\infty |\psi(r)|^2\, d\tau = 1$$

$d\tau$ is volume element and it is $d\tau = 4\pi r^2\, dr$

$$\therefore \qquad |A|^2 \int\limits_0^\infty e^{-2r/a_o}\, d\tau = 1$$

$d\tau$ is a typical volume element of space and it is $d\tau = 4\pi r^2\, d\tau$.

or $$\qquad |A|^2 \int\limits_0^\infty e^{-2r/a_o}\, 4\pi r^2 dr = 1$$

$$4\pi|A|^2 \int\limits_0^\infty r^2\, e^{-2r/a_o}\, dr = 1$$

$$4\pi|A|^2\, \frac{2!}{(2/a_o)^3} = 1$$

$$\therefore \qquad |A| = \frac{1}{\sqrt{\pi\, a_o^3}}$$

$$\therefore \qquad \psi(r) = \frac{1}{\sqrt{\pi\, a_o^3}}\, e^{-r/a_o}$$

The expectation value of r is given as

$$<r> = \int\limits_0^\infty r\, |\psi(r)|^2\, d\tau = \frac{1}{\pi\, a_o^3} \int\limits_0^\infty r\, e^{-2r/a_o}\, 4\pi r^2 dr$$

$$= \frac{1}{\pi\, a_o^3}\, 4\pi \int\limits_0^\infty r^3\, e^{-2r/a_o}\, dr = \frac{4}{a_o^3}\, \frac{3!}{(2/a_o)^4} = \frac{3}{2}\, a_o$$

Problem 2.11 : *The wave function of a certain particle is* $\psi = A \cos^2 x$ *for* $-\pi/2 < x < \pi/2$.

(a) Find the value of A.

(b) Find the probability that the particle be found between $x = 0$ and $x = \pi/4$.

Solution : (a) The condition for normalisation is

$$\int |\psi(x)|^2 \, dx = 1$$

$\therefore$ $$\int_{-\pi/2}^{\pi/2} |A|^2 \cos^4 x \, dx = 1$$

or $$|A|^2 \int_{-\pi/2}^{\pi/2} \cos^4 x \, dx = 1$$

$$|A|^2 \, 2 \int_{0}^{\pi/2} \cos^4 x \, dx = 1 \qquad \text{(as } \cos x \text{ is even function)}$$

We have general reduction formula

$$\int \cos^n x \, dx = \frac{\sin x \cos^{n-1} x}{n} + \frac{n-1}{n} \int \cos^{n-2} x \, dx$$

$\therefore$ $$\int \cos^4 x \, dx = \frac{\sin x \cos^3 x}{4} + \frac{3}{4} \int \cos^2 x \, dx$$

$$= \frac{\sin x \cos^3 x}{4} + \frac{3}{4} \int \cos^2 x \, dx$$

$$= \frac{\sin x \cos^3 x}{4} + \frac{3}{4} \left(\frac{\sin x \cos x}{2} + \frac{1}{2} \int dx \right)$$

$$= \frac{\sin x \cos^3 x}{4} + \frac{3}{4} \left(\frac{\sin x \cos x}{2} + \frac{1}{2} x \right)$$

$\therefore$ $$\int_{0}^{\pi/2} \cos^4 x \, dx = \left[\frac{\sin x \cos^3 x}{4} + \frac{3}{4} \left(\frac{\sin x \cos x}{2} + \frac{1}{2} x \right) \right]_{0}^{\pi/2}$$

$$= \frac{1}{4} \times 1 \times 0 + \frac{3}{4} \left(\frac{1}{2} \times 1 \times 0 + \frac{1}{2} \cdot \frac{\pi}{2} \right) - 0$$

$$= \frac{3\pi}{16}$$

Hence $$|A|^2 \, 2 \frac{3\pi}{16} = 1$$

$\therefore$ $$|A| = \sqrt{\frac{8}{3\pi}}$$

Therefore,

$$\psi(x) = \sqrt{\frac{8}{3\pi}}\cos^2 x$$

(b) The probability of particle finding in the range 0 to $\pi/4$ is

$$P(x) = \int_0^{\pi/4} |A|^2 \cos^4 x \, dx$$

$$= \frac{8}{3\pi} \int_0^{\pi/4} \cos^4 x \, dx$$

The reduction formula is

$$\int_0^{\pi/4} \cos^4 x \, dx = \left[\frac{\sin x \cos^3 x}{4} + \frac{3}{4}\left(\frac{\sin x \cos x}{2} + \frac{1}{2}x \right) \right]_0^{\pi/4}$$

$$= \frac{1}{4}\frac{1}{\sqrt{2}}\left(\frac{1}{\sqrt{2}}\right)^3 + \frac{3}{4}\left(\frac{1}{2}\frac{1}{\sqrt{2}}\frac{1}{\sqrt{2}} + \frac{1}{2}\frac{\pi}{4} \right) - 0$$

$$= \frac{1}{4}\left(\frac{1}{4} + \frac{3}{4} + \frac{3\pi}{8} \right) = \frac{8 + 3\pi}{32}$$

$\therefore$ $$P(x) = \frac{8}{3\pi} \times \frac{8 + 3\pi}{32}$$

or $$P(x) = 0.4623$$

Summary

1. The mathematical function which describes motion is the wave function $\psi(x, y, z, t)$.

2. The square of absolute magnitude of wave function $|\psi|^2$ (called probability density) evaluated at a particular place at a particular instant of time is proportional to the probability of finding the particle there at that time.

3. Probability of finding the particle in volume element dV is
$$P(r,t) \, dV = |\psi(r,t)|^2 dV$$

4. $$\int \psi\psi^* \, dV = 1$$

The integral in the above equation is carried out over the entire space. The above condition on ψ is called the *normalisation condition*.

5. The Schrödinger's time dependent equation is $i\hbar \dfrac{\partial \psi}{\partial t} = -\dfrac{\hbar^2}{2m}\dfrac{\partial^2 \psi}{\partial x^2} + V\psi$.

6. Schrödinger's one-dimensional time independent equation
$$\frac{d^2\psi}{dx^2} + \frac{2m}{\hbar^2}(E - V)\psi = 0$$

This is also called steady-state equation.

7. The requirements of wave function are

   $\psi(x)$ must be continuous, finite and single valued everywhere.

   And also $\dfrac{d\psi(x)}{dx}$ must be continuous, finite and single valued everywhere.

   The wave function which satisfies above condition are called as well behaved function.

8. Equation of continuity is $\nabla \cdot \vec{J} + \dfrac{\partial \rho}{\partial t} = 0$

9. $\vec{J} = \dfrac{\hbar}{2mi} [\psi^* \nabla \psi - \psi \nabla \psi^*]$

   $\vec{J}$ **is called probability current density.**

10. An operator $\hat{O}$ is a mathematical operation which may be applied to function $f(x)$, which changes the function $f(x)$ to another function $g(x)$. This can be represented as

$$\hat{O} f(x) = g(x)$$

11. Momentum operator is $\quad \hat{p} = -i\hbar\nabla$

12. The expectation value of any dynamical variable f obtained by wave function $\psi(x, t)$ is

$$<f> = \dfrac{\int \psi^* f \, \psi dx}{\int \psi^* \psi dx}$$

13. Ehrenfesf's theorems :

   1. First theorem : $m \dfrac{d<x>}{dt} = <p_x>$

      For all components, $m \dfrac{d<\vec{r}>}{dt} = <\vec{p}>$

   2. Second theorem :

   For conservative force field

$$\dfrac{d<p_x>}{dt} = \left\langle -\dfrac{dV}{dx} \right\rangle$$

   For all components, $\dfrac{d<\vec{p}>}{dt} = <-\nabla V>$

Exercises

(A) Short Answer Type Questions :

1. Define wave function.

2. State Schrödinger's time dependent and time independent equations.

3. When function is said to be well behaved ?
4. State equation of continuity.
5. Define operator.
6. Define expectation value.
7. Define eigen value and eigen function
8. State Ehrenfest theorems.
9. Define probability current density.

(B) Long Answer Type Questions :

1. Give the physical interpretation of the wave function.
2. Give the requirements of the wave function.
3. Obtain Schrödinger's time dependent equation.
4. Obtain Schrödinger's time independent equation from time dependent equation.
5. Show that time part of the wave function is $e^{-iEt/\hbar}$.
6. Obtain equation of continuity. Give the physical significance.
7. What is meant by eigen function and eigen values?
8. Define an operator. State the quantum mechanical operators.
9. How are the expectation values of physical quantities are obtained?
10. State and prove Ehrenfest first theorem.

(C) Unsolved Problems :

1. Normalise wave function $\psi(x) = A \exp(-k |x|)$ where k is a positive constant.

    $$(\textbf{Ans. } |A| = k^{1/2})$$

2. Normalise the wave function $\psi(x) = e^{-\alpha x^2}$ in the range $-\infty$ and $+\infty$.

    $$\left(\textbf{Ans. } \psi = \left(\frac{2\alpha}{\pi}\right)^{1/4} e^{-\alpha x^2}\right)$$

3. Normalise the wave function $\psi(x) = x\, e^{-\alpha x^2}$ in the range $-\infty$ and $+\infty$.

    $$\left(\textbf{Ans. } \psi = (4\alpha)^{1/2} \left(\frac{2\alpha}{\pi}\right)^{1/4} xe^{-\alpha x^2}\right)$$

4. Find the eigen value of the operator $\dfrac{d^2}{dx^2}$ for the eigen function $e^{-i\alpha x}$.

5. The eigen function for momentum operator is e^{ikx}. Find the eigen value.   (**Ans.** $\hbar k$)

6. Normalise the wave function

    $\psi(x) = e^{-|x|} \sin \alpha x$ in the range $-\infty$ to $+\infty$.

    $$\left(\textbf{Ans. } \text{Normalisation constant} = \sqrt{\frac{2(1 + \alpha^2)}{\alpha^2}}\right)$$

7. The state of a free particle is represented by

$$\psi(x) = A\, e^{-x^2/2a^2 + ikx}$$

(i) Find out the factor A.

(ii) In what region of space the particle is most likely to be found ?

$$\left(|N| = \frac{1}{a^{1/2}\, \pi^{1/4}}\ ,\ |\psi|^2 = |N|^2\, e^{-x^2/a^2} \right)$$

8. Find the expectation value of position and momentum whose wave function is

$$\psi(s) = N\, e^{-x^2/2s^2 + ikx}$$

(**Ans.** $<x> = 0$, $<p_x> = hx$)

9. Consider operator d^2/dx^2, check whether (i) e^{2x} and (ii) $\sin^2 x$ are eigen functions of the operator. Find corresponding eigen value in case of valid eigen functions.

(**Ans.** (i) Eigen value 4, (ii) Not eigen function)

10. Prove that in case of wave function $\psi(x) = [\exp(ikr)/r]$ the probability current density is given by $J = v/r^2$ where v is the velocity of particle.

❑❑❑

Chapter 3...
Applications of Schrödinger's Steady State Equation

It is wrong to think that the task of physics is to find out how Nature is. Physics concerns what we say about Nature.

— Niels Bohr

Niels Bohr
(1885-1962)

Niels Bohr was a Danish physicist who made foundational contributions to understand atomic structure and quantum theory for which he received Nobel Prize in 1922. He formulated correspondence principle. The correspondence principle states that the behaviour of system described by theory of quantum mechanics (or by old quantum theory) reproduces classical physics in the limit of large quantum numbers.

Introduction

- In the present chapter we shall obtain some interesting predictions concerning quantum mechanical phenomenon. We will consider some problems in which constraints are applied on the motion of particle. Constraints are applied by using different forms of potentials. The predictions corresponding to these constraints will be obtained by solving time-independent Schrödinger's equation. The eigen functions and eigen values will also be obtained. Quantization of energy is one of the very interesting features of quantum mechanical problems. Some problems involving quantization of energy will be studied in the chapter.

3.1 Free Particle or Zero Potential

- The simplest form of the time independent Schrödinger's equation is the case in which the particle is moving through constant potential *i.e.* V(x) = constant. Since the force $F = -\dfrac{dV}{dx}$ acting on the particle is zero, the particle is **a free particle**. We know that in classical mechanics a free particle is either at rest or moving with constant momentum *p*. In either case the total energy of the particle $E = \dfrac{p^2}{2m} + V = \dfrac{p^2}{2m}$ is constant.

- To predict the behaviour of the free particle quantum mechanically, we will solve Schrödinger's time independent equation. We have

$$\frac{d^2\psi}{dx^2} + \frac{2m}{\hbar^2}(E - V)\psi = 0$$

  With V = 0, we get

$$\frac{d^2\psi}{dx^2} + \frac{2mE}{\hbar^2}\psi = 0 \qquad \text{... (3.1)}$$

  Let

$$k^2 = \frac{2mE}{\hbar^2}$$

  ∴

$$\frac{d^2\psi}{dx^2} + k^2\psi = 0 \qquad \text{... (3.2)}$$

- The solutions of this equation are eigen functions. The possible solutions of equation (3.2) are e^{-ikx} and e^{ikx}.

- The solution of time part is given as $\phi(t) = e^{-iEt/\hbar}$. Since we have $E = \hbar\omega$, therefore, $\phi(t) = e^{-i\omega t}$. The wave function is

$$\psi(x, t) = \psi(x)\,\phi(t)$$

  ∴

$$\psi(x, t) = e^{ikx}\,e^{-i\omega t} = e^{i(kx - \omega t)} \qquad \text{... (3.3)}$$

  or

$$\psi(x, t) = e^{-ikx}\,e^{-i\omega t} = e^{-i(kx + \omega t)} \qquad \text{... (3.4)}$$

- Equation (3.3) represents the wave propagating along the positive x axis and equation (3.4) represents wave propagating along the negative x axis.

- Let us consider equation (3.3) and let A be the normalization constant, then a wave propagating along positive x axis is given by

$$\psi(x, t) = A\,e^{i(kx - \omega t)} \qquad \text{... (3.5)}$$

  The probability density is $\psi^*\psi = A^*A = $ constant

- Thus the particle is equally likely to be found anywhere and hence the uncertainty in the position is $\Delta x = \infty$. From $\Delta x\,\Delta p \geq \hbar/2$, we get $\Delta p = 0$ *i.e. the momentum of the particle is definite.* That is the particle has perfectly precise value of momentum as indicated by de Broglie equation $p = h/\lambda = \hbar k$. Since the particle can be found anywhere, there is infinite time available to measure the energy of the particle travelling over an infinite length.

From this uncertainty in time is $\Delta t = \infty$. From equation $\Delta E \Delta t \geq \hbar/2$, the uncertainty in energy $\Delta E = 0$. Thus, we get precise value of the energy. This is also indicated by de Broglie-Einstein equation $E = \hbar\omega$. As the wave function contains single value of k and ω, p and E are single valued.

- There is the difficulty in the normalization of free particle wave function. According to normalization condition,

$$\int_{-\infty}^{\infty} \psi^*\psi \, dx = AA^* \int_{-\infty}^{\infty} dx = 1$$

- The amplitude must be vanishingly small as $\int_{-\infty}^{\infty} dx$ has an infinite value. Therefore, the probability of finding the particle will be vanishingly small everywhere. Thus, there is difficulty in connection with the normalization of the free particle wave function. However, we should not worry too much about this mathematical difficulty because firstly, we cannot have a particle which is completely free from the forces. Secondly, in actual practice the range of motion of the particle is not infinite.

Energy spectrum of the free particle :

- The energy of the free particle is $E = \dfrac{p^2}{2m}$. For particle moving in the +X direction, p is positive and moving along –X axis, p is negative. But p^2 is always positive and can have any value between 0 and ∞. Therefore, range of energy is also from 0 to ∞. **Thus, the energy spectrum of the free particle is continuous.**

3.2 Particle in Infinitely Deep Potential Well (One Dimension)

- Let us consider one-dimensional motion along X-axis of a particle between two points x = 0 and x = a. The particle is free to move between 0 and a. But it cannot cross to the left of x = 0 and to the right of x = a. This situation is represented by the potential function V given by

$$V = \infty \qquad x \leq 0$$
$$V = 0 \qquad 0 < x < a$$
$$V = \infty \qquad x \geq a$$

- This potential has feature that it will bind the particle within x = 0 and x = a, with any finite energy $E \geq 0$. In classical mechanics any of these energies are possible and the energy spectrum is continuous. But in quantum mechanics as constrains are applied, it will be shown below that only certain discrete energy values are allowed. A particle moving under the influence of an infinite square well potential is often called a *particle in a one-dimensional rigid box*.

Fig. 3.1 represents infinitely deep potential well.

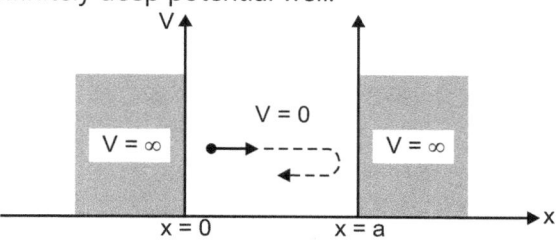

Fig. 3.1 : Graphical representation of infinite potential well

- In the region within the potential well the time-independent Schrödinger's equation can be solved to obtain eigen values of energy and corresponding eigen functions.

  Schrödinger's time independent equation is given as

  $$\frac{d^2\psi}{dx^2} + \frac{2m}{\hbar^2}(E - V)\psi = 0 \qquad \ldots (3.6)$$

  In the region $0 < x < a$, above equation takes the form

  $$\frac{d^2\psi}{dx^2} + \frac{2mE}{\hbar^2}\psi = 0 \qquad \ldots (3.7)$$

  Let $$k^2 = \frac{2mE}{\hbar^2}$$

  $\therefore$ $$\frac{d^2\psi}{dx^2} + k^2\psi = 0 \qquad \ldots (3.8)$$

- Equation (3.8) is a second order linear homogeneous differential equation in ψ. Its general solution may be written as

  $$\psi(x) = A \sin kx + B \cos kx \qquad \ldots (3.9)$$

  where A and B are arbitrary constants and can be obtained by using boundary conditions on ψ.

  Outside the region $0 < x < a$, the wave function $\psi(x) = 0$

  Also at the boundaries of the well, $\psi(x) = 0$

  Therefore, at $x = 0$, $\psi(x) = 0$, which gives

  $$B = 0$$

  Using in equation (3.9), we get

  $$\psi(x) = A \sin (kx) \qquad \ldots (3.10)$$

  At $x = a$, $\psi(x) = 0$, which gives

  $$A \sin (ka) = 0$$

- This is true if $A = 0$ or $\sin ka = 0$. But, $A \neq 0$, because otherwise $\psi = 0$ everywhere. This is not possible because then probability of finding the particle inside the well is zero. This contradicts the particle is present and moving between $x = 0$ and $x = a$.

- Therefore, only alternative is $\sin ka = 0$.

- Thus we choose k such that sin ka = 0. This is possible only if

$$ka = n\pi \text{ where } n = 1, 2, 3, 4, 5, ...$$

or

$$k = \frac{n\pi}{a} \qquad \qquad ... (3.11)$$

∴

$$\psi(x) = A \sin\left(\frac{n\pi}{a} x\right) \qquad \qquad ... (3.12)$$

Eigen Values of Energy : Since we have $k^2 = \dfrac{2mE}{\hbar^2}$,

∴

$$\frac{n^2 \pi^2}{a^2} = \frac{2mE}{\hbar^2}$$

Thus, we get energy eigen value

$$E = \frac{n^2\pi^2\hbar^2}{2ma^2}$$

Since energy E depends on index 'n', we may write

$$E_n = \frac{n^2\pi^2\hbar^2}{2ma^2} \qquad \qquad ... (3.13)$$

This equation shows that the eigen values of energy are discrete.

- Thus, we see that only certain values of energy are allowed as given by equation (3.13). As n is an integer, there is thus infinite sequence of discrete energy levels which correspond to positive integer n. This integer **n** is called a **quantum number.** The quantum state with lowest value of n (i.e. n = 1) is called the ground state. The levels corresponding to n = 2, 3 , 4 ... ... etc. are called excited states. Let us consider the energy for n = 1 level. The energy is

$$E_1 = \frac{\pi^2\hbar^2}{2ma^2} \qquad \qquad ... (3.14)$$

- This is the **lowest energy of particle called as zero-point energy.** Classically the lowest energy is zero. But quantum mechanically the ground state cannot have zero energy value. The phenomenon is basically a result of Heisenberg's uncertainty principle. If the particle is bound by the infinite potential well of width a, then the uncertainty in its position will be Δx = a. Consequently, the uncertainty in the momentum will be $\Delta p = \hbar/2a$ and hence have corresponding energy. Thus the uncertainty principle cannot allow the particle to be bound by the potential and having zero energy.

The higher energy levels are

$$E_2 = 4\frac{\pi^2\hbar^2}{2ma^2} = 4E_1$$

$$E_3 = 9\frac{\pi^2\hbar^2}{2ma^2} = 9E_1$$

and so on.

∴

$$E_n = n^2 E_1$$

The energy spectrum is shown in Fig. 3.2.

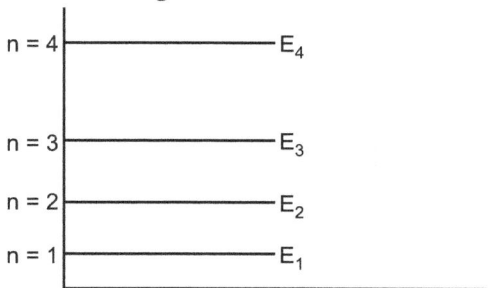

Fig. 3.2 : Energy spectrum

Wave functions :

* The wave functions are given by the equation (3.12). As it is characteristic of n, we may write

$$\psi_n(x) \ = \ A \sin\left(\frac{n\pi}{a} x\right) \qquad \dots (3.15)$$

* As the particle is confined to move between $x = 0$ and $x = a$, the condition for normalisation is

$$\int_0^a |\psi_n(x)|^2 \, dx \ = \ 1$$

$$\therefore \qquad \int_0^a |A|^2 \sin^2\left(\frac{n\pi}{a} x\right) dx \ = \ 1$$

$$|A|^2 \int_0^a \sin^2\left(\frac{n\pi}{a} x\right) dx \ = \ 1 \qquad \dots (3.16)$$

We have $\sin^2\theta = \frac{1}{2}(1 - \cos 2\theta)$, therefore, equation (3.16) becomes

$$|A|^2 \int_0^a \frac{1}{2}\left[1 - \cos\left(\frac{2n\pi}{a} x\right)\right] dx \ = \ 1$$

$$\frac{|A|^2}{2} \int_0^a \left[1 - \cos\left(\frac{2n\pi}{a} x\right)\right] dx \ = \ 1$$

$$\frac{|A|^2}{2} \int_0^a \left[dx - \cos\left(\frac{2n\pi}{a} x\right) dx\right] \ = \ 1$$

$$\frac{|A|^2}{2} \int_0^a \left[dx - \cos\left(\frac{2n\pi}{a}x\right) dx \right] = 1$$

$$\frac{|A|^2}{2} \left[x - \frac{\sin\left(\frac{2n\pi}{a}x\right)}{\frac{2n\pi}{a}} \right]_0^a = 1$$

$$\frac{|A|^2}{2} a = 1$$

$$\therefore \qquad |A| = \sqrt{\frac{2}{a}}$$

Thus, on normalisation, we get

$$\psi_n(x) = \sqrt{\frac{2}{a}} \sin\left(\frac{n\pi}{a}x\right) \qquad \qquad \text{... (3.17)}$$

This is the wave function corresponding to energy eigen value E_n.

The ground state function (n = 1) is

$$\psi_1(x) = \sqrt{\frac{2}{a}} \sin\left(\frac{\pi}{a}x\right) \qquad \qquad \text{... (3.18)}$$

- In Fig. 3.3 (a), first three wave functions ψ_1, ψ_2 and ψ_3 are shown and in Fig. 3.3 (b) corresponding probability densities $|\psi_1|^2$, $|\psi_2|^2$ and $|\psi_3|^2$ are shown.

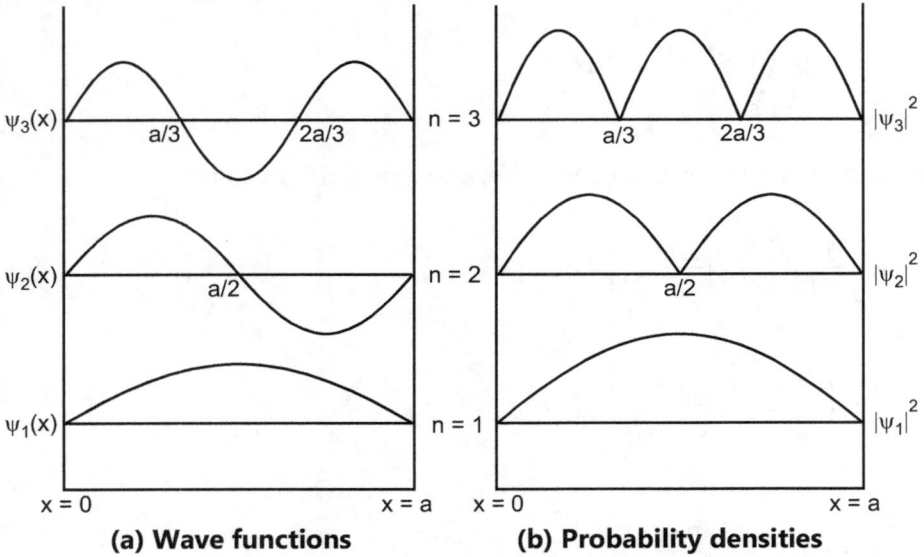

(a) Wave functions   (b) Probability densities

Fig. 3.3

- It is evident that ψ_1 has two modes at $x = 0$ and $x = a$. The wave function ψ_2 has three nodes at $x = 0$, $x = a/2$ and $x = a$. The wave function ψ_3 has four nodes at $x = 0$, $x = \dfrac{a}{3}$, $x = \dfrac{2a}{3}$ and $x = a$. Thus, wave function ψ_n will have $(n + 1)$ nodes.

3.3 Particle in Three Dimensional Rigid Box

- Now we shall consider the case of a particle enclosed in a rectangular box of sides a, b and c in length. The potential function V(x, y, z) is zero inside the box and outside the box the potential is infinite. As the potential is infinite outside the box, the particle is confined to move only inside the box and cannot come out of it. Thus, the box is called rigid box. Mathematically, the potential may be represented as

$$V = 0 \quad \begin{cases} 0 < x < a \\ 0 < y < b \\ 0 < z < c \end{cases}$$

$$V = \infty \qquad \textit{elsewhere}$$

- The rectangular box is shown in Fig. 3.4.

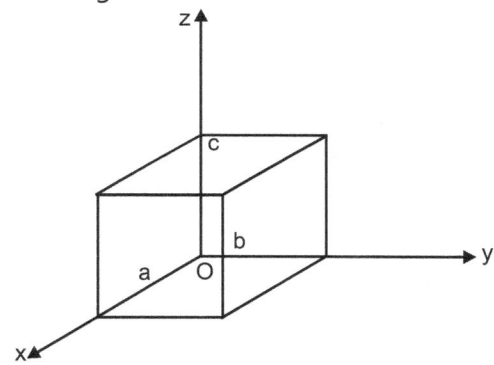

Fig. 3.4

- Three-dimensional time-independent Schrödinger's equation is given as

$$\nabla^2 \psi + \frac{2m}{\hbar^2} (E - V)\psi = 0$$

Inside the box, we have $V = 0$, therefore, the Schrödinger's equation takes the form

$$\nabla^2 \psi + \frac{2mE}{\hbar^2} \psi = 0 \qquad \text{... (3.19)}$$

where $\psi = \psi(x, y, z)$.

Equation (3.19) in Cartesian co-ordinate system may be written as

$$\frac{\partial^2 \psi}{\partial x^2} + \frac{\partial^2 \psi}{\partial y^2} + \frac{\partial^2 \psi}{\partial z^2} + \frac{2mE}{\hbar^2} \psi = 0 \qquad \text{... (3.20)}$$

Equation (3.20) can be solved by separation of variables method.

Let $\qquad\qquad \psi(x, y, z) = \psi_1(x)\,\psi_2(y)\,\psi_3(z)$ $\qquad\qquad$ ... (3.21)

Using equation (3.21) in equation (3.20), we get

$$\frac{\partial^2 \psi_1\psi_2\psi_3}{\partial x^2} + \frac{\partial^2 \psi_1\psi_2\psi_3}{\partial y^2} + \frac{\partial^2 \psi_1\psi_2\psi_3}{\partial z^2} + \frac{2mE}{\hbar^2}\,\psi_1\psi_2\psi_3 = 0$$

$$\therefore \qquad \psi_2\psi_3\frac{\partial^2 \psi_1}{\partial x^2} + \psi_1\psi_3\frac{\partial^2 \psi_2}{\partial y^2} + \psi_1\psi_2\frac{\partial^2 \psi_3}{\partial z^2} + \frac{2mE}{\hbar^2}\,\psi_1\psi_2\psi_3 = 0$$

- Dividing above equation throughout by $\psi_1\psi_2\psi_3$, we get

$$\frac{1}{\psi_1}\frac{\partial^2 \psi_1}{\partial x^2} + \frac{1}{\psi_2}\frac{\partial^2 \psi_2}{\partial y^2} + \frac{1}{\psi_3}\frac{\partial^2 \psi_3}{\partial z^2} + \frac{2mE}{\hbar^2} = 0$$

or $\qquad \dfrac{1}{\psi_1}\dfrac{d^2 \psi_1}{dx^2} + \dfrac{1}{\psi_2}\dfrac{d^2 \psi_2}{dy^2} + \dfrac{1}{\psi_3}\dfrac{d^2 \psi_3}{dz^2} + \dfrac{2mE}{\hbar^2} = 0$

$$\therefore \qquad \frac{1}{\psi_1}\frac{d^2 \psi_1}{dx^2} + \frac{1}{\psi_2}\frac{d^2 \psi_2}{dy^2} + \frac{1}{\psi_3}\frac{d^2 \psi_3}{dz^2} = -\frac{2mE}{\hbar^2} \qquad\qquad \text{... (3.22)}$$

Let $k^2 = \dfrac{2mE}{\hbar^2}$

$$\therefore \qquad \frac{1}{\psi_1}\frac{d^2 \psi_1}{dx^2} + \frac{1}{\psi_2}\frac{d^2 \psi_2}{dy^2} + \frac{1}{\psi_3}\frac{d^2 \psi_3}{dz^2} = -k^2 \qquad\qquad \text{... (3.23)}$$

- On LHS, the first term depends on x only, second term depends on y only and the third term depends on z only. On RHS the term $-k^2$ is constant. Since x, y, z are independent variables, each of the first three terms must be constant. Denoting them by $-k_1^2$, $-k_2^2$ and $-k_3^2$ respectively, we have

$$\frac{1}{\psi_1}\frac{d^2 \psi_1}{dx^2} = -k_1^2 \qquad\qquad \text{... (3.24)}$$

$$\frac{1}{\psi_2}\frac{d^2 \psi_2}{dy^2} = -k_2^2 \qquad\qquad \text{... (3.25)}$$

$$\frac{1}{\psi_3}\frac{d^2 \psi_3}{dz^2} = -k_3^2 \qquad\qquad \text{... (3.26)}$$

Using above three equations in equation (3.23), we get

$$k_1^2 + k_2^2 + k_2^2 = k^2 \qquad\qquad \text{... (3.27)}$$

Equations (3.24), (3.25) and (3.26) can be written as

$$\frac{d^2 \psi_1}{dx^2} + k_1^2\psi_1 = 0 \qquad\qquad \text{... (3.28)}$$

$$\frac{d^2 \psi_2}{dy^2} + k_2^2\psi_2 = 0 \qquad\qquad \text{... (3.29)}$$

$$\frac{d^2 \psi_3}{dz^2} + k_3^2\psi_3 = 0 \qquad\qquad \text{... (3.30)}$$

The general solution of equation (3.28) may be written as

$$\psi_1(x) = A_1 \sin k_1 x + B_1 \cos k_1 x \qquad \ldots (3.31)$$

where A_1 and B_1 are arbitrary constants and can be obtained by using boundary conditions on ψ.

Outside the region $0 < x < a$ the wave function $\psi_1(x) = 0$

Also at the boundaries of the rigid box, $\psi_1(x) = 0$

Thus, at $x = 0$, $\psi_1(x) = 0$. Substitution in equation (3.31) gives

$$\therefore \qquad\qquad B_1 = 0$$

Using in equation (3.31), we get

$$\psi_1(x) = A_1 \sin(k_1 x) \qquad \ldots (3.32)$$

At $x = a$, $\psi_1(x) = 0$, which gives

$$A_1 \sin(k_1 a) = 0$$

- In the above equation, $A_1 \neq 0$. Because then ψ_1 will be zero every inside the box between $x = 0$ and $x = a$. There is always some probability of finding the particle within $x = 0$ and $x = a$. Therefore, $\sin(k_1 a) = 0$.

$$\therefore \qquad\qquad k_1 a = n_1 \pi \text{ where } n_1 = 1, 2, 3, 4, 5, \ldots$$

$$\text{or} \qquad\qquad k_1 = \frac{n_1 \pi}{a} \qquad \ldots (3.33)$$

$$\therefore \qquad\qquad \psi_1(x) = A_1 \sin\left(\frac{n_1 \pi}{a} x\right) \qquad \ldots (3.34)$$

If we normalize the equation in the range 0 to a, we get

$$\psi_1(x) = \sqrt{\frac{2}{a}} \sin\left(\frac{n_1 \pi}{a} x\right) \qquad \ldots (3.35)$$

Similarly, solutions of equations (3.29) and (3.30) respectively can be written as

$$\psi_2(y) = \sqrt{\frac{2}{b}} \sin\left(\frac{n_2 \pi}{b} y\right) \text{ with } k_2 = \frac{n_2 \pi}{b}$$

$$\text{where } n_2 = 1, 2, 3, 4, \ldots \ldots$$

$$\psi_3(z) = \sqrt{\frac{2}{c}} \sin\left(\frac{n_3 \pi}{c} z\right) \text{ with } k_3 = \frac{n_3 \pi}{c}$$

$$\text{where } n_3 = 1, 2, 3, \ldots \ldots$$

- Using ψ_1, ψ_2 and ψ_3 in equation (3.21), we get resultant wave function ψ. As it depends on the integers n_1, n_2 and n_3, we may write

$$\psi_{n_1 n_2 n_3} = \sqrt{\frac{2}{a}} \sin\left(\frac{n_1 \pi}{a} x\right) \cdot \sqrt{\frac{2}{b}} \sin\left(\frac{n_2 \pi}{b} y\right) \cdot \sqrt{\frac{2}{c}} \sin\left(\frac{n_3 \pi}{c} z\right)$$

$$\text{or} \quad \psi_{n_1 n_2 n_3} = \sqrt{\frac{8}{abc}} \sin\left(\frac{n_1 \pi}{a} x\right) \cdot \sin\left(\frac{n_2 \pi}{b} y\right) \cdot \sin\left(\frac{n_3 \pi}{c} z\right) \qquad \ldots (3.36)$$

Using k_1, k_2 and k_3 in equation (3.27), we get

$$\frac{n_1^2 \pi^2}{a^2} + \frac{n_2^2 \pi^2}{b^2} + \frac{n_3^2 \pi^2}{c^2} = k^2$$

Since

$$k^2 = \frac{2mE}{\hbar^2}$$

$\therefore$

$$\pi^2 \left(\frac{n_1^2}{a^2} + \frac{n_2^2}{b^2} + \frac{n_3^2}{c^2} \right) = \frac{2mE}{\hbar^2}$$

$\therefore$

$$E = \frac{\hbar^2 \pi^2}{2m} \left(\frac{n_1^2}{a^2} + \frac{n_2^2}{b^2} + \frac{n_3^2}{c^2} \right) \qquad \text{... (3.37)}$$

Equation (3.37) gives the eigen values of energy.

Since energy eigen values depend on the indices n_1, n_2 and n_3, we may write

$$E_{n_1 n_2 n_3} = \frac{\hbar^2 \pi^2}{2m} \left(\frac{n_1^2}{a^2} + \frac{n_2^2}{b^2} + \frac{n_3^2}{c^2} \right) \qquad \text{... (3.38)}$$

The ground state of the system corresponds to $n_1 = n_2 = n_3 = 1$ and is given by

$$E_{111} = \frac{\hbar^2 \pi^2}{2m} \left(\frac{1}{a^2} + \frac{1}{b^2} + \frac{1}{c^2} \right)$$

- Let us consider the special case of motion of a particle in cubical box ($a = b = c$). For this case, we get

$$\psi_{n_1 n_2 n_3} = \sqrt{\frac{8}{a^3}} \sin \left(\frac{n_1 \pi}{a} x \right) \sin \left(\frac{n_2 \pi}{a} y \right) \sin \left(\frac{n_3 \pi}{a} z \right) \qquad \text{... (3.39)}$$

and energy eigen value $E_{n_1 n_2 n_3} = \dfrac{\hbar^2 \pi^2}{2ma^2} \left(n_1^2 + n_2^2 + n_3^2 \right)$ ... (3.40)

- The ground state energy or *zero point* energy can be obtained by using $n_1 = n_2 = n_3 = 1$ in equation (3.40), and it is $E_{111} = 3 \dfrac{\hbar^2 \pi^2}{2ma^2}$.

The ground state wave function is given as

$$\psi_{111} = \sqrt{\frac{8}{a^3}} \sin \left(\frac{\pi}{a} x \right) \sin \left(\frac{\pi}{a} y \right) \sin \left(\frac{\pi}{a} z \right) \qquad \text{... (3.41)}$$

- The next higher energy level *i.e.* first excited state energy corresponds to following three combinations of n_1, n_2 and n_3.

n_1	n_2	n_3
1	1	2
1	2	1
2	1	1

All these three combinations will have the same energy $E_{112} = E_{121} = E_{211} = 6 \dfrac{\hbar^2 \pi^2}{2ma^2}$

The wave functions corresponding to above three states are

$$\psi_{112} = \sqrt{\frac{8}{a^3}} \sin\left(\frac{\pi}{a}x\right) \sin\left(\frac{\pi}{a}y\right) \sin\left(\frac{2\pi}{a}z\right) \qquad \text{for } n_1 = 1, n_2 = 1, n_3 = 2$$

$$\psi_{121} = \sqrt{\frac{8}{a^3}} \sin\left(\frac{\pi}{a}x\right) \sin\left(\frac{2\pi}{a}y\right) \sin\left(\frac{\pi}{a}z\right) \qquad \text{for } n_1 = 1, n_2 = 2, n_3 = 1$$

$$\psi_{211} = \sqrt{\frac{8}{a^3}} \sin\left(\frac{2\pi}{a}x\right) \sin\left(\frac{\pi}{a}y\right) \sin\left(\frac{\pi}{a}z\right) \qquad \text{for } n_1 = 1, n_2 = 1, n_3 = 1$$

- Thus, it is clear that there are three possible states of the particle corresponding to the same energy value $E = 6\frac{\hbar^2\pi^2}{2ma^2}$.

- When there are more than one eigen functions corresponding to the same energy eigen value, the energy state of the particle is called **degenerate** and the order of degeneracy is equal to the number of eigen functions corresponding to the same energy. Thus, first excited state is *three fold degenerate*.

  Second excited state corresponds to the set of three combinations of n_1, n_2, n_3, which are

n_1	n_2	n_3
1	2	2
2	2	1
2	1	2

- This state is three fold degenerate corresponding to same energy eigen value $E = 9\frac{\hbar^2\pi^2}{2ma^2}$.

- The third excited state corresponds to $n_1 = 2$, $n_2 = 2$, $n_3 = 2$. This state is non-degenerate having energy $E = 12\frac{\hbar^2\pi^2}{2ma^2}$.

- In the above, we discussed the motion of a particle in a three-dimensional rigid box. We can also consider motion in two-dimensional box. The formula for energy in this case is

$$E_{n_1 n_2} = \frac{\hbar^2\pi^2}{2m}\left(\frac{n_1^2}{a^2} + \frac{n_2^2}{b^2}\right) \qquad \qquad \text{... (3.42)}$$

3.4 Step Potential

- The step potential function is defined as

$$\left. \begin{aligned} V(x) &= 0 \ \text{ for } x \le 0 \\ &= V_0 \ \text{for } x > 0 \end{aligned} \right\} \qquad \qquad \text{... (3.43)}$$

- Let a particle of energy E move from left to right, i.e. along the positive direction of x-axis. (Refer Fig. 3.5)

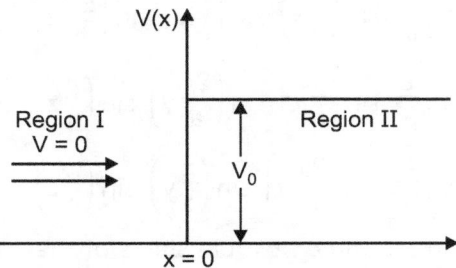

Fig. 3.5 : Step potential

We will first consider classical motion of a particle.

Classical treatment :

Case (I) : $E > V_0$: In region I, V = 0. Therefore, total energy E of particle is equal to its kinetic energy. If the particle with this kinetic energy arrives at x = 0 boundary, it will be able to cross over to the region II as $E > V_0$. As kinetic energy $(E - V_0)$ in region II is positive, the particle will move in forward direction. Thus for the case $E > V_0$, the reflection probability will be R = 0 and transmission probability T = 1.

Case (II) : $E < V_0$: Suppose a stream of particles is moving from region I towards region II. In region I, total energy E of particle is equal to its kinetic energy because V = 0. If the particle with this kinetic energy arrive at x = 0 boundary, it will not be able to cross over to the region II as $E < V_0$. Because kinetic energy $(E - V_0)$ in region II will be negative. Classically the particle with negative kinetic energy does not exist. Thus for the case $E < V_0$, the particle will definitely be reflected back at the boundary x = 0. Thus, the reflection probability will be R = 1 and transmission probability T = 0.

Now, we shall see what is prediction of quantum theory for this problem.

Quantum Mechanical Treatment :

As the potential is independent of time, we use time-independent Schrödinger's equation

$$\frac{d^2\psi}{dx^2} + \frac{2m}{\hbar^2}(E - V)\,\psi = 0 \qquad \qquad \ldots (3.44)$$

For region I, V = 0. Therefore, the Schrödinger's equation takes the form

$$\frac{d^2\psi_1}{dx^2} + \frac{2mE}{\hbar^2}\,\psi_1 = 0 \qquad \qquad \ldots (3.45)$$

Let $k_1^2 = \frac{2mE}{\hbar^2}$, therefore, equation (3.45) becomes

$$\frac{d^2\psi_1}{dx^2} + k_1^2\psi_1 = 0 \qquad \qquad \ldots (3.46)$$

The general solution of this equation is

$$\psi_1 = Ae^{ik_1x} + Be^{-ik_1x} \qquad \qquad \ldots (3.47)$$

Some particles may be reflected by the potential barrier and some transmitted. The first term $A\,e^{ik_1x}$ represents the *incident* wave and the second term $B\,e^{-ik_1x}$ represents *reflected wave*.

The Schrödinger's wave equation for region II is

$$\frac{d^2\psi_2}{dx^2} + \frac{2m}{\hbar^2}(E - V_0)\,\psi_2 = 0 \qquad \text{... (3.48)}$$

We will consider two cases viz. $E > V_0$ and $E < V_0$.

Case I : $E > V_0$:

Let $k_2^2 = \frac{2m}{\hbar^2}(E - V_0)$. With this equation (3.48) becomes

$$\frac{d^2\psi_2}{dx^2} + k_2^2\psi_2 = 0 \qquad \text{... (3.49)}$$

The general solution of equation (3.49) is given by

$$\psi_2 = C e^{ik_2x} + D e^{-ik_2x} \qquad \text{... (3.50)}$$

In region II, the term Ce^{ik_2x} represents a transmitted wave. There is no barrier after $x = 0$, and so no particles can flow to the left direction for $x > 0$. Thus, $D = 0$ in equation (3.50). So the solution in region II is

$$\psi_2 = C e^{ik_2x} \qquad \text{... (3.51)}$$

To determine constants A, B and C in equations (3.47) and (3.51), we use the boundary conditions on wave functions.

At $x = 0$, $\qquad\qquad [\psi_1]_{x=0} = [\psi_2]_{x=0}$

$\therefore \qquad\qquad\qquad A + B = C \qquad\qquad\qquad\qquad \text{... (3.52)}$

and $\qquad \left(\frac{d\psi_1}{dx}\right)_{x=0} = \left(\frac{d\psi_2}{dx}\right)_{x=0}$

$\therefore \qquad\qquad\qquad k_1(A - B) = k_2C \qquad\qquad\qquad \text{... (3.53)}$

Multiplying equation (3.52) by k_1 and adding to equation (3.53), we get

$$2k_1A = (k_1 + k_2)C$$

$\therefore \qquad\qquad\qquad C = \frac{2k_1}{k_1 + k_2}\,A \qquad\qquad\qquad \text{... (3.54)}$

Substituting this value in equation (3.52), we get

$$B = \frac{k_1 - k_2}{k_1 + k_2}\,A \qquad \text{... (3.55)}$$

The wave function for incident waves is given as

$$\psi_{in} = A e^{ik_1x}$$

Its complex conjugate is $\qquad \psi_{in}^* = A^* e^{-ik_1x}$

The equation of probability current density is given as,

$$\vec{J} = \frac{\hbar}{2mi}[\psi^*\nabla\psi - \psi\nabla\psi^*]$$

The current density for incident waves is

$$J_{in} = \frac{\hbar}{2mi}\left(\psi_{in}^*\frac{d\psi_{in}}{dx} - \psi_{in}\frac{d\psi_{in}^*}{dx}\right)$$

Using ψ_{in} and ψ_{in}^* in J_{in}, we get

$$J_{in} = \frac{\hbar k_1}{m}|A|^2 \qquad \qquad \ldots (3.56)$$

The wave function for reflected waves is given as

$$\psi_{ref} = Be^{-ik_1x}$$

Its complex conjugate is $\psi_{ref}^* = B^* e^{ik_1x}$

The current density for reflected waves is

$$J_{ref} = \frac{\hbar}{2mi}\left(\psi_{ref}^*\frac{d\psi_{ref}}{dx} - \psi_{ref}\frac{d\psi_{ref}^*}{dx}\right)$$

Using ψ_{ref} and ψ_{ref}^* in J_{ref}, we get

$$J_{ref} = \frac{\hbar k_1}{m}|B|^2 \qquad \qquad \ldots (3.57)$$

The transmitted wave is given as

$$\psi_2 = \psi_{tr} = C e^{ik_2x}$$

So the current density for *transmitted wave* will be

$$J_{tr} = \frac{\hbar k_2}{m}|C|^2 \qquad \qquad \ldots (3.58)$$

The probability of transmission T is given by

$$T = \frac{J_{tr}}{J_{in}}$$

Using equations (3.58) and (3.56), we get

$$T = \frac{k_2|C|^2}{k_1|A|^2}$$

Using value of C from equation (3.54), we get

$$T = \frac{k_2}{k_1} \cdot \frac{4k_1^2}{(k_1 + k_2)^2}$$

or $$T = \frac{4k_1k_2}{(k_1 + k_2)^2} \qquad \qquad \ldots (3.59)$$

The probability of reflection R is given by

$$R = \frac{J_{ref}}{J_{in}}$$

Using equations (3.57) and (3.56), we get

$$R = \frac{|B|^2}{|A|^2}$$

Using equation (3.55) in above equation, we get

$$R = \frac{(k_1 - k_2)^2}{(k_1 + k_2)^2} \qquad \qquad \dots (3.60)$$

From equations (3.59) and (3.60), we get

$$R + T = \frac{(k_1 - k_2)^2}{(k_1 + k_2)^2} + \frac{4k_1k_2}{(k_1 + k_2)^2}$$

$$\therefore \qquad \qquad R + T = 1$$

Case II : E < V$_0$:

Under this condition, equation (3.58) becomes

$$\frac{d^2\psi_2}{dx^2} - \frac{2m}{\hbar^2}(V_0 - E)\,\psi_2 = 0 \qquad \qquad \dots (3.61)$$

Let

$$\alpha^2 = \frac{2m}{\hbar^2}(V_0 - E)$$

$$\therefore \qquad \qquad \frac{d^2\psi_2}{dx^2} - \alpha^2\,\psi_2 = 0 \qquad \qquad \dots (3.62)$$

The transmitted wave equation is the solution of equation (3.62) in forward direction, which will be

$$\psi_2 = \psi_{tr} = C\,e^{-\alpha x} \qquad \qquad \dots (3.63)$$

The current density for transmitted waves is

$$J_{tr} = \frac{\hbar}{2mi}\left(\psi_{tr}^* \frac{d\psi_{tr}}{dx} - \psi_{tr}\frac{d\psi_{tr}^*}{dx}\right)$$

We have

$$\psi_{tr}^* = C\,e^{-\alpha x}$$

Using ψ_{tr} and ψ_{tr}^* in J_{tr}, we get

$$J_{tr} = 0$$

Hence, T = 0

By definition, R + T = 1. Therefore, R = 1.

Thus there is complete reflection.

The wave functions in regions I and II for $E \geq V_0$ and $E < V_0$ are shown in Fig. 3.6.

- Classically, for $E < V_0$, $R = 1$ and $T = 0$. Thus, quantum mechanical results are the same as those of classical results for this case. However, the function has tail into the *classically forbidden region*. This tail is represented by the term $e^{-\alpha x}$ (Refer Fig. 3.6). The tail becomes shorter and shorter as E becomes smaller and smaller as compared to V_0. There is some probability even though small in finding the particle in the region $x > 0$. This phenomenon is called b*arrier penetration*. It may be noted that $T = 0$ does not contradict with the fact that there is some probability of finding the particle in region II, because there is no wave travelling continuously along +x axis in region II. We may say that the particle penetrates through the potential barrier at $x = 0$. However, it returns back into the region I after spending short time in region II.

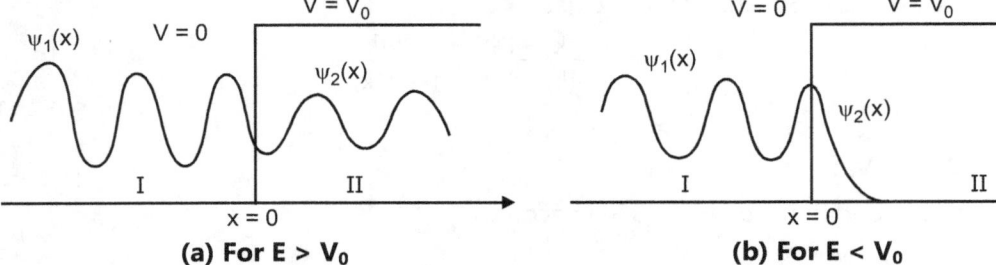

(a) For $E > V_0$ 　　　　　 (b) For $E < V_0$

Fig. 3.6

3.5 Potential Barrier (Qualitative Discussion)

- In this section, we consider a potential barrier, illustrated in Fig. 3.7.

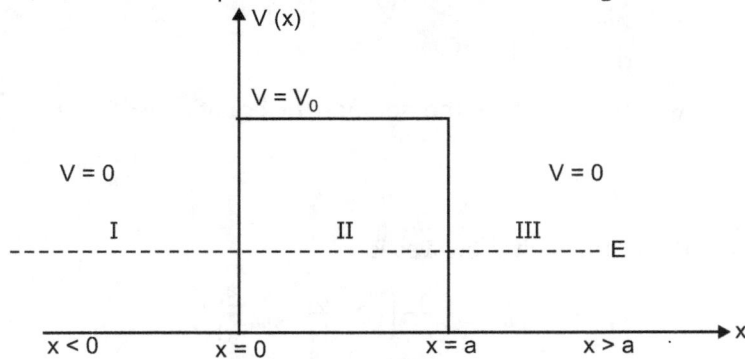

Fig. 3.7 : Potential barrier

- The potential can be written as follows :

$$V = 0 \qquad\qquad x < 0$$
$$V = V_0 \qquad\qquad 0 \leq x \leq a$$
$$V = 0 \qquad\qquad x > a$$

Classical motion : Suppose a particle of total energy E is moving from left to right in region I ($x < 0$). When it is incident on the barrier at $x = 0$, there are two possibilities. First, if the energy of particle $E < V_0$, the particle is reflected back and second, if $E > V_0$ the particle crosses over through the barrier into the region II ($x > a$).

Quantum Mechanical motion : Now, we will see quantum mechanical results.

We have one-dimensional time-independent Schrödinger's equation

$$\frac{d^2\psi}{dx^2} + \frac{2m}{\hbar^2}(E - V)\psi = 0 \qquad \ldots (3.64)$$

In region I (V = 0), above equation becomes

$$\frac{d^2\psi_1}{dx^2} + \frac{2mE}{\hbar^2}\psi_1 = 0 \qquad \ldots (3.65)$$

In region II (V = V_0), equation (3.64) becomes

$$\frac{d^2\psi_2}{dx^2} + \frac{2m}{\hbar^2}(E - V_0)\psi_2 = 0 \qquad \ldots (3.66)$$

In region III (V = 0), equation (3.64) becomes

$$\frac{d^2\psi_3}{dx^2} + \frac{2mE}{\hbar^2}\psi_3 = 0 \qquad \ldots (3.67)$$

Consider two cases.

Case I : E > V_0 :

Let

$$k^2 = \frac{2mE}{\hbar^2} \qquad \ldots (3.68)$$

and

$$\alpha^2 = \frac{2m(E - V_0)}{\hbar^2} \qquad \ldots (3.69)$$

With above two equations, equations (3.65), (3.66) and (3.67) become

$$\frac{d^2\psi_1}{dx^2} + k^2\psi_1 = 0 \qquad \ldots (3.70)$$

$$\frac{d^2\psi_2}{dx^2} + k^2\psi_2 = 0 \qquad \ldots (3.71)$$

and

$$\frac{d^2\psi_3}{dx^2} + k^2\psi_3 = 0 \qquad \ldots (3.72)$$

The general solution of equation (3.70) is given by

$$\psi_1(x) = A\,e^{ikx} + B\,e^{-ikx} \qquad \ldots (3.73)$$

In equation (3.73), the term $A\,e^{ikx}$ represents the wave incident along +X direction towards the barrier at x = 0 and $B\,e^{-ikx}$ represents reflected wave *i.e.*

$$\psi_{in} = A\,e^{ikx} \text{ and } \psi_{ref} = B\,e^{-ikx}$$

The general solution of equation (3.71) is given by

$$\psi_2(x) = F\,e^{i\alpha x} + G\,e^{-i\alpha x}$$

The general solution of equation (3.72) is given by

$$\psi_3(x) = C\,e^{ikx} + D\,e^{-ikx}$$

Once the particle is transmitted in the region III, there will be wave propagating along +x axis only. Hence we set D = 0 in the above equation. Thus, the wave function in the region III will be

$$\psi_3(x) = C e^{ikx} \qquad \qquad \dots (3.74)$$

It also represents the transmitted wave. Thus,

$$\psi_{tr} = C e^{ikx}$$

A, B, C, D, F and G are constants. Their values can be calculated by using the boundary conditions. These values are as under :

$$A = \frac{(k + \alpha)}{2k} F + \frac{(k - \alpha)}{2k} G$$

$$\therefore \qquad B = \frac{(k - \alpha)}{2k} F + \frac{(k + \alpha)}{2k} G$$

$$\therefore \qquad F = \frac{(k + \alpha)}{2\alpha} C e^{ika} e^{-i\alpha a}$$

$$\therefore \qquad G = \frac{(\alpha - k)}{2\alpha} C e^{ika} e^{i\alpha a}$$

Using these constants, we can obtain coefficient of transmission and coefficient of reflection. Coefficient of transmission can be given as,

$$T = \frac{J_{tr}}{J_{in}} = \frac{|C|^2}{|A|^2} = \frac{CC^*}{AA^*}$$

Solving this equation, $\qquad T = \dfrac{1}{\left[1 + \dfrac{V_0^2 \sin^2 \alpha a}{4E (E - V_0)} \right]} \qquad \dots (3.75)$

Similarly, the coefficient of reflection is given as

$$R = \frac{J_{ref}}{J_{in}} = \frac{|B|^2}{|A|^2} = \frac{BB^*}{AA^*}$$

Solving this equation,

$$R = \frac{1}{\left[\dfrac{4 E(E - V_0)}{V_0^2 \sin^2 \alpha a} + 1 \right]} \qquad \dots (3.76)$$

This is the formula for reflection coefficient.

We can prove that R + T = 1. Using equations (3.75) and (3.76), we have

$$R + T = \frac{1}{\left[1 + \dfrac{V_0^2 \sin^2 \alpha a}{4E(E - V_0)} \right]} + \frac{1}{\left[\dfrac{4 E(E - V_0)}{V_0^2 \sin^2 \alpha a} + 1 \right]}$$

$$= \frac{4E(E - V_0)}{[4E(E - V_0) + V_0^2 \sin^2 \alpha a]} + \frac{V_0^2 \sin^2 \alpha a}{[4E(E - V_0) + V_0^2 \sin^2 \alpha a]}$$

$$\therefore \quad R + T = 1$$

It is seen from equation (3.75) that, in general, T is less than unity. Therefore, there is general partial reflection and partial transmission across the potential barrier between x = 0 and x = a. However, sin αa = 0 for those values of energies for which αa = π, 2π, 3π etc. Then T = 1 *i.e.* there is *perfect* transmission through the barrier. This means that all the particles pass through the barrier as if it was absent. This is a very interesting phenomenon. However, kinetic energy of the particles will be reduced as long as the particles are in region II.

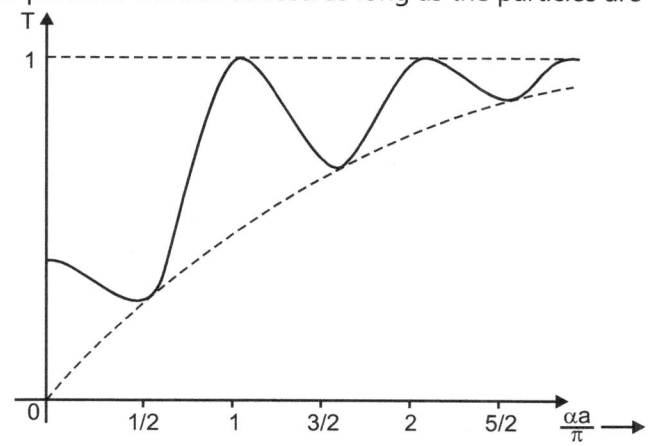

Fig. 3.8: T is a function of αa/π

The appearance of maxima and minima in the flux of particles is similar to the interference phenomenon in the case of light waves.

Case II : E < V₀ :

The case for E < V₀ can be easily derived from the case E > V₀. From equation (3.69), we have

$$\alpha^2 = \frac{2m(E - V_0)}{\hbar^2}$$

$$\therefore \qquad \alpha^2 = -\frac{2m(V_0 - E)}{\hbar^2}$$

Let $\beta^2 = \dfrac{2m(V_0 - E)}{\hbar^2}$. For $V_0 > E$, β^2 is positive.

$$\therefore \qquad \alpha^2 = -\beta^2$$

or $\qquad \alpha = i\beta.$

Using $\alpha = i\beta$ in equations (3.75) and (3.76), we get R and T for E < V₀. Therefore,

$$T = \frac{1}{\left[1 + \dfrac{V_0^2 \sin^2 i\beta a}{4E(E - V_0)} \right]} \qquad \qquad ... (3.77)$$

and $\qquad\qquad R = \dfrac{1}{\left[\dfrac{4 E(E - V_0)}{V_0^2 \sin^2 i\beta a} + 1 \right]} \qquad\qquad ... (3.78)$

We have $\sin i\theta = i \sin h\theta$ where $\sin h\theta$ represents the hyperbolic function.

$\therefore$

$$T = \cfrac{1}{\left[1 + \cfrac{V_0{}^2 (i)^2 \sinh^2 \beta a}{4E(E - V_0)} \right]}$$

or

$$T = \cfrac{1}{\left[1 + \cfrac{V_0{}^2 \sinh^2 \beta a}{4E(V_0 - E)} \right]} \qquad \text{... (3.79)}$$

and

$$R = \cfrac{1}{\left[\cfrac{4 E(V_0 - E)}{V_0{}^2 \sinh^2 \beta a} + 1 \right]} \qquad \text{... (3.80)}$$

- It is seen that for $E < V_0$ there is always some probability of transmission. Classically, the probability of transmission for $E < V_0$ is $T = 0$, *i.e.* there is no transmission. Thus, this type of transmission is completely quantum mechanical phenomenon. This is also called as *tunneling effect*.

Barrier penetration and tunneling effect :

- Quantum tunneling is a quantum mechanical phenomenon where particles tunnel through a barrier that classically could not surmount. To understand the phenomenon, particles attempting to travel between potential barriers can be compared to a ball trying to roll over a hill. Classically the particles that do not have sufficient energy to rise above the hill will not able to reach the other side. Thus a ball without sufficient energy to surmount the hill would roll back (reflection). In quantum mechanics these particles can, with a small probability, tunnel through other side, thus crossing the barrier.

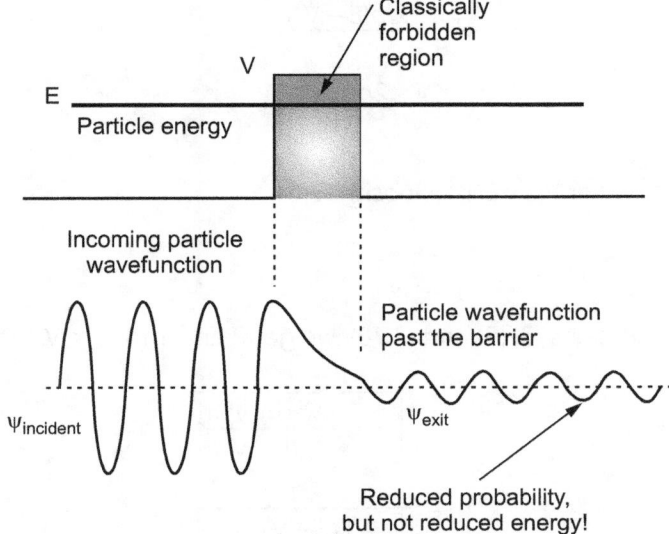

Fig. 3.9 : Quantum tunneling

- The reason for this difference comes from behavior of matter in quantum mechanics having properties of waves and particles. If a particle impinging on the potential barrier with energy less than the height of the potential barrier, there is always some probability of transmission through the barrier. This probability of crossing the barrier is called the tunneling effect (Refer Fig. 3.9).
- According to classical physics, a particle of energy E less than the height V of a barrier could not penetrate - the region inside the barrier is classically forbidden. But the wave function associated with a free particle must be continuous at the barrier and will show an exponential decay inside the barrier. The wave function must also be continuous on the far side of the barrier, so there is a finite probability that the particle will tunnel through the barrier. As a particle approaches the barrier, it is described by a free particle wave function. When it reaches the barrier, it must satisfy the Schrödinger equation in the form

$$\frac{d^2\psi}{dx^2} + \frac{2m}{\hbar^2}(E - V)\psi = 0$$

which has the solution $\psi(x) = A\,e^{-\alpha x}$ where $\alpha = \sqrt{\dfrac{2m(E - V_0)}{\hbar^2}}$

There are several phenomena that have same behavior as quantum tunneling.

Applications : Tunneling effect provides explanation for following phenomena :
(i)   the field of emission of electron from a cold metallic surface (cold emission)
(ii)   the electrical breakdown of insulator.
(iii)   the reverse breakdown of semiconductor diode.
(iv)   the switching action of tunnel diode used in high speed devices.
(v)   the emission of α particle from a radioactive element (radioactive decay).
(vi)   Spontaneous mutation of DNA occurs when normal DNA replication takes place after a particular significant proton has defied the odds in quantum tunneling (quantum biology).
(vii) The scanning tunneling microscope (STM) operates by taking advantage of relation between quantum tunneling with distance.

3.6 One-Dimensional Harmonic Oscillator

- First we will consider the classical motion of one-dimensional simple harmonic oscillator.

Classical motion :

- In linear simple harmonic motion, the restoring force F is proportional to the displacement of a particle from the mean position and directed towards the mean position, so that

$$F = -kx$$

∴ $m\dfrac{d^2x}{dt^2} = -kx$

or $\dfrac{d^2x}{dt^2} + \omega^2 x = 0$

where $\omega^2 = k/m$ or $k = m\omega^2$

The solution of above equation is

$$x = a \sin (\omega t + \phi)$$

where a is the amplitude of oscillation.

- Thus, particle oscillates between + a and − a with frequency

$$\nu = \frac{1}{2\pi} \sqrt{\frac{k}{m}}$$

The total energy of the oscillator is

$$E = \frac{1}{2} k a^2$$

where a is amplitude called classical limit. It is different for different energies.

- We can say that the particle must be moving around in the classically allowed region : $|x| < a$ where $a = (2E/k)^{1/2}$. All subdivisions within the classically allowed region are not equally probable, as the particle is whizzing through equilibrium, while spending more time in the parts through which it is slowly moving. The time (dt) that a particle spends in a small region dx depends on its speed and is given by dt = dx/v. The probability (dP) of finding the particle in dx is then proportional to the time it spends there is dP = 2dt/T, where T is the period of oscillations.

$$\therefore \qquad dP = \frac{2\,dt}{T} = \frac{2}{T} \frac{dt}{dx} dx$$

$$= \frac{2}{T} \left(\frac{1}{v} \right) dx$$

$\because$ $v = \omega^2 \sqrt{a^2 - x^2}$ and T = 2π/ω, we get

$$dP = \frac{1}{\pi \sqrt{a^2 - x^2}} dx = P(x)\,dx \qquad\qquad ... (3.81)$$

where $P(x) = \dfrac{1}{\pi \sqrt{a^2 - x^2}}$ is called the probability density.

- The plot of classical probability density against displacement is shown in Fig. 3.10.

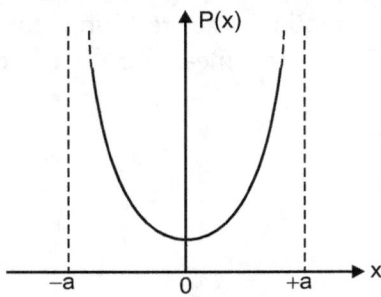

Fig. 3.10 : Classical probability density plot

Quantum mechanical motion :

- The simple harmonic oscillator has potential energy

$$V = \frac{1}{2} kx^2$$

- The plot of potential energy against displacement is shown in Fig. 3.11.

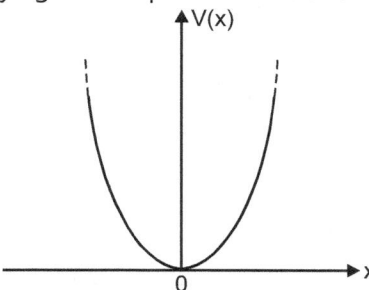

Fig. 3.11 : Potential energy

The Schrödinger's equation for harmonic oscillator is

$$\frac{d^2\psi}{dx^2} + \frac{2m}{\hbar^2}\left(E - \frac{1}{2}kx^2\right)\psi = 0 \qquad \qquad \text{... (3.82)}$$

- It is convenient to simplify equation (3.82) by introducing the dimensionless quantities. Let us introduce dimensionless variable

$$\xi = \alpha x \qquad \qquad \text{... (3.83)}$$

where α is a constant having dimensions of inverse of length.

$$\therefore \qquad \frac{d\psi}{dx} = \frac{d\psi}{d\xi}\frac{d\xi}{dx}$$

$$\therefore \qquad \frac{d\psi}{dx} = \alpha\,\frac{d\psi}{d\xi}$$

and $\quad \dfrac{d^2\psi}{dx^2} = \dfrac{d}{dx}\!\left(\dfrac{d\psi}{dx}\right) = \dfrac{d}{dx}\!\left(\alpha\dfrac{d\psi}{d\xi}\right) = \dfrac{d\xi}{dx}\dfrac{d}{d\xi}\!\left(\alpha\,\dfrac{d\psi}{d\xi}\right) = \alpha^2\dfrac{d^2\psi}{d\xi^2}$

Using these values in equation (3.82), we get

$$\alpha^2\frac{d^2\psi}{d\xi^2} + \frac{2m}{\hbar^2}\left(E - \frac{1}{2}k\frac{\xi^2}{\alpha^2}\right)\psi = 0$$

$$\therefore \qquad \alpha^2\frac{d^2\psi}{d\xi^2} + \left(\frac{2mE}{\hbar^2} - \frac{mk\xi^2}{\hbar^2\alpha^2}\right)\psi = 0$$

Dividing throughout by α^2, we get

$$\frac{d^2\psi}{d\xi^2} + \left(\frac{2mE}{\hbar^2\alpha^2} - \frac{mk\xi^2}{\hbar^2\alpha^4}\right)\psi = 0 \qquad \qquad \text{... (3.84)}$$

Since α is constant, let us choose α in such a way that

$$\frac{mk}{\hbar^2\alpha^4} = 1 \ \text{ or } \ \alpha^4 = \frac{mk}{\hbar^2} \ \textit{i.e. } \alpha = \left(\frac{mk}{\hbar^2}\right)^{1/4}$$

We also introduce another constant λ, defined as,

$$\lambda = \frac{2mE}{\hbar^2\alpha^2} \qquad \qquad \text{... (3.85)}$$

Using $k = m\omega^2$ in equation (3.85), we get

$$\alpha = \left(\frac{m\omega}{\hbar}\right)^{1/2} \qquad \qquad \text{... (3.86)}$$

and

$$\lambda = \frac{2E}{\hbar\omega} \qquad \qquad \text{... (3.87)}$$

Therefore, equation (3.84) will take the form

$$\frac{d^2\psi}{d\xi^2} + (\lambda - \xi^2)\psi = 0 \qquad \qquad \text{... (3.88)}$$

- We desire to obtain solutions $\psi(\xi)$ which satisfy equation (3.88) throughout the region $-\infty$ to $+\infty$ for ξ, and which are acceptable functions *i.e.*, each function must be continuous, single valued and finite throughout the region.

- Let us consider asymptotic solution *i.e.* $\xi \to \infty$. When ξ is large we can neglect λ in comparison with ξ. Then equation (3.88) becomes

$$\frac{d^2\psi}{d\xi^2} - \xi^2\psi = 0$$

The general solution of the above equation will be of the form

$$\psi(\xi) = A\,e^{-\xi^2/2} + B\,e^{\xi^2/2}$$

As $\xi \to \infty$, $e^{-\xi^2/2} \to 0$ and $e^{\xi^2/2} \to \infty$. Thus acceptable solution will be

$$\psi(\xi) = A\,e^{-\xi^2/2}$$

- We proceed to obtain the solution of wave equation (3.88) throughout the configuration space $(-\infty < \xi < +\infty)$, based upon the asymptotic solution. Let us assume that the solution is of the form

$$\psi(\xi) = A\,H(\xi)\,e^{-\xi^2/2} \qquad \qquad \text{... (3.89)}$$

where A is constant, and $H(\xi)$ is some function of ξ.

From equation (3.89),

$$\frac{d\psi}{d\xi} = AH'(\xi)\,e^{-\xi^2/2} - \xi\,AH(\xi)\,e^{-\xi^2/2}$$

and 　$\dfrac{d^2\psi}{d\xi^2} = AH''(\xi)\,e^{-\xi^2/2} - \xi AH'(\xi)\,e^{-\xi^2/2} - AH(\xi)e^{-\xi^2/2} - \xi AH'(\xi)\,e^{-\xi^2/2} + \xi^2\,AH(\xi)e^{-\xi^2/2}$

$$\therefore \quad \frac{d^2\psi}{d\xi^2} = AH''(\xi)\,e^{-\xi^2/2} - 2\xi AH'(\xi)\,e^{-\xi^2/2} - AH(\xi)e^{-\xi^2/2} + \xi^2\,AH(\xi)e^{-\xi^2/2}$$

Using $\dfrac{d^2\psi}{d\xi^2}$ and $\psi(\xi)$ in equation (3.88), we get

$$AH''(\xi)\,e^{-\xi^2/2} - 2\xi AH'(\xi)\,e^{-\xi^2/2} - AH(\xi)e^{-\xi^2/2} + \xi^2 AH(\xi)e^{-\xi^2/2} + (\lambda - \xi^2)\,AH(\xi)e^{-\xi^2/2} = 0$$

$\therefore \quad A\,e^{-\xi^2/2}\left[H''(\xi) - 2\xi H(\xi) + (\lambda - 1)H(\xi)\right] = 0 \qquad \ldots (3.90)$

As $e^{-\xi^2/2}$ is an arbitrary function, we get

$\qquad H''(\xi) - 2\xi H'(\xi) + (\lambda - 1)H(\xi) = 0$

or $\qquad H'' - 2\xi H' + (\lambda - 1)H = 0 \qquad \ldots (3.91)$

where primes denote differentiation with respect to ξ.

- Equation (3.91) is the Hermite differential equation for 'H' in the variable 'ξ'. We try to obtain the solution of this equation in the form of Frobenius power series.

Let, $\qquad\qquad\qquad\qquad H(\xi) = \displaystyle\sum_{m=0}^{\infty} a_m \xi^m$

$\therefore \qquad\qquad\qquad\qquad H'(\xi) = \displaystyle\sum_{m=1}^{\infty} a_m\, m\, \xi^{m-1}$

and $\qquad\qquad\qquad\qquad H''(\xi) = \displaystyle\sum_{m=2}^{\infty} a_m\, m(m-1)\, \xi^{m-2}$

- Using all these values in equation (3.91), we get

$$\sum_{m=2}^{\infty} a_m\, m(m-1)\, \xi^{m-2} - 2\xi \sum_{m=1}^{\infty} a_m\, m\, \xi^{m-1} + (\lambda - 1) \sum_{m=0}^{\infty} a_m \xi^m = 0$$

$$\sum_{m=2}^{\infty} a_m\, m(m-1)\, \xi^{m-2} - 2 \sum_{m=1}^{\infty} a_m\, m\, \xi^{m} + (\lambda - 1) \sum_{m=0}^{\infty} a_m \xi^m = 0$$

In above equation, replace m by m+2 in first term. Therefore,

$$\sum_{m=0}^{\infty} a_{m+2}\, (m+2)(m+1)\, \xi^m - 2 \sum_{m=0}^{\infty} a_m\, m\, \xi^m + (\lambda - 1) \sum_{m=0}^{\infty} a_m \xi^m = 0$$

$\therefore \quad \displaystyle\sum_{m=0}^{\infty} \left[a_{m+2}\,(m+2)m - 2a_m m + (\lambda - 1)a_m\right] \xi^m = 0 \qquad \ldots (3.92)$

- Since 'ξ' is arbitrary, the coefficient of each and every power of ξ in the above equation must be zero. Therefore, considering coefficient of ξ^m, we get

$\qquad a_{m+2}\,(m+2)(m+1) - 2a_m m + (\lambda - 1)a_m = 0$

$\therefore \qquad\qquad\qquad a_{m+2} = \dfrac{(2m + 1 - \lambda)}{(m+1)(m+2)}\, a_m \qquad \ldots (3.93)$

- This expression is called *recursion formula*. If we know a_0, we can calculate a_2, a_4, a_6 etc. Similarly if we know a_1, we can find a_3, a_5, a_7 etc. Thus $H(\xi)$ is an infinite power series of odd and even powers of ξ such as

$$H(\xi) = [a_0 + a_2\xi^2 + a_4\xi^4 + \text{... ... ..}] + [a_1\xi + a_3\xi^3 + a_5\xi^5 + \text{... ...}]$$

- For arbitrary values of the energy parameter λ, the above given series consists of an infinite number of terms and does not correspond to satisfactory wave function. Let us examine the convergence of the power series solution defined by equation (3.93), as $m \to \infty$.

Consider

$$\lim_{m\to\infty} \frac{a_{m+2}}{a_m} = \lim_{m\to\infty} \frac{(2m + 1 - \lambda)}{(m + 1)(m + 2)} = \frac{2}{m} \qquad \text{... (3.94)}$$

Considering the series expansion of e^{ξ^2}, we have

$$e^{\xi^2} = 1 + \xi^2 + \frac{\xi^4}{2!} + \frac{\xi^6}{3!} + \text{... ... ...} + \frac{\xi^m}{(m/2)!} + \frac{\xi^{m+2}}{(m/2 + 1)!} + \text{... ... .}$$

$$= b_0 + b_2\xi^2 + b_4\xi^4 + \text{... ... ..} + b_m\xi^m + b_{m+2}\xi^{m+2} + \text{... ... .}$$

From this series, we get

$$\frac{b_{m+2}}{b_m} = \frac{\dfrac{1}{(m/2+1)!}}{\dfrac{1}{(m/2)!}} = \frac{2}{2 + m}$$

Therefore, for limit $m \to \infty$, we have

$$\lim_{m\to\infty} \frac{b_{m+2}}{b_m} = \lim_{m\to\infty} \frac{2}{2+m} = \frac{2}{m} \qquad \text{... (3.95)}$$

- Equations (3.94) and (3.95) show the behavior of $H(\xi)$ and e^{ξ^2} respectively, which shows that $H(\xi)$ diverges approximately as e^{ξ^2} and therefore $\psi(\xi) = AH(\xi)e^{-\xi^2/2} = Ae^{\xi^2} e^{-\xi^2/2} = Ae^{\xi^2/2}$. This gives that as $\xi \to +\infty$ or $-\infty$ the wave function $\psi(\xi) \to \infty$, thus making it unacceptable as a wave function.

- The only way in which this situation can be avoided is to choose λ in equation (3.93) in such a way that the coefficients of powers of ξ vanish after certain value of $m = n$ making $H(\xi)$ a polynomial in ξ instead of an infinite series.

- Thus, after a_n all coefficients are zero, this is possible if for $m = n$ in equation (3.93), it gives

$$a_{n+2} = \frac{(2n + 1 - \lambda)}{(n + 1)(n + 2)} a_n = 0$$

But $a_n \neq 0$, therefore, $2n + 1 - \lambda = 0$

or $\lambda = 2n + 1$.

From equation (3.87), we have

$$\lambda = \frac{2E}{\hbar\omega}$$

$$\therefore \qquad \frac{2E}{\hbar\omega} = (2n + 1)$$

$$E = \frac{1}{2}(2n + 1)\hbar\omega$$

or $\qquad E = \left(n + \frac{1}{2}\right)\hbar\omega$ where n = 0, 1, 2, 3, 4, 5 ... .

Since, the allowed energies are different for different 'n', we may write

$$E_n = \left(n + \frac{1}{2}\right)\hbar\omega \qquad\qquad ... (3.96)$$

- Above equation gives the energy spectrum of one-dimensional harmonic oscillator. About the energy spectrum of harmonic oscillator, we note the following :

  (1) The energy spectrum is *discrete*. There are infinite number of energy levels corresponding to n = 0, 1, 2, 3, 4 .... However, the classical theory predicts the energy spectrum to be continuous.

  (2) The lowest energy level (corresponding to n = 0) has energy $E_0 = \frac{1}{2}\hbar\omega$, called the ground state energy or *zero-point energy*. Classically, the lowest energy is zero, which corresponds to state of rest. Quantum mechanically, the lowest energy is not zero but $\frac{1}{2}\hbar\omega$. This is consequence of uncertainty principle.

  The energy spectrum is shown in Fig. 3.12. It is seen that the separation between successive energy levels is the same and is equal to $\hbar\omega$.

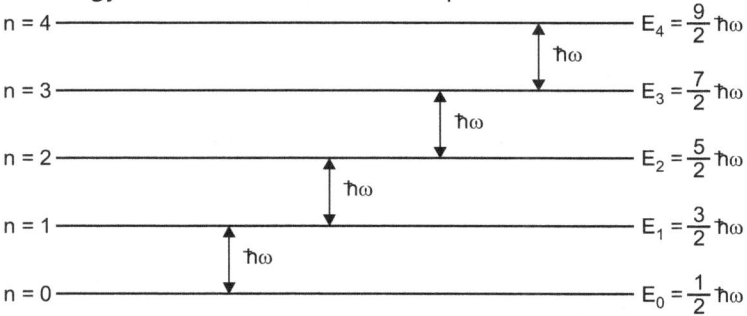

Fig. 3.12 : Energy spectrum of one-dimensional oscillator

Normalization of wave function :

The wave function for one-dimensional harmonic oscillator is given as

$$\psi(\xi) = AH(\xi)\, e^{-\xi^2/2}, \text{ where A is constant called normalization constant.}$$

Since $\xi = \alpha x$

$$\therefore \qquad\qquad \psi(x) = A\, H(\alpha x)\, e^{-\alpha^2 x^2/2}$$

Since energy depends on the integer n, the wave function corresponding to different energy levels E_n is expressed as

$$\psi_n(\xi) = A_n H_n(\xi) e^{-\xi^2/2} \qquad \ldots (3.97)$$

or $\qquad\qquad \psi_n(x) = A_n H_n(\alpha x)\, e^{-\alpha^2 x^2/2} \qquad \ldots (3.98)$

We determine A_n, using normalization condition

$$\int_{-\infty}^{+\infty} \psi \psi^* dx = 1$$

i.e. $\qquad\qquad \int_{-\infty}^{+\infty} |\psi(x)|^2 dx = 1$

$\therefore \qquad \int_{-\infty}^{+\infty} |A_n|^2 H_n^2(\alpha x)\, e^{-\alpha^2 x^2} dx = 1$

$\therefore \qquad |A_n|^2 \int_{-\infty}^{+\infty} H_n^2(\alpha x)\, e^{-\alpha^2 x^2} dx = 1$

We have $\qquad \int_{-\infty}^{+\infty} H_n^2(\alpha x)\, e^{-\alpha^2 x^2} dx = \dfrac{1}{\alpha} \int_{-\infty}^{+\infty} H_n^2(\xi)\, e^{-\xi^2} d\xi$

But the integral $\int_{-\infty}^{+\infty} H_n^2(\xi)\, e^{-\xi^2} d\xi = \sqrt{\pi}\, 2^n\, n!$

$\therefore \qquad\qquad |A_n|^2 \dfrac{\sqrt{\pi}\, 2^n\, n!}{\alpha} = 1$

This gives $\qquad\qquad A_n = \left(\dfrac{\alpha}{\sqrt{\pi}\, 2^n\, n!} \right)^{1/2}$

Therefore the normalized wave function for the harmonic oscillator is

$$\psi_n(x) = \left(\dfrac{\alpha}{\sqrt{\pi}\, 2^n\, n!} \right)^{1/2} H_n(\alpha x)\, e^{-\alpha^2 x^2/2} \qquad \ldots (3.99)$$

where n = 0, 1, 2, 3, 4,... .

For n = 0, the wave function is called *ground state wave function*.

The Hermite Polynomials are given as follows :

Order	$H_n(\xi)$	$H_n(\alpha x)$
0	$H_0(\xi) = 1$	$H_0(\alpha x) = 1$
1	$H_1(\xi) = 2\xi$	$H_1(\alpha x) = 2\alpha x$
2	$H_2(\xi) = 4\xi^2 - 2$	$H_2(\alpha x) = 4\alpha^2 x^2 - 2$
3	$H_3(\xi) = 8\xi^3 - 12\xi$	$H_3(\alpha x) = 8\alpha^3 x^3 - 12\alpha x$
4	$H_4(\xi) = 16\xi^4 - 48\xi^2 + 12$	$H_4(\alpha x) = 16\alpha^4 x^4 - 48\alpha^2 x^2 + 12$

The wave functions for different states are given as follows :

(1) Ground state function :

$$\psi_0(x) = \left(\frac{\alpha}{\sqrt{\pi}}\right)^{1/2} H_0(\alpha x) \, e^{-\alpha^2 x^2/2}$$

or

$$\psi_0(x) = \left(\frac{\alpha}{\sqrt{\pi}}\right)^{1/2} e^{-\alpha^2 x^2/2} \qquad \dots (3.100)$$

The probability density is

$$|\psi_0(x)|^2 = \left(\frac{\alpha}{\sqrt{\pi}}\right) e^{-\alpha^2 x^2} \qquad \dots (3.101)$$

(2) First excited state wave function :

$$\psi_1(x) = \left(\frac{\alpha}{2\sqrt{\pi}}\right)^{1/2} H_1(\alpha x) \, e^{-\alpha^2 x^2/2}$$

or

$$\psi_1(x) = \left(\frac{\alpha}{2\sqrt{\pi}}\right)^{1/2} (2\alpha x) \, e^{-\alpha^2 x^2/2} \qquad \dots (3.102)$$

The probability density is

$$|\psi_1(x)|^2 = \left(\frac{\alpha}{2\sqrt{\pi}}\right) 4\alpha^2 x^2 \, e^{-\alpha^2 x^2} \qquad \dots (3.103)$$

* The wave function and probability density for ground state and first four excited states are graphically plotted as shown in Fig. 3.13.

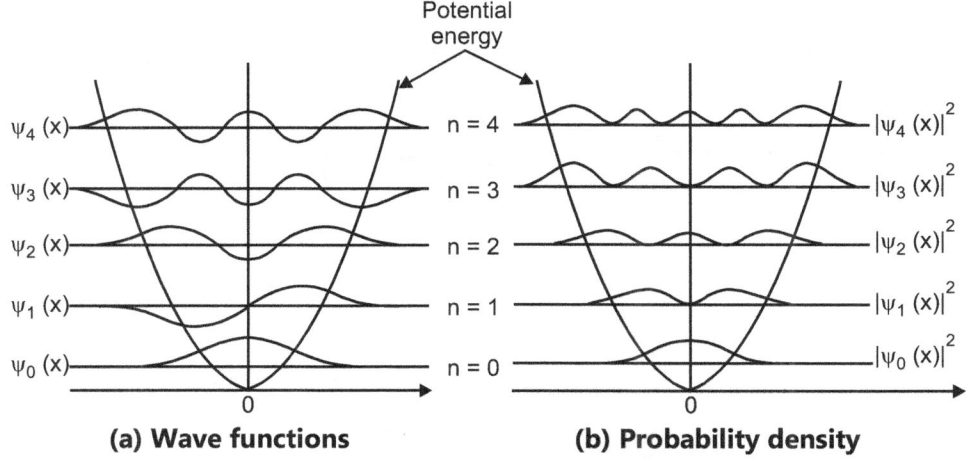

(a) Wave functions   **(b) Probability density**

Fig. 3.13

Physical interpretation of harmonic oscillator wave functions :

* Wave functions of first four states and their corresponding probability densities are shown in Fig. 3.14 (a). The dotted curves in Fig. 3.14 (b) represent classical probability densities. Fig. 3.14 (b) shows that the quantum mechanical probability density curves do not match with the classical ones for smaller values of n.

The classical probability density is $P(x) = \dfrac{1}{\pi\sqrt{a^2 - x^2}} \rightarrow \infty$ as $x \rightarrow \pm a$

where a is the amplitude of the oscillator whose energy is equal to quantum mechanical energy eigen value.

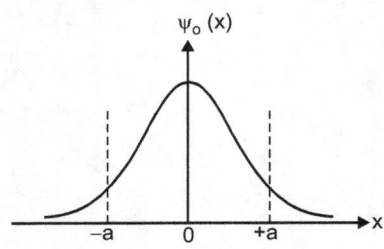
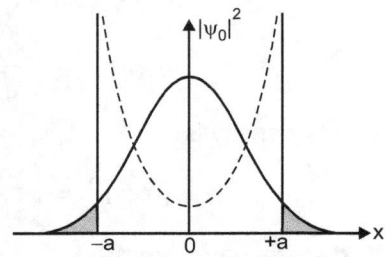

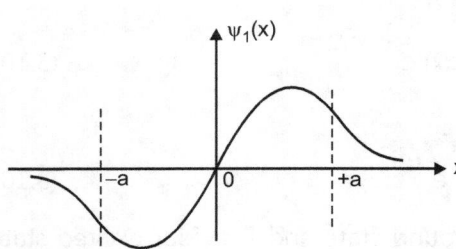
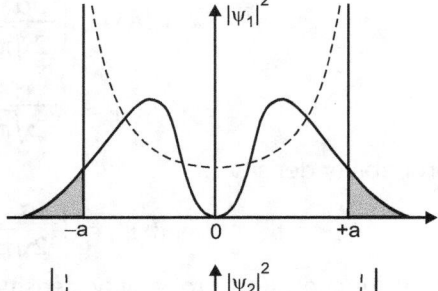

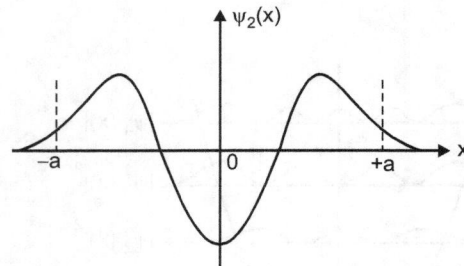
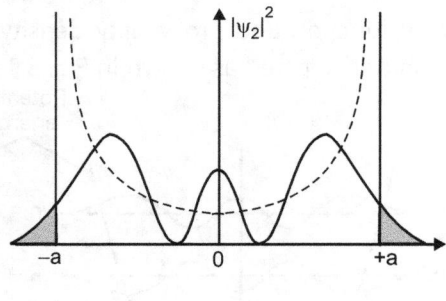

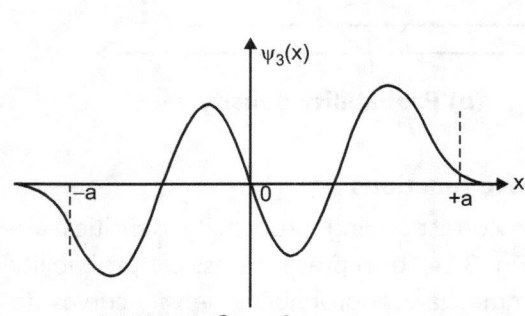
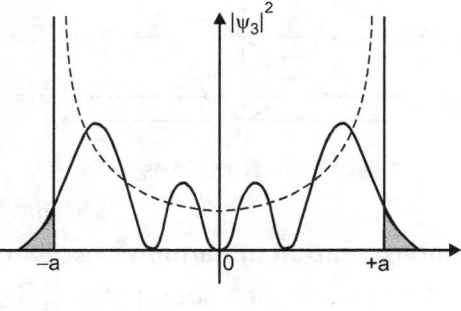

(a) Wave functions   **(b) Probability densities**

Fig. 3.14

- According to classical theory, for a given energy, there is a limit beyond which oscillator cannot go, and classical probability density approaches infinity at that limit. The probability density is maximum because the particle spends more time at the extreme points, as its velocity tends to zero. The particle spends least time at the mean position because its velocity is maximum and hence less probability of finding the particle at the mean position.

- On the other hand, quantum mechanically, there is a small probability outside the classical limits as shown by shaded portion in Fig. 3.14 (b). This is because the wave function has a 'tail' in the classically forbidden region. This existence of particle outside the classical limits i.e. in the classically forbidden region is called *tunneling effect*.

Correspondence principle :

- The **correspondence principle** states that the behavior of systems described by the theory of quantum mechanics (or by the old quantum theory) reproduces classical physics in the limit of large quantum numbers.

- It is apparent from Fig. 3.14 (b) that the probability densities $|\psi_n(x)|^2$ associated with lower states have very little agreement to the corresponding classical densities for the classical harmonic oscillator. However, the agreement between classical and quantum mechanical probability densities improves rapidly as the quantum number n increases.

- Fig. 3.15 shows graphs of probability density $|\psi_n(x)|^2$ for large n (in Fig. 3.15 (a) for n = 10 and in (b) n = 16). It is seen that quantum mechanical probability density function is an oscillating function. The points of minima correspond to $|\psi_n(x)|^2 = 0$. The maxima are of varying heights. The height of maxima is least at x = 0 and it increases on either side of x = 0.

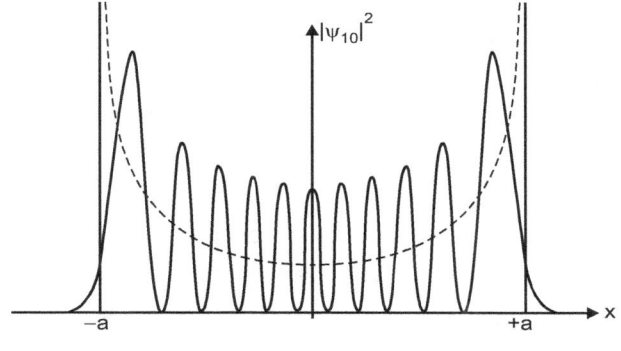

(a) For n = 10

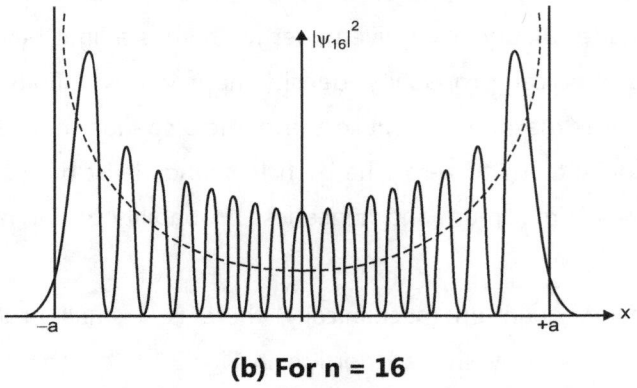

(b) For n = 16

Fig. 3.15 : The probability distribution function $|\psi_n(x)|^2$

- The dotted curve shows the averaged out behaviour of probability density. It is observed that this curve has the same nature as the classical probability curve. Thus, for large 'n' it is seen that the quantum mechanical probability curve (averaged out) is in agreement with the classical probability curve. This is consistent with **Bohr's correspondence principle** which states that as the quantum number which characterizes the system $n \to \infty$ the quantum mechanical results are the same as those predicted by the classical theory.

Parity of the wave function :

The wave function of the simple harmonic oscillator is given as

$$\psi_n(x) = \left(\frac{\alpha}{\sqrt{\pi}\, 2^n\, n!}\right)^{1/2} H_n(\alpha x)\, e^{-\alpha^2 x^2/2}$$

Replacing x by $-x$ in the above equation, we get

$$\psi_n(-x) = \left(\frac{\alpha}{\sqrt{\pi}\, 2^n\, n!}\right)^{1/2} H_n(-\alpha x)\, e^{-\alpha^2 x^2/2}$$

From the property of Hermite polynomial, we have $H_n(-x) = (-1)^n H_n(x)$

Therefore, above equation can be written as

$$\psi_n(-x) = (-1)^n \left(\frac{\alpha}{\sqrt{\pi}\, 2^n\, n!}\right)^{1/2} H_n(\alpha x)\, e^{-\alpha^2 x^2/2}$$

or
$$\psi_n(-x) = (-1)^n \psi_n(x)$$

- Thus, if n is even $\psi_n(-x) = \psi_n(x)$ and if n is odd, $\psi_n(-x) = -\psi_n(x)$. Hence even order solutions *i.e.* $\psi_0(x)$, $\psi_2(x)$, $\psi_4(x)$ ... . are even parity functions and odd order functions *i.e.* $\psi_1(x)$, $\psi_3(x)$, ... are *odd parity functions*. Thus, eigen functions of simple harmonic oscillator have definite parity, which is either even or odd.

Solved Problems

Problem 3.1 : *Find lowest energy of an electron confined to move in a one dimension potential box of 1 A°. (Given m = 9.11 ×10⁻³¹ kg, ħ = 1.054 ×10⁻³⁴ Js, 1 eV = 1.6 ×10⁻¹⁹ J).*

Solution : We have,

$$E_1 = \frac{1^2\pi^2\hbar^2}{2ma^2} = \frac{\pi^2 \times (1.054 \times 10^{-34})^2}{2 \times 9.11 \times 10^{-31} \times (10^{-10})^2} = 6 \times 10^{-18} \text{ J}$$

$$= \frac{6 \times 10^{-18}}{1.6 \times 10^{-19}} = \textbf{37.5 eV} \qquad \textbf{... Ans.}$$

Problem 3.2 : *The wave function for a particle in infinite potential well is given as*

$$\psi_n(x) = A \sin\left(\frac{n\pi}{a} x\right) \text{ where } 0 \leq x \leq a. \text{ Find } <x> \text{ and } <p_x>.$$

Solution : A is normalization constant and it is easy to show that its value is $A = \sqrt{\dfrac{2}{a}}$

$$\therefore \qquad \psi_n(x) = \sqrt{\frac{2}{a}} \sin\left(\frac{n\pi}{a}x\right)$$

(a) Expectation value of x is given as

$$<x> = \int_0^a x |\psi_n(x)|^2 \, dx$$

$$\therefore \quad <x> = \int_0^a x |A|^2 \sin^2\left(\frac{n\pi}{a}x\right) dx = \frac{2}{a} \int_0^a x \sin^2\left(\frac{n\pi}{a}x\right) dx$$

$$= \frac{2}{a} \int_0^a \frac{x}{2}\left(1 - \cos\left(2\frac{n\pi}{a}x\right)\right) dx = \frac{1}{a}\int_0^a \left(x - x\cos\left(2\frac{n\pi}{a}x\right)\right) dx$$

$$= \frac{1}{a}\left(\int_0^a x \, dx - \int_0^a x\cos\left(2\frac{n\pi}{a}x\right) dx\right) = \frac{1}{a}\left(\frac{x^2}{2}\Big|_0^a - \int_0^a x\cos\left(2\frac{n\pi}{a}x\right) dx\right)$$

Integrating second term by parts, we get

$$\int_0^a x\cos\left(2\frac{n\pi}{a}x\right) dx = x\frac{\sin\left(2\frac{n\pi}{a}x\right)}{2n\pi/a} - \int_0^a \cos\left(2\frac{n\pi}{a}x\right) dx$$

$$= \left[x\frac{\sin\left(2\frac{n\pi}{a}x\right)}{2n\pi/a} - \frac{\sin\left(2\frac{n\pi}{a}x\right)}{2n\pi/a}\right]_0^a = 0$$

This gives $\displaystyle\int_0^a x \cos\left(2\,\frac{n\pi}{a}\,x\right) dx = 0$

$\therefore$ $\qquad\qquad\qquad\qquad <x> = \dfrac{1}{a}\dfrac{a^2}{2}$

or $\qquad\qquad\qquad\qquad <x> = \dfrac{a}{2}$ **... Ans.**

(b) Expectation value of p_x is given as

$$<p_x> = \int_0^a \psi_n{}^*\left(-i\hbar\frac{d}{dx}\right)\psi_n\, dx = -i\hbar\int_0^a \psi_n{}^*\frac{d\psi}{dx}dx$$

$$= -i\hbar\frac{2}{a}\int_0^a \sin\left(\frac{n\pi}{a}x\right)\frac{d}{dx}\sin\left(\frac{n\pi}{a}x\right) dx$$

$$= -i\hbar\frac{2}{a}\frac{n\pi}{a}\int_0^a \sin\left(\frac{n\pi}{a}x\right)\cos\left(\frac{n\pi}{a}x\right) dx = \frac{-i\hbar n\pi}{a^2}\int_0^a \sin\left(\frac{2n\pi}{a}x\right) dx$$

$$= \frac{i\hbar n\pi}{a^2}\left[\frac{\cos\left(\frac{2n\pi}{a}x\right)}{2n/\pi}\right]_0^a$$

$\therefore$ $\qquad\qquad <p_x> = 0$ **... Ans.**

Problem 3.3 : *A small object of mass 1.00 µg is confined to move between two rigid walls separated by a distance of 1.00 mm. (a) Calculate the minimum speed of the object. (b) If the speed is 3 × 10⁶ m/s, find the corresponding value of n.*

Solution : When a particle is confined to one-dimensional rigid box, the energy eigen values are given by

$$E_n = \frac{n^2\pi^2\hbar^2}{2ma^2} \text{ where } n = 1, 2, 3, \ldots$$

(a) If the particle is in n = 1 state *i.e.* in the ground state then it has the lowest energy and hence the minimum speed.

Thus,

$$E_1 = \frac{\pi^2\hbar^2}{2ma^2}$$

We have

$$a = 1.00 \text{ mm} = 1 \times 10^{-3} \text{ m}$$
$$m = 1.00 \text{ μg} = 1 \times 10^{-6} \text{ g} = 10^{-9} \text{ kg.}$$
$$\hbar = 1.055 \times 10^{-34} \text{ J-sec}$$

∴

$$E_1 = \frac{3.14^2 \times (1.055 \times 10^{-34})^2}{2 \times 10^{-9} \times (10^{-3})^2}$$

$$= 5.486 \times 10^{-53} \text{ J}$$

The particle has only the kinetic energy, since V = 0.

∴

$$E_1 = \frac{1}{2} mv^2$$

∴

$$v = \sqrt{\frac{2E}{m}} = \left(\frac{2 \times 5.486 \times 10^{-53}}{10^{-9}}\right)^2 = (10.972 \times 10^{-44})^{1/2}$$

$$= \mathbf{3.31 \times 10^{-22} \text{ m/s}} \qquad \textbf{... Ans.}$$

The velocity is so small that the particle is treated at rest *i.e.* in ground state. The particle will require time 3.021×10^{18} seconds or 9.57×10^{10} years to cover the distance equal to width of one-dimensional rigid box.

(b) Let the particle be in level n with speed v = 3×10^6 m/sec.

We have

$$E_n = \frac{n^2 \pi^2 \hbar^2}{2ma^2}$$

∴

$$\frac{1}{2} mv^2 = \frac{n^2 \pi^2 \hbar^2}{2ma^2}$$

or

$$n^2 = \frac{m^2 a^2 v^2}{\pi^2 \hbar^2}$$

or

$$n = \frac{m \, a \, v}{\pi \, \hbar} = \frac{10^{-9} \times 10^{-3} \times 3 \times 10^6}{3.14 \times 1.055 \times 10^{-34}} = 0.905 \times 10^{28}$$

∴

$$n = \mathbf{9 \times 10^{27}} \qquad \textbf{... Ans.}$$

n is very high, so the particle cannot be treated quantum mechanically.

Problem 3.4 : *A proton is confined to move in a one-dimensional box of width 0.200 nm. (a) Find the lowest possible energy of the proton. (b) What is the lowest possible energy of an electron confined to the same box ?*

Solution : When particle is confined to one-dimensional rigid box, the energy eigen value is given by

$$E_n = \frac{n^2 \pi^2 \hbar^2}{2ma^2}$$

(a) If the particle is in n = 1 *i.e.* in the ground state it has the lowest energy. Thus,

$$E_1 = \frac{\pi^2 \hbar^2}{2ma^2}$$

We have $\qquad$ a = 0.200 nm = 0.200×10^{-9} m = 2×10^{-10} m

For proton, $\qquad$ m = 1.66×10^{-27} kg

$\qquad$ $\hbar$ = 1.055×10^{-34} J-sec

$\therefore$ $\qquad$ $E_1 = \dfrac{3.14^2 \times (1.055 \times 10^{-34})^2}{2 \times 1.66 \times 10^{-27} \times (2 \times 10^{-10})^2}$

$\qquad\qquad$ = 0.826×10^{-21} J = **5.16×10^{-3} eV** $\qquad$ ... Ans.

(b) Now, let us work out the problem for electron.

$$E_1 = \frac{\pi^2 \hbar^2}{2ma^2}$$

We have $\qquad$ a = 0.200 nm = 0.2×10^{-9} m

$\qquad$ m = 9.1×10^{-31} kg

$\qquad$ $\hbar$ = 1.055×10^{-34} J-sec

$\therefore$ $\qquad$ $E_1 = \dfrac{3.14^2 \times (1.055 \times 10^{-34})^2}{2 \times 9.1 \times 10^{-31} \times (2 \times 10^{-10})^2}$

$\qquad\qquad$ = 0.1507×10^{-17} = 1.507×10^{-18} J = **9.42 eV** $\qquad$ ... Ans.

Problem 3.5 : *A ruby laser emits light of wavelength 693.4 nm. If this light is due to transition from n = 2 to n = 1 state of an electron in a one-dimensional box, find the width of the box.*

Solution : The energy in the nth level is given by

$$E_n = \frac{n^2 \pi^2 \hbar^2}{2ma^2}$$

When electron jumps from n = 2 to n = 1, the energy difference is

$$E_2 - E_1 = 4\frac{\pi^2 \hbar^2}{2ma^2} - \frac{\pi^2 \hbar^2}{2ma^2} = 3\frac{\pi^2 \hbar^2}{2ma^2}$$

This energy difference is emitted in the form of photon with frequency ν. Then

$$E_2 - E_1 = h\nu$$

$\therefore$ $\qquad$ $h\nu = 3\dfrac{\pi^2 \hbar^2}{2ma^2}$

or $\qquad$ $\dfrac{hc}{\lambda} = 3\dfrac{\pi^2 \hbar^2}{2ma^2}$

or $\qquad$ $a^2 = \dfrac{3\pi^2 \hbar^2 \lambda}{2mhc}$

Since $\qquad$ $h = \dfrac{\hbar}{2\pi}$, we get

$\qquad$ $a = \dfrac{3h\lambda}{8mc}$

Given : $\lambda = 693.4 \text{ nm} = 693.4 \times 10^{-9} \text{ m}$

$c = 3 \times 10^8 \text{ m/sec}$

$m = 9.1 \times 10^{-31} \text{ kg}$

$h = 6.625 \times 10^{-34} \text{ J-sec}$

$\therefore$ $a^2 = \dfrac{3 \times 6.625 \times 10^{-34} \times 693.4 \times 10^{-9}}{8 \times 9.1 \times 10^{-31} \times 3 \times 10^8}$

$= 63.1 \times 10^{-20} \text{ m}^2$

$\therefore$ $a = 7.94 \times 10^{-10} \text{ m} = \textbf{7.94 A°}$ **... Ans.**

Problem 3.6 : *Using ground state function of the simple harmonic oscillator, show that the ground state energy is $\dfrac{1}{2}\hbar\omega$*

Solution : Ground state function of the simple harmonic oscillator is given as

$$\psi_0(x) = \left(\dfrac{\alpha}{\sqrt{\pi}}\right)^{1/2} e^{-\alpha^2 x^2/2} = Ae^{-\alpha^2 x^2/2}$$

where $\alpha = \sqrt{\dfrac{m\omega}{\hbar}}$

Schrödinger's equation for harmonic oscillator is given by

$$\dfrac{d^2\psi}{dx^2} + \dfrac{2m}{\hbar^2}\left(E - \dfrac{1}{2}kx^2\right)\psi = 0$$

In ground state,

$$\dfrac{d^2\psi_0}{dx^2} + \dfrac{2m}{\hbar^2}\left(E - \dfrac{1}{2}kx^2\right)\psi_0 = 0 \qquad \text{... (i)}$$

$$\dfrac{d\psi_0}{dx} = \dfrac{d}{dx}\left(Ae^{-\alpha^2 x^2/2}\right) = -\alpha^2 x\, Ae^{-\alpha^2 x^2/2}$$

$\therefore$ $$\dfrac{d^2\psi_0}{dx^2} = \dfrac{d}{dx}\dfrac{d\psi_0}{dx} = \dfrac{d}{dx}\left(-\alpha^2 xAe^{-\alpha^2 x^2/2}\right) = \alpha^4 x^2 Ae^{-\alpha^2 x^2/2} - \alpha^2 Ae^{-\alpha^2 x^2/2}$$

or $$\dfrac{d^2\psi_0}{dx^2} = (\alpha^4 x^2 - \alpha^2)\psi_0$$

Using in equation (i), we get

$$(\alpha^4 x^2 - \alpha^2)\psi_0 + \dfrac{2m}{\hbar^2}\left(E - \dfrac{1}{2}kx^2\right)\psi_0 = 0$$

or $$(\alpha^4 x^2 - \alpha^2)\psi_0 + \dfrac{2mE}{\hbar^2}\psi_0 - \dfrac{mk}{\hbar^2}x^2\psi_0 = 0$$

We have $k = m\omega^2$

$\therefore$ $$(\alpha^4 x^2 - \alpha^2)\psi_0 + \dfrac{2mE}{\hbar^2}\psi_0 - \dfrac{m^2\omega^2}{\hbar^2}x^2\psi_0 = 0$$

$$\left[(\alpha^4 x^2 - \alpha^2) + \dfrac{2mE}{\hbar^2} - \dfrac{m^2\omega^2}{\hbar^2}x^2\right]\psi_0 = 0$$

Here ψ_0 is the ground state function of harmonic oscillator, it is not zero.

Therefore, we have

$$\alpha^4 x^2 - \alpha^2 + \frac{2mE}{\hbar^2} - \frac{m^2\omega^2}{\hbar^2} x^2 = 0$$

Using $\alpha = \sqrt{\dfrac{m\omega}{\hbar}}$, we get

$$\frac{m^2\omega^2}{\hbar^2} x^2 - \frac{m\omega}{\hbar} + \frac{2mE}{\hbar^2} - \frac{m^2\omega^2}{\hbar^2} x^2 = 0$$

$$\therefore \qquad\qquad -\frac{m\omega}{\hbar} + \frac{2mE}{\hbar^2} = 0$$

or $$\qquad\qquad \frac{2mE}{\hbar^2} = \frac{m\omega}{\hbar}$$

$$\therefore \qquad\qquad E = \frac{1}{2}\hbar\omega \qquad\qquad\qquad \text{... Ans.}$$

Problem 3.7 : *Using the ground state wave function of the simple harmonic oscillator, find* <x>, <x^2> *and* <p$_x$>.

Solution : Ground state function of the simple harmonic oscillator is given as

$$\psi_0(x) = \left(\frac{\alpha}{\sqrt{\pi}}\right)^{1/2} e^{-\alpha^2 x^2/2}$$

(a) The expectation value of x is given as

$$<x> = \int_{-\infty}^{\infty} x\,|\psi_0(x)|^2\,dx$$

$$\therefore \qquad <x> = \int_{-\infty}^{\infty} x\left(\frac{\alpha}{\sqrt{\pi}}\right) e^{-\alpha^2 x^2}\,dx = \left(\frac{\alpha}{\sqrt{\pi}}\right)\int_{-\infty}^{\infty} x\,e^{-\alpha^2 x^2}\,dx$$

The integral on RHS is an odd integral. Hence the integral vanishes over the entire range $(-\infty, \infty)$.

$$\therefore \qquad\qquad\qquad <x> = 0 \qquad\qquad\qquad \text{... Ans.}$$

(b) The expectation value of x^2 is given as

$$<x^2> = \int_{-\infty}^{\infty} x^2\,|\psi_0(x)|^2\,dx$$

$$\therefore \qquad <x^2> = \int_{-\infty}^{\infty} x^2\left(\frac{\alpha}{\sqrt{\pi}}\right) e^{-\alpha^2 x^2}\,dx = \left(\frac{\alpha}{\sqrt{\pi}}\right)\int_{-\infty}^{\infty} x^2\,e^{-\alpha^2 x^2}\,dx$$

We have general integral $\int\limits_{-\infty}^{\infty} x^2 \, e^{-\beta x^2} \, dx = \dfrac{1}{2\beta}\sqrt{\dfrac{\pi}{\beta}}$

$\therefore$ $<x^2> = \left(\dfrac{\alpha}{\sqrt{\pi}}\right)\dfrac{1}{2\alpha^2}\sqrt{\dfrac{\pi}{\alpha^2}}$

$\therefore$ $<x^2> = \dfrac{1}{2\alpha^2}$

$\because$ $\alpha = \sqrt{\dfrac{m\omega}{\hbar}}$

$\therefore$ $\mathbf{<x^2> = \dfrac{\hbar}{2m\omega}}$ ... **Ans.**

(c) Expectation value of p_x is given as

$$<p_x> = \int\limits_{-\infty}^{\infty} \psi_0{}^*\left(-i\hbar\dfrac{d}{dx}\right)\psi_0 \, dx = -i\hbar\int\limits_{-\infty}^{\infty}\psi_0{}^*\dfrac{d\psi_0}{dx} \, dx$$

$$= -i\hbar\left(\dfrac{\alpha}{\sqrt{\pi}}\right)\int\limits_{-\infty}^{\infty} e^{-\alpha^2 x^2}\dfrac{d}{dx}e^{-\alpha^2 x^2} \, dx$$

$$= -i\hbar\left(\dfrac{\alpha}{\sqrt{\pi}}\right)\int\limits_{-\infty}^{\infty} e^{-\alpha^2 x^2}(-\alpha^2 x)\,e^{\alpha^2 x^2} \, dx$$

$$= i\hbar\,\alpha^2\left(\dfrac{\alpha}{\sqrt{\pi}}\right)\int\limits_{-\infty}^{\infty} x\,e^{-\alpha^2 x^2} \, dx$$

The integral on RHS is an odd integral over the entire range $(-\infty, \infty)$. Hence the integral vanishes.

$\therefore$ $<p_x> = 0$ ... **Ans.**

Problem 3.8 : *For a particle in a one-dimensional rigid box, show that the fractional difference in the energy between adjacent eigen values is*

$$\dfrac{\Delta E_n}{E_n} = \dfrac{2n+1}{n^2}$$

Use this result to discuss the classical limit of the system.

Solution : The energy eigen value in the nth state of one-dimensional rigid box is given as

$$E_n = \dfrac{n^2\pi^2\hbar^2}{2ma^2}$$

The energy eigen value in the $(n + 1)^{th}$ state is given as

$$E_{n+1} = \frac{(n+1)^2 \pi^2 \hbar^2}{2ma^2}$$

Difference between the eigen values is

$$\Delta E_n = E_{n+1} - E_n$$

$$= \frac{(n+1)^2 \pi^2 \hbar^2}{2ma^2} - \frac{n^2 \pi^2 \hbar^2}{2ma^2}$$

$$= [(n+1)^2 - n^2] \frac{\pi^2 \hbar^2}{2ma^2}$$

$$\therefore \quad \frac{\Delta E_n}{E_n} = \frac{(n+1)^2 - n^2}{n^2}$$

$$= \frac{n^2 + 2n + 1 - n^2}{n^2}$$

$$\therefore \quad \frac{\Delta E_n}{E_n} = \frac{2n + 1}{n^2}$$

For classical limit, $n \to \infty$. Therefore,

$$\lim_{n \to \infty} \frac{\Delta E_n}{E_n} = \lim_{n \to \infty} \frac{2n+1}{n^2} = \lim_{n \to \infty} \frac{2 + 1/n}{n} = \lim_{n \to \infty} \frac{2}{n} \to 0 \text{ as } n \to \infty.$$

$$\therefore \quad \lim_{n \to \infty} \frac{\Delta E_n}{E_n} = 0$$

or $\Delta E_n \to 0$ as $n \to \infty$ *i.e.* the energy levels are continuous.

Problem 3.9 : *The restoring force constant k for the vibrations of the interatomic spacing of the diatomic molecule is 10^3 J/m². If mass of the molecule is 4.9×10^{-26} kg estimate the zero point energy of the oscillator.*

Solution : Given :

$$m = 4.9 \times 10^{-26} \text{ kg}$$

$$k = 10^3 \text{ J/m}^2$$

The zero-point energy of the oscillator is $E = \frac{1}{2} \hbar \omega$

For the oscillator of mass *m* and force constant k, the angular frequency is

$$\omega = \sqrt{\frac{k}{m}}$$

$$= \sqrt{\frac{10^3}{4.9 \times 10^{-26}}} = \sqrt{\frac{10^{29}}{4.9}} = \sqrt{\frac{10^{30}}{49}} = \frac{10^{15}}{7}$$

$$\therefore \quad E = \frac{1}{2} \times 1.055 \times 10^{-34} \times \frac{1}{7} \times 10^{15} = \frac{1}{14} \times 1.055 \times 10^{-19}$$

or $\qquad E = 0.0754 \times 10^{-19}$ J

$\therefore \qquad E = \mathbf{0.0471}$ **eV**   **... Ans.**

Problem 3.10 : *Calculate the most probable distance of the particle in the first excited state of the simple harmonic oscillator.*

Solution : The wave function in the first excited state of the oscillator is given by

$$\psi_1(x) = \left(\frac{\alpha}{2\sqrt{\pi}}\right)^{1/2} H_1(\alpha x) \, e^{-\alpha^2 x^2/2}$$

or

$$\psi_1(x) = \left(\frac{\alpha}{2\sqrt{\pi}}\right)^{1/2} (2\alpha x) \, e^{-\alpha^2 x^2/2} \qquad \text{(since } H_1(\alpha x) = 2\alpha x\text{)}$$

The probability density is

$$P(x) = |\psi_1(x)|^2 = \left(\frac{\alpha}{2\sqrt{\pi}}\right) 4\alpha^2 x^2 \, e^{-\alpha^2 x^2}$$

The distance at which the probability is maximum is called the most probable distance. It can be obtained by differentiating P(x) w.r.t. x and equating to zero.

$$\frac{dP}{dx} = \left(\frac{\alpha}{2\sqrt{\pi}}\right) 4\alpha^2 \frac{d}{dx}\left(x^2 \, e^{-\alpha^2 x^2}\right)$$

$$= \left(\frac{\alpha}{2\sqrt{\pi}}\right) 4\alpha^2 \left(-2\alpha^2 x^3 e^{-\alpha^2 x^2} + 2x e^{-\alpha^2 x^2}\right)$$

$\frac{dP}{dx} = 0$ gives

$$\left(\frac{\alpha}{2\sqrt{\pi}}\right) 4\alpha^2 \left(-2\alpha^2 x^3 e^{-\alpha^2 x^2} + 2x e^{-\alpha^2 x^2}\right) = 0$$

or

$$\left(-2\alpha^2 x^3 e^{-\alpha^2 x^2} + 2x e^{-\alpha^2 x^2}\right) = 0$$

$$(-2\alpha^2 x^3 + 2x) e^{-\alpha^2 x^2} = 0$$

or

$$-2\alpha^2 x^3 + 2x = 0$$

$$\therefore \qquad x^2 = \frac{1}{\alpha^2}$$

or

$$x = \pm\frac{1}{\alpha} \qquad \qquad \text{... Ans.}$$

Thus, the particle is most likely to be found at positions $x = \dfrac{1}{\alpha}$ and $x = -\dfrac{1}{\alpha}$.

Problem 3.11 : *For one-dimensional harmonic oscillator in its ground state, obtain the expectation value of the potential energy.*

Solution : The expectation value of the potential energy is given by

$$<V> = \int_{-\infty}^{\infty} \psi_0 {}^* V \psi_0 \, dx$$

$$\because \qquad V = \frac{1}{2} kx^2$$

$$\therefore \quad <V> = \int_{-\infty}^{\infty} \psi_0^* \frac{1}{2} kx^2 \, \psi_0 \, dx = \frac{1}{2} k \int_{-\infty}^{\infty} \psi_0^* x^2 \, \psi_0 \, dx$$

$$= \frac{1}{2} k \int_{-\infty}^{\infty} x^2 \left(\frac{\alpha}{\sqrt{\pi}} \right) e^{-\alpha^2 x^2} \, dx = \left(\frac{\alpha}{\sqrt{\pi}} \right) \int_{-\infty}^{\infty} x^2 \, e^{-\alpha^2 x^2} \, dx$$

We have general integral $\int_{-\infty}^{\infty} x^2 \, e^{-\beta x^2} \, dx = \frac{1}{2\beta} \sqrt{\frac{\pi}{\beta}}$

$$\therefore \quad <V> = \frac{1}{2} k \left(\frac{\alpha}{\sqrt{\pi}} \right) \frac{1}{2\alpha^2} \sqrt{\frac{\pi}{\alpha^2}} = \frac{1}{2} k \frac{1}{2\alpha^2}$$

$$\because \quad k = m\omega^2 \text{ and } \alpha = \sqrt{\frac{m\omega}{\hbar}}$$

$$\therefore \quad <V> = \frac{1}{4} m\omega^2 \times \frac{\hbar}{m\omega} = \frac{1}{4} \hbar\omega \qquad \text{... Ans.}$$

Problem 3.12 : *Calculate the probability of finding the simple harmonic oscillator outside the classical limit when it is in the ground state.*

Solution : The ground state eigen function of the oscillator is given by

$$\psi_0(x) = \left(\frac{\alpha}{\sqrt{\pi}} \right)^{1/2} e^{-\alpha^2 x^2/2}$$

The classical limit of the oscillator is ± a, where a is the amplitude.

The classical energy of the oscillator $E = \frac{1}{2} ka^2 = \frac{1}{2} m\omega^2 a^2$

Quantum mechanical ground state energy is $E = \frac{1}{2} \hbar\omega$

$$\therefore \quad \frac{1}{2} \hbar\omega = \frac{1}{2} m\omega^2 a^2$$

Which gives $a = \pm \sqrt{\frac{\hbar}{m\omega}} = \pm \frac{1}{\alpha}$

The probability of finding the particle outside the classical region is

$$p(x) = \int_{-1/\alpha}^{-\infty} |\psi_0(x)|^2 \, dx + \int_{1/\alpha}^{\infty} |\psi_0(x)|^2 \, dx$$

$$= \int_{-1/\alpha}^{-\infty} \left(\frac{\alpha}{\sqrt{\pi}} \right) e^{-\alpha^2 x^2} \, dx + \int_{1/\alpha}^{\infty} \left(\frac{\alpha}{\sqrt{\pi}} \right) e^{-\alpha^2 x^2} \, dx = \frac{\alpha}{\sqrt{\pi}} \left[\int_{-1/\alpha}^{-\infty} e^{-\alpha^2 x^2} \, dx + \int_{1/\alpha}^{\infty} e^{-\alpha^2 x^2} \, dx \right]$$

Since the integrals are even integrals, we can write $\displaystyle\int_{-1/\alpha}^{-\infty} e^{-\alpha^2 x^2}\, dx = \int_{1/\alpha}^{\infty} e^{-\alpha^2 x^2}\, dx$

$\therefore$ $\displaystyle p(x) = \frac{\alpha}{\sqrt{\pi}} \cdot 2 \int_{1/\alpha}^{\infty} e^{-\alpha^2 x^2}\, dx$

Let $\alpha x = t$ $\therefore$ $dx = \dfrac{dt}{\alpha}$

When $x = 1/\alpha$, we get $t = 1$

And when $x = \infty$, we get $t = \infty$

$\therefore$ $\displaystyle p(x) = \frac{\alpha}{\sqrt{\pi}}\,\frac{2}{\alpha} \int_{1}^{\infty} e^{-t^2}\, dt = \frac{2}{\sqrt{\pi}} \int_{1}^{\infty} e^{-t^2}\, dt$

$\therefore$ $\displaystyle p(x) = \frac{2}{\sqrt{\pi}} \left[\int_{0}^{\infty} e^{-t^2}\, dt - \int_{0}^{1} e^{-t^2}\, dt \right]$

We have $\displaystyle \int_{0}^{\infty} e^{-t^2}\, dt = \frac{\sqrt{\pi}}{2}$

$\therefore$ $\displaystyle p(x) = \frac{2}{\sqrt{\pi}} \left[\frac{\sqrt{\pi}}{2} - \int_{0}^{1} e^{-t^2}\, dt \right] = 1 - \frac{2}{\sqrt{\pi}} \int_{0}^{1} e^{-t^2}\, dt$ ... (i)

Consider the integral $\displaystyle\int_{0}^{1} e^{-t^2}\, dt$. We use the infinite series expansion for e^{-t^2}.

$$\int_{0}^{1} e^{-t^2}\, dt = \int_{0}^{1} \left(1 - t^2 + \frac{t^4}{2!} - \frac{t^6}{3!} + \frac{t^8}{4!} - \cdots \right) dt$$

$$= \left[t - \frac{t^3}{3} + \frac{t^5}{2! \times 5} - \frac{t^7}{3! \times 7} + \frac{t^9}{4! \times 9} - \cdots \right]_{0}^{1}$$

$$= \left[1 - \frac{1}{3} + \frac{1}{2! \times 5} - \frac{1}{3! \times 7} + \frac{1}{4! \times 9} - \cdots \right]$$

$$= \left[1 - \frac{1}{3} + \frac{1}{2 \times 5} - \frac{1}{6 \times 7} + \frac{1}{24 \times 9} - \cdots \right]$$

$$= 0.74244$$

Using in equation (i), we get the probability of finding the particle outside the classical limits.

$$P(x) = 1 - \frac{2}{\sqrt{\pi}} \times 0.74244$$

$$= 1 - 0.837966$$

$$= \textbf{0.16203 approximately} \qquad \textbf{... Ans.}$$

Consequently the probability of finding the particle inside the classical limit will be 0.837966 or 84%.

Problem 3.13 : *An electron is trapped in an infinitely deep potential well 3.0 A° in length. If the electron is in the ground state, what is the probability of finding it within the 1.0 A° of the left hand wall ?*

Solution : The eigen function for the particle in a deep potential well of width a is given as

$$\psi_n(x) = \sqrt{\frac{2}{a}} \, \sin\left(\frac{n\pi}{a} x\right) \text{ for } 0 < x < a$$

The ground state wave function is

$$\psi_0(x) = \sqrt{\frac{2}{a}} \, \sin\left(\frac{\pi}{a} x\right)$$

The probability of finding the particle in the region from 0 to a/3 *i.e.* upto the distance $1/3^{rd}$ of total width from the left wall is

$$p(x) = \int_0^{a/3} |\psi_0(x)|^2 \, dx = \int_0^{a/3} \frac{2}{a} \sin^2\left(\frac{\pi}{a} x\right) dx = \frac{2}{a} \int_0^{a/3} \sin^2\left(\frac{\pi}{a} x\right) dx$$

We have $\sin^2\theta = \frac{1}{2}(1 - \cos 2\theta)$, therefore, above equation becomes

$$p(x) = \frac{2}{a} \int_0^{a/3} \frac{1}{2}\left[1 - \cos\left(\frac{2\pi}{a} x\right)\right] dx = \frac{1}{a} \int_0^{a/3} \left[1 - \cos\left(\frac{2\pi}{a} x\right)\right] dx$$

$$= \frac{1}{a} \int_0^{a/3} \left[dx - \cos\left(\frac{2\pi}{a} x\right) dx\right] = \frac{1}{a}\left[x - \frac{\sin\left(\frac{2\pi}{a} x\right)}{\frac{2\pi}{a}}\right]_0^{a/3}$$

$$= \frac{1}{a}\left[\frac{a}{3} - \frac{a}{2\pi} \sin\left(\frac{2\pi}{a} \frac{a}{3}\right)\right] = \left[\frac{1}{3} - \frac{1}{2\pi} \sin\left(\frac{2\pi}{3}\right)\right]$$

$$= 0.3333 - 0.1370 = 0.1963$$

$$\therefore \qquad p(x) = \textbf{19.63 \%} \qquad \textbf{... Ans.}$$

Summary

1. The particle will be free when force $F = -\dfrac{dv}{dx}$ acting on the particle is zero. Energy spectrum of free particle is continuous.

2. For infinitely deep potential well,

$$V = \infty \qquad x \leq 0 \text{ and } x \geq a$$
$$V = 0 \qquad x < x < a$$

Eigen value of energy for such situation is $E_n = \dfrac{\pi^2 \hbar^2}{2ma^2}$.

3. For particle in 3D rigid box,

$$E = \frac{\hbar^2 \pi^2}{2m}\left(\frac{n_1^2}{a^2} + \frac{n_2^2}{b^2} + \frac{n_3^2}{c^2}\right)$$

4. When there are more than one eigen function corresponding to same energy eigen value, the energy state of particle is called degenerate state.

5. Step potential is defined as

$$V(x) = 0 \quad \text{for } x \leq 0$$
$$= V_0 \text{ for } x > 0$$

For region $E < V_0$, $R = 1$ and $T = 0$.

6. The function has tail into classical forbidden region (represented by term $e^{-\alpha x}$). This tail becomes shorter and shorter as E becomes smaller and smaller as compared to V_0. There is small probability of finding the particle in region $x < 0$. This is called barrier penetration.

7. In case of potential barrier for $E > V_0$,

$$T = \cfrac{1}{\left[1 + \cfrac{V_0^2 \sin^2 \alpha a}{4E\,(E - V_0)}\right]} \text{ and } R = \cfrac{1}{\left[\cfrac{4E\,(E - V_0)}{V_0^2 \sin^2 \alpha a} + 1\right]}$$

8. If a particle impinging on the potential barrier with energy less than the height of potential barrier, there is always some probability of transmission through the barrier. This phenomenon of crossing barrier is called tunneling effect.

9. Energy of harmonic oscillator $E = \left(n + \dfrac{1}{2}\right)\hbar\omega$. The energy spectrum is discrete.

   The lowest energy level (for $n = 0$) is called ground state energy $E_0 = \dfrac{1}{2}\hbar\omega$.

10. Ground state wave function for harmonic oscillator is

$$\psi_o(x) = \left(\frac{\alpha}{\sqrt{\pi}}\right)^{1/2} e^{-\alpha^2 x^2/2}$$

11. The **correspondence principle** states that the behavior of systems described by the theory of quantum mechanics (or by the old quantum theory) reproduces classical physics in the limit of large quantum numbers. For large value of n quantum mechanical probability curve for SHO is in agreement with the classical probability curve.

Exercises

(A) Short Answer Type Questions :

1. What is free particle?
2. Represent situation of particle in infinitely deep potential well in one dimension mathematically.
3. Write expression for zero point energy in case of particle in infinitely deep potential well.
4. Draw plot of first three wave functions and their probability density for particle in infinitely deep potential well.
5. When energy state of particle is said to be degenerate ?
6. Show second excited state of particle in 3D rigid box is three fold degenerate.
7. Represent step potential mathematically.
8. What is potential barrier ?
9. Define tunneling effect.
10. State four applications of tunneling effect.
11. Plot graph of variation of coefficient of transmission w.r.t. $\alpha a/\pi$ in case of potential barrier.
12. Plot graph of wave function and probability density in case of simple harmonic oscillator.

(B) Long Answer Type Questions :

1. Explain quantum mechanical motion of a particle through constant potential.
2. With the help of time independent Schrödinger's equation, obtain the energy eigen values and eigen functions for a particle in one-dimensional deep potential well.
3. A particle is enclosed in a three-dimensional rigid box. Using the Schrödinger's steady state equation, obtain the eigen values of energy of the particle. What are degenerate states ?
4. Show that particle in one-dimensional infinite well will have discrete energy states. Plot the first three eigen functions.
5. Obtain eigen value of energy for particle in three-dimensional rigid box.
6. A particle travelling with energy E > 0, has a potential barrier defined as

$$V = \begin{cases} 0 & x \leq 0 \\ V_0 & 0 < x < a \\ 0 & x \geq a \end{cases}$$

Write formulae for the transmission coefficient and reflection coefficient.

7. Discuss potential barrier qualitatively for $E < V_0$.

8. Write down the steady-state Schrödinger's equation for one-dimensional harmonic oscillator. Solve the same to show that the energy eigen values are given by $E_n = \left(n + \dfrac{1}{2}\right)\hbar\omega$.

9. Draw the first three eigen functions of the one-dimensional harmonic oscillator.

10. Explain the classical and quantum mechanical correspondence in the case of one-dimensional simple harmonic oscillator.

(C) Unsolved Problems :

1. A beam of monoenergetic electrons each with energy 0.08 eV is incident on a potential step of height 0.04 eV. Calculate the probability of reflection from the potential wall. **(Ans. 0.027)**

2. A particle is confined between rigid walls separated by a distance a. Find the probability that it will be found within distances a/3 and 2a/3 from left wall.

(Ans. 60 % approx.)

3. Calculate the probability of finding the simple harmonic oscillator within the classical limit when it is in the ground state. **(Ans. 84%)**

4. Using first excited state function of the simple harmonic oscillator, show that the energy eigen value is $\dfrac{3}{2}\hbar\omega$.

5. Calculate the ground state energy of the harmonic oscillator of mass of 1 gm is fixed to a spring which is stretched by 1 cm by a force of 10,000 dynes along the x axis.

(Ans. 5.273×10^{-24} erg)

6. Calculate the probability of transmission for a 1 MeV proton to be transmitted through a potential barrier of height 4 MeV and width 0.01 A°. **(Ans. 1.5×10^{-24})**

7. Find the probability that a particle in a one-dimensional rigid box of width a can be found between x = 0 to x = a/n, when it is in the nth state. **(Ans. 1/n)**

8. The wave function for a particle in infinite potential well is given as

$$\psi_n(x) = A \sin\left(\dfrac{n\pi}{a}x\right) \text{ where } 0 < x < a$$

Find $<x^2>$. **(Ans. $\dfrac{a^2}{12}\left(1 - \dfrac{6}{n^2\pi^2}\right)$)**

9. Find lowest possible energy of a neutron confined to a nucleus of size 10^{-14} m. Given mass of neutron = 1.67×10^{-27} kg. **(Ans. 2.05 MeV)**

10. Find the lowest energy of an electron confined in a cubical box of each side 1 A°.

(Ans. 18.03×10^{-18} J)

Chapter 4...
Spherically Symmetric Potentials

> *"There are only two ways to live your life. One is as though nothing is a miracle. The other is as though everything is a miracle."*
> — *Albert Einstein*

Albert Einstein
(1879-1955)

Albert Einstein was German born theoretical physicist. He developed the general theory of relativity. He is best known for his mass-energy relation $E = mc^2$. He received Nobel price in 1921 for his discovery of law of photoelectric effect, a pivotal step in the evaluation of quantum theory.

Introduction

- In the previous topics we have seen how quantum mechanics can be used to describe motion in one dimension. For the applications in atomic physics, solid-state physics and nuclear physics we need three dimensional treatment and also in spherical polar co-ordinate system. In the present topic, we will study Schrödinger's equation in spherical polar co-ordinate system. We will also apply it to spherically symmetric potential and study the quantization of energy.

- Hydrogen atom problem will be discussed in qualitative way. Because of its simplicity, hydrogen atom has advantage that its properties can be calculated exactly and without approximation, which has permitted comparison between prediction and experiment for a variety of physical theories from quantum mechanics.

4.1 Schrödinger's Equation in Spherical Polar Co-ordinates

- Schrödinger's equation in Cartesian co-ordinate system is given as

$$\nabla^2 \psi + \frac{2m}{\hbar^2} [E - V]\psi = 0$$

where $\nabla^2 = \dfrac{\partial^2}{\partial x^2} + \dfrac{\partial^2}{\partial y^2} + \dfrac{\partial^2}{\partial z^2}$ is the Laplacian operator.

- The transformation equations from Cartesian to spherical polar co-ordinate system are

$$x = r \sin \theta \cos \phi$$
$$y = r \sin \theta \sin \phi$$
$$z = r \cos \theta$$

- With these transformations, the Laplacian operator becomes

$$\nabla^2 = \frac{1}{r^2} \frac{\partial}{\partial r} \left(r^2 \frac{\partial}{\partial r} \right) + \frac{1}{r^2 \sin \theta} \frac{\partial}{\partial \theta} \left(\sin \theta \frac{\partial}{\partial \theta} \right) + \frac{1}{r^2 \sin^2 \theta} \frac{\partial^2}{\partial \phi^2}$$

Schrödinger's equation in spherical polar co-ordinate system is

$$\frac{1}{r^2} \frac{\partial}{\partial r} \left(r^2 \frac{\partial \psi}{\partial r} \right) + \frac{1}{r^2 \sin \theta} \frac{\partial}{\partial \theta} \left(\sin \theta \frac{\partial \psi}{\partial \theta} \right) + \frac{1}{r^2 \sin^2 \theta} \frac{\partial^2 \psi}{\partial \phi^2} + \frac{2m}{\hbar^2} [E - V] \psi = 0 \qquad \ldots (4.1)$$

where $V = V(r, \theta, \phi)$ and $\psi = \psi(r, \theta, \phi)$.

4.2 Rigid Rotator (Free Axis)

- *A rigid rotator is a system of two particles connected by a light rigid rod i.e. distance between the particles is always constant.* Fig. 4.1 shows the rigid rotator of masses m_1 and m_2 at a distance r apart.

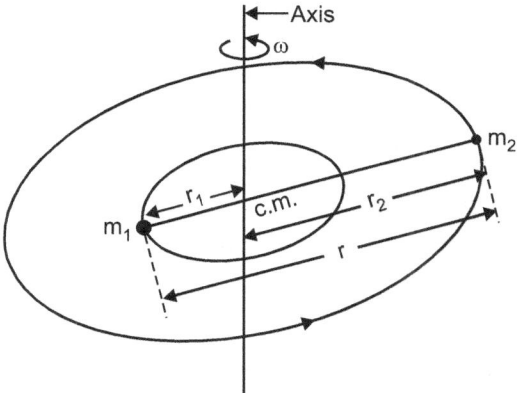

Fig. 4.1 : Rigid rotator

- The axis of rotation is passing through the centre of mass of rigid rotator and perpendicular to the length of the rod. The orientation of axis of rotation in space can be along any direction, so this is called free axis rigid rotator. The moment of inertia about an axis passing through centre of mass and perpendicular to the line joining of m_1 and m_2 is

$$I = m_1 r_1^2 + m_2 r_2^2 \qquad \ldots (4.2)$$

where r_1 and r_2 are distances of m_1 and m_2 respectively from centre of mass. Since the mass is equally distributed about centre of mass, we have

$$m_1 r_1 = m_2 r_2$$

and $$r = r_1 + r_2$$

$\therefore$

$$r_1 = \frac{m_2}{m_1} r_2$$

and

$$r = \frac{m_2}{m_1} r_2 + r_2 = \frac{m_1 + m_2}{m_1} r_2$$

or

$$r_2 = \frac{m_1}{m_1 + m_2} r$$

Similarly

$$r_1 = \frac{m_2}{m_1 + m_2} r$$

Using r_1 and r_2 in equation (4.2), we get

$$I = \frac{m_1 m_2}{m_1 + m_2} r^2$$

The reduced mass of the system is

$$\mu = \frac{m_1 m_2}{m_1 + m_2} \qquad \qquad \dots (4.3)$$

and moment of inertia of the system about the free axis is

$$I = \mu \, r^2 \qquad \qquad \dots (4.4)$$

- Equation (4.4) states that the rotation of a rigid rotator is equivalent to the rotation of a single particle of mass μ at perpendicular distance r from the axis of rotation.

Classically the kinetic energy of rotation is

$$E = \frac{1}{2} I \omega^2$$

where ω is the angular velocity.

Since angular momentum is $L = I\omega$, we can write

$$E = \frac{L^2}{2I} \qquad \qquad \dots (4.5)$$

- The rigid rotator can have any value of ω between 0 to ∞. Therefore, energy spectrum is continuous.

- Now, we will solve the problem quantum mechanically.

Schrödinger's time independent equation in spherical polar co-ordinates is given as

$$\frac{1}{r^2} \frac{\partial}{\partial r} \left(r^2 \frac{\partial \psi}{\partial r} \right) + \frac{1}{r^2 \sin \theta} \frac{\partial}{\partial \theta} \left(\sin \theta \frac{\partial \psi}{\partial \theta} \right) + \frac{1}{r^2 \sin^2 \theta} \frac{\partial^2 \psi}{\partial \phi^2} + \frac{2\mu}{\hbar^2} [E - V] \, \psi = 0$$

Multiplying throughout by r^2, we get

$$\frac{\partial}{\partial r} \left(r^2 \frac{\partial \psi}{\partial r} \right) + \frac{1}{\sin \theta} \frac{\partial}{\partial \theta} \left(\sin \theta \frac{\partial \psi}{\partial \theta} \right) + \frac{1}{\sin^2 \theta} \frac{\partial^2 \psi}{\partial \phi^2} + \frac{2\mu r^2}{\hbar^2} [E - V] \, \psi = 0$$

- Since the rigid rotator is free to rotate in any plane and no force acting on it, its potential energy V = 0. Therefore,

$$\frac{\partial}{\partial r} \left(r^2 \frac{\partial \psi}{\partial r} \right) + \frac{1}{\sin \theta} \frac{\partial}{\partial \theta} \left(\sin \theta \frac{\partial \psi}{\partial \theta} \right) + \frac{1}{\sin^2 \theta} \frac{\partial^2 \psi}{\partial \phi^2} + \frac{2\mu r^2 E}{\hbar^2} \, \psi = 0$$

- But r = constant, therefore, the first term on right hand side of above equation is $\frac{\partial}{\partial r}\left(r^2 \frac{\partial \psi}{\partial r}\right) = 0$. Hence we get

$$\frac{1}{\sin\theta}\frac{\partial}{\partial\theta}\left(\sin\theta\frac{\partial\psi}{\partial\theta}\right) + \frac{1}{\sin^2\theta}\frac{\partial^2\psi}{\partial\phi^2} + \frac{2\mu r^2 E}{\hbar^2}\psi = 0 \qquad \ldots (4.6)$$

Since $I = \mu r^2$, we get

$$\frac{1}{\sin\theta}\frac{\partial}{\partial\theta}\left(\sin\theta\frac{\partial\psi}{\partial\theta}\right) + \frac{1}{\sin^2\theta}\frac{\partial^2\psi}{\partial\phi^2} + \frac{2IE}{\hbar^2}\psi = 0 \qquad \ldots (4.7)$$

Equation (4.7) can be solved by separation of variables method. Let us assume

$$\psi(\theta,\phi) = F(\theta)\, G(\phi) = FG \qquad \ldots (4.8)$$

Using in equation (4.6), we get

$$\frac{1}{\sin\theta}\frac{\partial}{\partial\theta}\left(\sin\theta\frac{\partial FG}{\partial\theta}\right) + \frac{1}{\sin^2\theta}\frac{\partial^2 FG}{\partial\phi^2} + \frac{2IE}{\hbar^2}FG = 0$$

Let, $\qquad \lambda = \dfrac{2IE}{\hbar^2} \qquad\qquad\qquad\qquad\qquad \ldots (4.9)$

Therefore, $\dfrac{1}{\sin\theta}\dfrac{\partial}{\partial\theta}\left(\sin\theta\dfrac{\partial FG}{\partial\theta}\right) + \dfrac{1}{\sin^2\theta}\dfrac{\partial^2 FG}{\partial\phi^2} + \lambda FG = 0$

$$\frac{G}{\sin\theta}\frac{\partial}{\partial F}\left(\sin\theta\frac{\partial F}{\partial\theta}\right) + \frac{F}{\sin^2\theta}\frac{\partial^2 G}{\partial\phi^2} + \lambda FG = 0$$

Multiplying above equation throughout by $\sin^2\theta$ and dividing by FG, we get

$$\frac{\sin\theta}{F}\frac{\partial}{\partial\theta}\left(\sin\theta\frac{\partial F}{\partial\theta}\right) + \frac{1}{G}\frac{\partial^2 G}{\partial\phi^2} + \lambda\sin^2\theta = 0$$

or $\qquad \dfrac{\sin\theta}{F}\dfrac{\partial}{\partial\theta}\left(\sin\theta\dfrac{\partial F}{\partial\theta}\right) + \lambda\sin^2\theta = -\dfrac{1}{G}\dfrac{\partial^2 G}{\partial\phi^2} \qquad \ldots (4.10)$

- Left hand side of above equation depends upon θ only and right hand side depends on ϕ only. This is possible only when both sides are equal to some constant say m_l^2. Therefore, we get

$$\frac{\sin\theta}{F}\frac{d}{d\theta}\left(\sin\theta\frac{dF}{d\theta}\right) + \lambda\sin^2\theta = m_l^2 \qquad \ldots (4.11)$$

and $\qquad -\dfrac{1}{G}\dfrac{d^2 G}{d\phi^2} = m_l^2 \qquad\qquad\qquad\qquad \ldots (4.12)$

Equation (4.12) can be written as

$$\frac{d^2 G}{d\phi^2} + m_l^2 G = 0 \qquad \ldots (4.13)$$

The general solution of equation (4.13) can be written as

$$G(\phi) = A\, e^{im_l\phi} \qquad \ldots (4.14)$$

where m_l can be positive or negative integer. The range of ϕ is from 0 to 2π. The constant A can be obtained by normalisation condition *i.e.*

$$\int_0^{2\pi} G^*G\,d\phi = 1$$

$$\therefore \quad \int_0^{2\pi} A^* e^{-im_l\phi}\, A\, e^{im_l\phi}\,d\phi = 1$$

$$|A|^2 \int_0^{2\pi} d\phi = 1$$

or $\quad |A|^2\, 2\pi = 1$

This gives $\quad |A| = \dfrac{1}{\sqrt{2\pi}}$

$$\therefore \quad G(\phi) = \frac{1}{\sqrt{2\pi}}\, e^{im_l\phi} \qquad\qquad ...(4.15)$$

- As the wave function (4.15) must be acceptable solution (*i.e.* single valued and continuous), then we must have $G(\phi) = G(\phi + 2\pi)$. Because rotating ϕ by 2π, we are again at the same point.

$$\therefore \quad \frac{1}{\sqrt{2\pi}}\, e^{im_l\phi} = \frac{1}{\sqrt{2\pi}}\, e^{im_l(\phi + 2\pi)}$$

or $\quad e^{i2\pi m_l} = 1$

$\therefore \quad \cos(2\pi m_l) + i\sin(2\pi m_l) = 1$

This gives $\quad \cos(2\pi m_l) = 1$ and $\sin(2\pi m_l) = 0$

This is possible only when

$$2\pi m_l = 0, \pm 2\pi, \pm 4\pi, \pm 6\pi \,......$$

$$\therefore \quad m_l = 0, \pm 1, \pm 2, \pm 3,........ \qquad\qquad ... (4.16)$$

Equation (4.11) can be written as

$$\frac{1}{\sin\theta}\frac{d}{d\theta}\left(\sin\theta\frac{dF}{d\theta}\right) + \left(\lambda - \frac{m_l^2}{\sin^2\theta}\right)F = 0 \qquad\qquad ... (4.17)$$

This equation can be solved by following substitution.

$$\cos\theta = x, \text{ then } -\sin\theta\, d\theta = dx$$

or $\quad -\dfrac{d}{dx} = \dfrac{1}{\sin\theta}\dfrac{d}{d\theta}$

$$\therefore \quad \sin\theta\frac{dF}{d\theta} = \frac{\sin^2\theta}{\sin\theta}\frac{dF}{d\theta} = -(1-x^2)\frac{dF}{dx}$$

Using in equation (4.17), we get

$$-\frac{d}{dx}\left(-(1-x^2)\frac{dF}{dx}\right) + \left[\lambda - \frac{m_l^2}{(1-x^2)}\right] = 0$$

or

$$(1-x^2)\frac{d^2F}{dx^2} - 2x\frac{dF}{dx} + \left[\lambda - \frac{m_l^2}{(1-x^2)}\right] = 0 \qquad \dots (4.18)$$

- This is associated Legendre's equation. For a given value of m_l, it has acceptable solution only when $\lambda = l(l+1)$, where l is a positive integer given as

$$l = |m_l|, \quad |m_l| + 1, \quad |m_l| + 2, \quad |m_l| + 3, \dots\dots$$

With equation (4.16), we get

$$l = 0, 1, 2, 3, 4, \dots\dots \qquad \dots (4.19)$$

Therefore, we can write equation (4.18) as

$$(1-x^2)\frac{d^2F}{dx^2} - 2x\frac{dF}{dx} + \left[l(l+1) - \frac{m_l^2}{(1-x^2)}\right] = 0$$

The general solution of above equation is associated Legendre polynomials $P_l^{m_l}(x)$ given as

$$P_l^{m_l}(x) = (1-x^2)^{|m_l|/2}\frac{d^{|m_l|}}{dx^{|m_l|}} P_l(x)$$

where $P_l(x)$ are Legendre polynomials.

Hence general solution of equation (4.17) is

$$F_l^{m_l}(\theta) = B\, P_l^{m_l}(\cos\theta) \qquad \dots (4.20)$$

where B is normalization constant and is given by

$$B = \sqrt{\frac{(2l+1)}{2}\frac{(l-|m_l|)!}{(l+|m_l|)!}}$$

Thus, the total wave function is

$$\psi(\theta, \phi) = F_l^{m_l}(\theta)\, G_{m_l}(\phi)$$

or

$$\psi(\theta, \phi) = \frac{1}{\sqrt{2\pi}}\sqrt{\frac{(2l+1)}{2}\frac{(l-|m_l|)!}{(l+|m_l|)!}}\; P_l^{m_l}(\cos\theta)\; e^{im_l\phi} \qquad \dots(4.21)$$

From equation (4.9), we have

$$\lambda = \frac{2IE}{\hbar^2}$$

$$\therefore \qquad \frac{2IE}{\hbar^2} = l(l+1)$$

Thus the corresponding eigen value is

$$E_l = \frac{l(l+1)\hbar^2}{2I} \qquad \dots (4.22)$$

When

$l = 0$, $E_0 = 0$

$l = 1$, $E_1 = 2\dfrac{\hbar^2}{2I} = 2B$

$l = 2$, $E_1 = 6\dfrac{\hbar^2}{2I} = 6B$

$l = 3$, $E_1 = 12\dfrac{\hbar^2}{2I} = 12B$

and so on...

where $B = \dfrac{\hbar^2}{2I}$.

- The energy level E_0 is called the ground state energy of rigid rotator. The subsequent levels E_1, E_2, E_3 etc. are called first, second, third etc. energy levels.

  The energy level diagram is shown in Fig. 4.2.

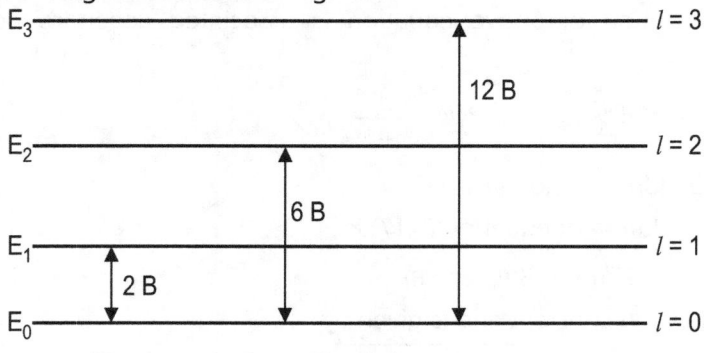

Fig. 4.2

- It is seen that the difference between successive energy levels increases with increase in l. Also the spectrum is discrete one. The discrete nature energy levels is confirmed experimentally.

4.3 Hydrogen Atom (Qualitative Discussion)

- The solution of the Schrodinger's equation for the hydrogen atom is a formidable mathematical problem, but is of such fundamental importance that it will be treated in outline here. The solution is managed by separating the variables.

- Hydrogen atom is a system consisting of an electron and proton (nucleus) bound by an electrostatic attraction given by Coulomb's force. Coulomb's force of attraction is

$$F = \frac{1}{4\pi\varepsilon_o}\frac{Ze^2}{r^2}$$

and hence the potential energy is

$$V(r) = -\frac{1}{4\pi\varepsilon_o}\frac{Ze^2}{r} \qquad \qquad ...(4.23)$$

where   Ze = nuclear charge (Z = 1 for hydrogen)

   – e = electronic charge

   ε_o = permittivity of free space

$\therefore$ $$V(r) = -\frac{1}{4\pi\varepsilon_o}\frac{e^2}{r}$$ ...(4.24)

• Let M and m be the masses of nucleus and electron respectively. The reduced mass of the system is

$$\mu = \frac{Mm}{M + m}$$

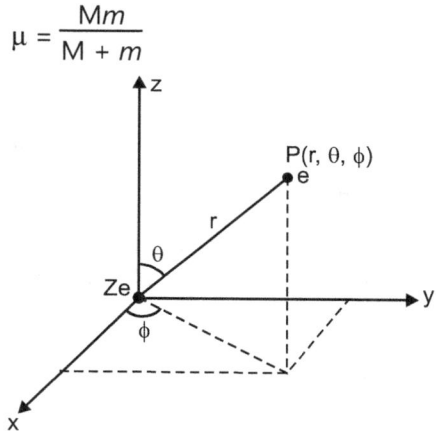

Fig. 4.3

• Potential energy V is a function of r i.e. potential is spherically symmetric. We will apply Schrödinger's equation in spherical co-ordinate system and it is given as

$$\frac{1}{r^2}\frac{\partial}{\partial r}\left(r^2\frac{\partial\psi}{\partial r}\right) + \frac{1}{r^2\sin\theta}\frac{\partial}{\partial\theta}\left(\sin\theta\frac{\partial\psi}{\partial\theta}\right) + \frac{1}{r^2\sin^2\theta}\frac{\partial^2\psi}{\partial\phi^2} + \frac{2\mu}{\hbar^2}[E - V(r)]\,\psi = 0 \qquad ... (4.25)$$

• Using $\psi(r, \theta, \phi) = R(r)F(\theta)G(\phi)$ in equation (4.25) and solving by separation of variables method, we get three equations :

(1) Radial equation :

$$\frac{1}{r^2}\frac{d}{dr}\left(r^2\frac{dR}{dr}\right) + \frac{2\mu}{\hbar^2}\left[E - V(r) - \frac{l(l + 1)}{r^2}\right]R = 0 \qquad ... (4.26)$$

In order to separate the equations, the radial part is set equal to a constant and the form of the constant on the right above reflects the nature of the solution. Solution of these equations under the constraints placed on the wave function leads to series solutions in the form of polynomials called the associated Laguerre functions. In order to fit the physical boundary conditions, these solutions contain a parameter n which can take only positive integer values; this parameter is called the principal quantum number.

(2) θ-part equation :

$$\frac{1}{\sin\theta}\frac{d}{d\theta}\left(\sin\theta\frac{dF}{d\theta}\right) + \left(l(l + 1) - \frac{m_l^2}{\sin^2\theta}\right)F = 0 \qquad ... (4.27)$$

(3) φ-part equation :

$$\frac{d^2 G}{d\phi^2} + m_l^2 G = 0 \qquad \ldots (4.28)$$

Solution of φ-part equation is given as

$$G(\phi) = \frac{1}{\sqrt{2\pi}} e^{im_l \phi} \qquad \ldots (4.29)$$

The constant m_l must be positive or negative integer. This is because G and its derivative must be continuous and single valued in the domain $0 \leq \phi \leq 2\pi$.

We have $m_l = 0, \pm 1, \pm 2, \pm 3, \pm 4, \ldots\ldots$ ...(4.30)

m_l is known as *magnetic quantum number*.

As we know that equation (4.27) is associated Legendre equation, its solution is

$$F_l^{m_l}(\theta) = B P_l^{m_l}(\cos \theta) \qquad \ldots (4.31)$$

where $P_l^{m_l}(\cos \theta)$ is associated Legendre polynomials and B is normalization constant. B can be obtained by condition of normalization of equation (4.31) in the range $0 \leq \theta < \leq \pi$. It is given by

$$B = \sqrt{\frac{(2l + 1)}{2} \frac{(l - |m_l|)!}{(l + |m_l|)!}} \qquad \ldots (4.32)$$

and l is positive integer given as

$$l = |m_l|, \quad |m_l| + 1, \quad |m_l| + 2, \quad |m_l| + 3, \ldots\ldots\ldots \qquad \ldots (4.33)$$

Substituting equation (4.30) in equation (4.32), we get

$$\frac{1}{r^2} \frac{d}{dr} \left(r^2 \frac{dR}{dr} \right) + \frac{2\mu}{\hbar^2} \left[E + \frac{e^2}{4\pi\varepsilon_o r} - \frac{l(l + 1)}{r^2} \right] R = 0 \qquad \ldots (4.34)$$

The effective potential is

$$V_{eff} = -\frac{e^2}{4\pi\varepsilon_o r} + \frac{l(l + 1)}{r^2}$$

- With the given value of l, it is found that there are bound state solutions for equation (4.34) which are acceptable (*i.e.* single valued, continuous and finite) solutions only if the total energy E has one of the values E_n, where

$$E_n = -\frac{\mu e^4}{(4\pi\varepsilon_o)^2 2\hbar^2 n^2} \qquad \ldots (4.35)$$

where n is the integer and can have values

$$n = l + 1, l + 2, l + 3, \ldots\ldots\ldots \qquad \ldots (4.36)$$

With l from equation (4.33) and m_l from equation (4.30), we get

$$n = 1, 2, 3, 4, 5, \ldots\ldots\ldots\ldots \qquad \ldots (4.37)$$

The acceptable solution of radial part equation (4.34) is more conveniently be written as

$$R_{nl}(r) = C e^{-\alpha r} (\alpha r)^l L(\alpha r) \qquad \ldots (4.38)$$

where

$L(\alpha r)$ is polynomial in (αr)

$\alpha = \dfrac{1}{na_0}$ where a_0 is Bohr's radius given by $a_0 = \dfrac{4\pi\varepsilon_0\hbar^2}{\mu e^2}$

and   C is normalization constant.

Therefore the general eigen function of the hydrogen atom is

$$\psi(r, \theta, \phi) = N\, e^{-\alpha r}(\alpha r)^l\, L(\alpha r)\, P_l^{m_l}(\cos\theta)\, e^{im_l\phi} \qquad \text{...(4.39)}$$

where N is normalization constant and is given by

$$N = \sqrt{\left(\frac{2}{na_0}\right)^3 \frac{(n-l-1)!}{2n\{(n+l)!\}^3}} \cdot \sqrt{\frac{(2l+1)}{2}\frac{(l-|m_l|)!}{(l+|m_l|)!}} \cdot \frac{1}{\sqrt{2\pi}}$$

Some of the eigen functions are listed in Table 4.2.

Table 4.2

n	l	m_l	$\psi_{nlm}\,(r, \theta, \phi)$	
1	0	0	$\psi_{100} = \dfrac{1}{\sqrt{\pi a_0^3}}\, e^{-r/a_0}$	Ground state
2	0	0	$\psi_{200} = \dfrac{1}{4\sqrt{2\pi a_0^3}}\left(2 - \dfrac{r}{a_0}\right) e^{-r/2a_0}$	First excited state
2	1	0	$\psi_{210} = \dfrac{1}{4\sqrt{2\pi a_0^3}}\left(\dfrac{r}{a_0}\right) e^{-r/2a_0}\cos\theta$	First excited state
2	1	± 1	$\psi_{21\pm1} = \dfrac{1}{8\sqrt{\pi a_0^3}}\left(\dfrac{r}{a_0}\right) e^{-r/2a_0}\sin\theta\, e^{\pm i\phi}$	
3	0	0	$\psi_{300} = \dfrac{1}{81\sqrt{3\pi a_0^3}}\left(27 - 18\dfrac{r}{a_0} + 2\dfrac{r^2}{a_0^2}\right) e^{-r/2a_0}$	Second excited state
3	1	0	$\psi_{310} = \dfrac{\sqrt{2}}{81\sqrt{\pi a_0^3}}\left(6 - \dfrac{r}{a_0}\right)\dfrac{r}{a_0}\, e^{-r/2a_0}\cos\theta$	Second excited state
3	1	± 1	$\psi_{31\pm1} = \dfrac{1}{81\sqrt{\pi a_0^3}}\left(6 - \dfrac{r}{a_0}\right)\dfrac{r}{a_0}\, e^{-r/2a_0}\sin\theta\, e^{\pm i\phi}$	

Eigen values :

- The solution of radial part of the hydrogen atom shows that the allowed values of total energy of bound state is

$$E_n = -\frac{\mu e^4}{(4\pi\varepsilon_o)^2 \, 2\hbar^2 n^2} = -\frac{13.6}{n^2} \, eV$$

which is same as predicted by Bohr's theory. Both quantum mechanical predictions and Bohr's predictions are in exact agreement with the experimental results.

Quantum numbers :

- The energy eigen values depend on the quantum number 'n' only. But the eigen functions depend on three quantum numbers n, l, m_l since they are products of three functions $R_{nl}(r)$, $F_l^{m_l}(\theta)$ and $G_{m_l}(\phi)$. These three quantum numbers arise because Schrödinger's time independent equation contains three variables r, θ and ϕ, one for each space co-ordinate.

From equations (4.30), (4.33) and (4.36), the conditions for three quantum numbers

$$m_l = 0, \pm 1, \pm 2, \pm 3, \pm 4, \ldots\ldots$$

$$l = |m_l|, \ |m_l| + 1, \ |m_l| + 2, \ |m_l| + 3, \ldots\ldots\ldots$$

and

$$n = l + 1, l + 2, l + 3, \ldots\ldots\ldots$$

These conditions are conveniently can be written as

$$n = 0, 1, 2, 3, 4, \ldots\ldots\ldots\ldots$$

$$l = 0, 1, 2, 3, \ldots\ldots (n - 1)$$

and

$$m_l = -l, -l + 1, -l + 2, \ldots\ldots -1, 0, +1, \ldots\ldots l + 1, l.$$

1. **Principal quantum number :** The role of 'n' is in specifying the energy eigen value E_n as given by equation (4.35), it is sometimes called principal quantum number. It may assume values 1, 2, 3 … ∞. The principal quantum number of a particle prescribes its energy value.

2. **Orbital quantum number :** As the orbital angular momentum number depends on quantum number l, it is also called orbital quantum number. Thus, for a given n, l takes values as 0, 1, 2, …...(n – 1). For an electron, in a particular bound state of atom, l governs the degree with which it is attached to nucleus; larger is the value of l, weaker is the bond with which electron is maintained in the nucleus.

3. **Magnetic quantum number :** If an atom is placed in an external magnetic field, its energy depends on m_l. Consequently m_l is also called magnetic quantum number. For a given l, m_l takes values as $-l, -l + 1, -l + 2, \ldots\ldots -1, 0, +1, \ldots\ldots l + 1, l.$

4. Another quantum number is spin quantum number. It has two possible values of orientation $m_s = \pm\frac{1}{2}$.

Degeneracy :

- For a given value of principal quantum number n, the energy of the atomic level is fixed as predicted by the Bohr's theory. But for a given value of n there are generally several different values of l and for each l there are different values of m_l. Thus there are several possible wave function for a given energy value (n fixed). As the eigen functions depend on n, l and m_l, we have a number of possible eigen functions corresponding to a given energy eigen value E_n. Behaviour of the atom is described by the eigen functions. So the atom has different states for given n with the same energy eigen values. This is referred as *degeneracy* of the level, and the eigen functions corresponding to the same energy are called *degenerate*.

- As m_l takes values $- l, - l + 1, - l + 2, ... -1, 0, +1, ... l + 1, l$ that is $(2l + 1)$ values. Each l takes values as 0, 1, 2, ... (n – 1). Therefore, for each n the number of independent eigen functions will be

$$\sum_{l=0}^{n-1} (2l + 1) = 2\sum_{l=0}^{n-1} l + \sum_{l=0}^{n-1} 1 = n^2$$

Thus for each n there are n^2 corresponding degenerate eigen functions.

- If we take into account spin quantum number (s), which has two possible values of orientation $m_s = \pm 1/2$ there are $2n^2$ degenerate state corresponding to each energy eigen value En.

- Table 4.3 shows possible values of quantum numbers for n = 1, 2, 3 and number of degenerate eigen functions.

Table 4.3

n	1	2		3		
l	0	0	1	0	1	2
m_l	0	0	–1, 0, +1	0	–1, 0, +1	–2, –1, 0, 1, 2
Number of degenerate eigen functions for each l	1	1	3	1	3	5
Number of degenerate eigen functions for each n	1	4		9		

Solved Problems

Problem 4.1 : *The moment of inertia of CO molecule is 1.46×10^{-46} kg-m². Calculate the rotational energy and angular velocity in the lowest level of CO molecule.*

Solution : The rotational energy level is given as

$$E_l = \frac{l(l + 1)\hbar^2}{2I}$$

For the lowest rotational energy level $l = 1$, therefore,

$$E_1 = \frac{2\hbar^2}{2I} = \frac{\hbar^2}{I}$$

$\hbar = 1.055 \times 10^{-34}$ J-sec, $I = 1.46 \times 10^{-46}$ kg-m²

$\therefore$ $$E_1 = \frac{(1.055 \times 10^{-34})^2}{1.46 \times 10^{-46}}$$

or $$E_1 = 7.62 \times 10^{-23} \text{ J}$$

$\therefore$ $$E_1 = \frac{7.62 \times 10^{-23}}{1.6 \times 10^{-19}} \text{ eV}$$

$$= 4.763 \times 10^{-4} \text{ eV}$$

We have $$E = \frac{1}{2} I\omega^2$$

$\therefore$ $$\omega = \sqrt{\frac{2E}{I}} = \sqrt{\frac{2 \times 7.62 \times 10^{-23}}{1.46 \times 10^{-46}}}$$

$$= \mathbf{3.23 \times 10^{11} \text{ rad/sec}} \qquad \text{... Ans.}$$

Problem 4.2 : *Compute the expectation value of r in the ground state of the hydrogen atom. Also compute the most probable value of r in this state, given that*

$$\Psi_{100} = \frac{1}{\sqrt{\pi a_0^3}} e^{-r/a_0} \qquad \text{where } a_0 \text{ is Bohr radius.}$$

Solution : (a) The expectation value of r is given as

$$<r> = \int_0^\infty r|\Psi_{100}|^2 \, d\tau$$

where $d\tau$ is volume element and for spherically symmetric system, $d\tau = 4\pi r^2 dr$

$\therefore$ $$<r> = \frac{1}{\pi a_0^3} \int_0^\infty r e^{-2r/a_0} 4\pi r^2 \, dr$$

$$= \frac{4}{a_0^3} \int_0^\infty r^3 e^{-2r/a_0} \, dr$$

We have the general integral $\int\limits_{0}^{\infty} x^n e^{-\beta x} dx = \dfrac{n!}{(\beta)^{n+1}}$

$\therefore \qquad\qquad <r> = \dfrac{4}{a_0^3} \dfrac{3!}{(2/a_0)^4}$

$\therefore \qquad\qquad <r> = \dfrac{3}{2} a_0$

(b) Most probable distance can be obtained by differentiating probability density w.r.t. r and equating to zero.

The radial probability density is given as

$$P(r) = 4\pi r^2 \, | \, \psi_{100}|^2$$

$$P(r) = \dfrac{4}{a_0^3} r^2 e^{-2r/a_0}$$

$\therefore \qquad \dfrac{dP}{dr} = \dfrac{4}{a_0^3}\left[-\dfrac{2}{a_0} e^{-2r/a_0} r^2 + 2r \, e^{-2r/a_0} \right]$

$$\qquad\qquad = \dfrac{4}{a_0^3} 2r \left(1 - \dfrac{r}{a_0} \right) e^{-2r/a_0}$$

For most probable distance, $\dfrac{dP}{dr} = 0$

$\therefore \qquad\qquad \dfrac{4}{a_0^3} 2r \left(1 - \dfrac{r}{a_0} \right) e^{-2r/a_0} = 0$

or $\qquad\qquad 1 - \dfrac{r}{a_0} = 0$

or $\qquad\qquad$ **$r = a_0$** $\qquad\qquad\qquad\qquad\qquad$ ... **Ans.**

This is the location of maximum in the radial probability density.

Problem 4.3 : *Calculate the expectation value of the potential energy in the ground state of the hydrogen atom.*

Solution : The ground state of the hydrogen atom is given as

$$\psi_{100} = \dfrac{1}{\sqrt{\pi a_0^3}} e^{-r/a_0} \qquad\qquad \text{where } a_0 \text{ is the Bohr radius.}$$

The potential energy of the hydrogen atom is

$$V = -\dfrac{1}{4\pi\varepsilon_0} \dfrac{e^2}{r}$$

The expectation value of V is given as

$$<V> = \int\limits_{0}^{\infty} V |\psi_{100}|^2 \, d\tau$$

where $d\tau$ is the volume element and for spherically symmetric system, $d\tau = 4\pi r^2 dr$

$$\therefore \qquad <V> = \frac{1}{\pi a_0{}^3} \int_0^\infty \left(-\frac{e^2}{4\pi\varepsilon_0\, r}\right) e^{-2r/a_0}\, 4\pi r^2\, dr$$

$$= -\frac{4}{a_0{}^3}\, \frac{e^2}{4\pi\varepsilon_0} \int_0^\infty r\, e^{-2r/a_0}\, dr$$

We have the general integral $\int_0^\infty x^n\, e^{-\beta x}\, dx = \frac{n!}{(\beta)^{n+1}}$

$$\therefore \qquad <V> = -\frac{4}{a_0{}^3}\, \frac{e^2}{4\pi\varepsilon_0}\, \frac{1!}{(2/a_0{}^2)}$$

$$= -\frac{1}{4\pi\varepsilon_0}\, \frac{e^2}{a_0}$$

$$\therefore \qquad a_0 = \frac{4\pi\varepsilon_0 \hbar^2}{\mu e^2}$$

$$\therefore \qquad <V> = -\frac{\mu e^4}{(4\pi\varepsilon_0)^2 \hbar^2} \qquad\qquad\qquad \textbf{... Ans.}$$

Problem 4.4 : *The radial part solution for ground state hydrogen atom is given as*

$$R_{10}(r) = \frac{1}{\sqrt{\pi a_0{}^3}}\, e^{-r/a_0}$$

Show that its ground state energy is $-\dfrac{\mu e^4}{(4\pi\varepsilon_0)^2\, 2\hbar^2}$

Solution : The radial part equation of hydrogen atom is given as

$$\frac{1}{r^2}\frac{d}{dr}\left(r^2 \frac{dR}{dr}\right) + \frac{2m}{\hbar^2}\left[E + \frac{e^2}{4\pi\varepsilon_0 r} - \frac{l(l+1)}{r^2}\right]R = 0$$

For ground state $R(r) = R_{10}(r)$ and $l = 0$

$$\therefore \qquad \frac{1}{r^2}\frac{d}{dr}\left(r^2 \frac{dR_{10}}{dr}\right) + \frac{2\mu}{\hbar^2}\left[E + \frac{e^2}{4\pi\varepsilon_0 r}\right]R_{10} = 0$$

or $\qquad \dfrac{d^2R_{10}}{dr^2} + \dfrac{2}{r}\dfrac{dR_{10}}{dr} + \dfrac{2\mu}{\hbar^2}\left[E + \dfrac{e^2}{4\pi\varepsilon_0 r}\right]R_{10} = 0 \qquad\qquad$ ...(i)

We have $\qquad R_{10} = \dfrac{1}{\sqrt{\pi a_0{}^3}}\, e^{-r/a_0}$

$$\therefore \qquad \frac{dR_{10}}{dr} = -\frac{1}{\sqrt{\pi a_0{}^3}}\, \frac{1}{a_0}\, e^{-r/a_0}$$

and $\qquad \dfrac{d^2R_{10}}{dr^2} = \dfrac{1}{\sqrt{\pi a_0{}^3}}\, \dfrac{1}{a_0{}^2}\, e^{-r/a_0}$

Using in equation (i), we get

$$\frac{1}{\sqrt{\pi a_0{}^3}}\frac{1}{a_0{}^2}e^{-r/a_0} - \frac{2}{r}\frac{1}{\sqrt{\pi a_0{}^3}}\frac{1}{a_0}e^{-r/a_0} + \frac{2\mu}{\hbar^2}\left[E + \frac{e^2}{4\pi\varepsilon_o r}\right]\frac{1}{\sqrt{\pi a_0{}^3}}e^{-r/a_0} = 0$$

$$\therefore \quad \frac{1}{a_0{}^2} - \frac{2}{r a_0} + \frac{2\mu}{\hbar^2}\left[E + \frac{e^2}{4\pi\varepsilon_o r}\right] = 0$$

or

$$\frac{1}{a_0{}^2} + \frac{2\mu E}{\hbar^2} = -\frac{2\mu e^2}{4\pi\varepsilon_o \hbar^2 r} + \frac{2}{r a_0}$$

Using $a_0 = \frac{4\pi\varepsilon_o\hbar^2}{\mu e^2}$ in above equation, we get

$$\frac{\mu^2 e^4}{(4\pi\varepsilon_o)^2\hbar^4} + \frac{2\mu E}{\hbar^2} = -\frac{2\mu e^2}{4\pi\varepsilon_o \hbar^2 r} + \frac{2\mu e^2}{4\pi\varepsilon_o\hbar^2 r}$$

$$\frac{\mu^2 e^4}{(4\pi\varepsilon_o)^2\hbar^4} + \frac{2\mu E}{\hbar^2} = 0$$

$$\therefore \quad E = -\frac{\mu e^4}{(4\pi\varepsilon_o)^2\,2\hbar^2} \qquad\qquad \text{... Proved.}$$

This is the required result.

Problem 4.5 : *How much more likely an electron in ground state in a hydrogen atom to be at the distance a_0 from the nucleus than at the distance $a_0/2$?*

Solution : Ground state wave function of hydrogen atom is

$$\psi_{100} = \frac{1}{\sqrt{\pi a_0{}^3}}e^{-r/a_0}$$

The radial probability density is given as

$$P(r) = 4\pi r^2 \,|\,\psi_{100}\,|^2 = \frac{4}{a_0{}^3}r^2\,e^{-2r/a_0}$$

$$\therefore \quad \frac{P(r_1)}{P(r_2)} = \frac{r_1{}^2\,e^{-2r_1/a_0}}{r_2{}^2\,e^{-2r_2/a_0}}$$

Here $r_1 = a_0$ and $r_2 = a_0/2$

$$\therefore \quad \frac{P(a_0)}{P(a_0/2)} = \frac{(a_0)^2\,e^{-2}}{(a_0/2)^2\,e^{-1}} = \frac{4}{e} = 1.470$$

$$\therefore \quad P(a_0) = 1.47\,P(a_0/2)$$

Thus the electron is 47 % more likely to be at a_0 than $a_0/2$.   **... Ans.**

Problem 4.6 : *How many hydrogen atom states are there with n = 5 ? How are they distributed among the subshells ?*

Solution : For every n level there are n^2 sublevels. Thus, for n = 5 there are 25 subshells.

They are obtained as follows.

l takes values as 0, 1, 2, ...(n − 1)

For each l, m_l takes values from $-l$ to $+ l$ i.e. (2l + 1) values.

For n = 5

l	0	1	2	3	4
m_l	0	+ 1, 0, –1	2, 1, 0, –1, –2	3, 2, 1, 0, –1, –2, –3	4, 3, 2, 1, 0, –1, –2, –3, –4
No. of sublevels	1	3	5	7	9
	2s	5p	5d	5f	5g

Problem 4.7 : For HCl molecule, if internuclear distance is 1.29×10^{-8} cm, $m_{Cl} = 35\ m_H$ and $m_H = 1.68 \times 10^{-24}$ gm, calculate the separation of the lines in the far infra-red region. Given : $h = 6.625 \times 10^{-27}$ erg.s, $c = 3 \times 10^{10}$ cm/s

Solution : Reduced formula for HCl is

$$\mu = \frac{m_{Cl}\ m_H}{m_H + m_{Cl}} = \frac{35\ m_H \cdot m_H}{36\ m_H} \qquad (\because m_{Cl} = 35\ m_H)$$

$$= \frac{35}{36}\ m_H = \frac{35}{36} \times 1.68 \times 10^{-24}\ gm$$

$$I = \mu r^2 = \frac{35}{36} \times 1.68 \times 10^{-24}\ gm \times (1.29 \times 10^{-8}\ cm)^2$$

The separation between the lines is given as

$$B = \frac{h}{4\pi^2\ I \cdot c} = \frac{6.625 \times 10^{-27} \times 36}{4 \times (3.14)^2 \times 35 \times 1.68 \times 10^{-24} \times (1.29 \times 10^{-8})^2 \times 3 \times 10^{10}}$$

$$= \mathbf{20.68\ cm^{-1}} \qquad\qquad \textbf{... Ans.}$$

Summary

1. Schrödinger's equation in spherical polar co-ordinate system is

$$\frac{1}{r^2}\frac{\partial}{\partial r}\left(r^2\frac{\partial\psi}{\partial r}\right) + \frac{1}{r^2\sin\theta}\frac{\partial}{\partial\theta}\left(\sin\theta\frac{\partial\psi}{\partial\theta}\right) + \frac{1}{r^2\sin^2\theta}\frac{\partial^2\psi}{\partial\phi^2} + \frac{2m}{\hbar^2}[E - V]\ \psi = 0$$

2. A rigid rotator is a system of two particles connected by light rigid rod (i.e. distance between particle is constant).

In case of free axis rigid rotator, eigen value of energy

$$E_l = \frac{l(l+1)\hbar^2}{2I}$$

3. Energy eigen value for rigid rotator

$$E = \frac{m_l^2\hbar^2}{2I}$$

4. In case of hydrogen atom, we have three equations :

(a) Radial equation : $\dfrac{1}{r^2}\dfrac{d}{dr}\left(r^2\dfrac{dR}{dr}\right) + \dfrac{2\mu}{\hbar^2}\left[E - V(r) - \dfrac{l(l+1)}{r^2}\ R\right] = 0$

(b) θ part equation : $\dfrac{1}{\sin\theta}\dfrac{d}{d\theta}\left(\sin\theta\dfrac{dF}{d\theta}\right) + \left(l(l+1) - \dfrac{m_l^2}{\sin^2\theta}\right)F = 0$

(c) ϕ part equation : $\dfrac{d^2G}{d\phi^2} + m_l^2G = 0$

5. Ground state wave function for hydrogen atom is $\psi_{100} = \dfrac{1}{\sqrt{\pi a_0{}^3}} e^{-r/a_0}$

6. Quantum numbers :
   (i)   Principal quantum number (n)
   (ii) Orbital quantum number (l)
   (iii) Magnetic quantum number (m_l)
   (iv) Spin quantum number (m_s).

7. Degeneracy means number of possible eigen functions corresponding to a given energy eigen value E_n and the eigen functions corresponding to the same energy are called *degenerate*.

Exercises

(A) Short Answer Type Questions :
1. Write the Schrödinger's time independent equation in spherical polar co-ordinate system.
2. What is rigid rotator?
3. Draw energy level diagram of free axis rigid rotator.
4. State quantum numbers.
5. Define degeneracy.

(B) Long Answer Type Questions :
1. Obtain Schrödinger's equation for a rigid rotator with free axis and solve it to obtain eigen values and eigen functions.
2. Discuss qualitatively the radial part, θ part and ϕ part of Schrödinger's equation for hydrogen atom .
3. What do you mean by degeneracy of the level? Explain in the case of hydrogen atom.
4. State quantum numbers. What is their significance?

(C) Unsolved Problems :
1. The moment of inertia of HCl molecule is 2.7×10^{-40} gm-cm^2. What would be the separation between $l = 0$ and $l = 1$ energy levels ?   (**Ans.** 4.05×10^{-15} erg)
2. The OH radical has a moment of inertia 1.48×10^{-40} gm-cm^2. Calculate angular velocity in $l = 5$ state.   (**Ans.** 3.90×10^{13} rad/sec)
3. Write down the quantum numbers for all the hydrogen atom states belonging to the subshell for which n = 4 and l = 3.
4. Compute the expectation value of $\dfrac{1}{r}$ in the ground state of the hydrogen atom.

    (**Ans.** $1/a_0$)
5. For hydrogen atom in its ground state, calculate the probability density of finding the electron between two spheres of radii $1.0a_0$ and $1.01a_0$.
6. Find the expectation value of r^2 in the ground state of the hydrogen atom.   (**Ans.** $3a_0^2$)

❑❑❑

Chapter **5**...

Operators in Quantum Mechanics

> *One could perhaps describe the situation by saying that God is a mathematician of a very high order, and he used very advanced mathematics in constructing the universe. Our feeble attempts at mathematics enable us to understand a bit of the universe, and as we proceed to develop higher and higher mathematics we can hope to understand the universe better.*
>
> *— P. A. M. Dirac (1963)*

Paul A. M. Dirac
(1902-1984)

Paul Adrien Maurice Dirac was an English theoretical physicist. He made fundamental contribution to the development of both quantum mechanics and quantum electrodynamics. He formulated Dirac equation which describe behaviour of fermions and predicted existence of antimatter. He shared Nobel prize in physics for 1933 with Erwin Schrödinger.

Introduction

- Operator is a mathematical term which is used in operation on a function such that it is transferred to another function. In this chapter, we will study some properties of operators. Also, the concept of commutation brackets used in quantum mechanics is introduced. The commutation relations involving position and momentum co-ordinates are of basic importance in quantum mechanics. These relations are to be derived in the present topic.

5.1 Hermitian Operator

- If $\hat{A}$ is the operator corresponding to certain observable quantity and ψ is a wave function of the system then the expectation value is given by,

$$<A> = \int_\tau \psi^* \hat{A} \psi \ d\tau$$

$<A>$ is a real number. Consequently, $\hat{A}$ must satisfy the condition

$$\int_\tau \psi^* \hat{A} \psi \ d\tau = \int_\tau (\psi^* \hat{A} \psi)^* \ d\tau = \int_\tau (\hat{A}\psi)^* \psi \ d\tau \qquad \text{... (5.1)}$$

for every ψ to which it may be applied. The operator which obeys above condition (given in equation 5.1) is called *hermitian operator*.

Problem 5.1 : *Prove that eigen values of the hermitian operator are real.*

Solution : Eigen value equation for any operator $\hat{A}$ has the following form

$$\hat{A} \psi = \lambda \psi$$

where λ is the eigen value of the operator $\hat{A}$ corresponding to the function ψ. Then,

$$\int_\tau \psi^* \hat{A} \psi \ d\tau = \int_\tau \psi^* (\lambda \psi) \ d\tau = \lambda \int_\tau \psi^* \psi d\tau$$

If the eigen function is normalised $\int_\tau \psi^* \psi d\tau = 1$, then

$$\int_\tau \psi^* \hat{A} \psi \ d\tau = \lambda$$

Also

$$\int_\tau (\hat{A}\psi)^* \psi \ d\tau = \int_\tau (\lambda^* \psi^*) \psi \ d\tau = \lambda^* \int_\tau \psi^* \psi \ d\tau = \lambda^*$$

where λ^* is the complex conjugate of λ. For hermitian operator, we have

$$\int_\tau \psi^* \hat{A} \psi \ d\tau = \int_\tau (\hat{A}\psi)^* \psi \ d\tau$$

$\therefore \qquad\qquad\qquad\qquad \lambda = \lambda^* \qquad\qquad\qquad\qquad \text{... (5.2)}$

This is possible only when λ is real. Thus, eigen value of the hermitian operator is real.

Problem 5.2 : *Show that the momentum operator $-i\hbar \dfrac{\partial}{\partial x}$ is hermitian operator. Obtain eigen function for momentum operator.*

Solution : For hermitian operator, we have

$$\int_\tau \psi^* \hat{A} \psi \ d\tau = \int_\tau (\hat{A}\psi)^* \psi \ d\tau \qquad \text{... (i)}$$

If momentum operator is hermitian, it should satisfy the following condition :

$$\int_{-\infty}^{\infty} \psi^* \left(-i\hbar \frac{\partial \psi}{\partial x} \right) dx = \int_{-\infty}^{\infty} \left(-i\hbar \frac{\partial \psi}{\partial x} \right)^* \psi \, dx$$

or

$$-i\hbar \int_{-\infty}^{\infty} \psi^* \frac{\partial \psi}{\partial x} dx = i\hbar \int_{-\infty}^{\infty} \frac{\partial \psi^*}{\partial x} \psi \, dx \qquad \text{... (ii)}$$

Consider the integral

$$\int_{-\infty}^{\infty} \psi^* \left(-i\hbar \frac{\partial \psi}{\partial x} \right) dx = -i\hbar \int_{-\infty}^{\infty} \psi^* \frac{\partial \psi}{\partial x} dx \qquad \text{... (iii)}$$

Integration by parts of the following integral is

$$\int_{a}^{b} u(x) \frac{dv(x)}{dx} dx = \left[u(x)v(x) \right]_{a}^{b} - \int_{a}^{b} \frac{du(x)}{dx} v(x) \, dx$$

Thus,

$$\int_{-\infty}^{\infty} \psi^* \frac{\partial \psi}{\partial x} dx = \left[\psi^* \psi \right]_{-\infty}^{\infty} - \int_{-\infty}^{\infty} \frac{\partial \psi^*}{\partial x} \psi \, dx$$

Both ψ^* and $\psi \to 0$ at infinity ($\psi^* \psi) \to 0$. Hence

$$\int_{-\infty}^{\infty} \psi^* \frac{\partial \psi}{\partial x} dx = - \int_{-\infty}^{\infty} \frac{\partial \psi^*}{\partial x} \psi \, dx$$

Using the above equation on R.H.S. of equation (iii), we get

$$\int_{-\infty}^{\infty} \psi^* \left(-i\hbar \frac{\partial \psi}{\partial x} \right) dx = i\hbar \int_{-\infty}^{\infty} \frac{\partial \psi^*}{\partial x} \psi \, dx$$

$$= \int_{-\infty}^{\infty} \left(i\hbar \frac{\partial \psi^*}{\partial x} \right) \psi \, dx$$

$$\int_{-\infty}^{\infty} \psi^* \left(-i\hbar \frac{\partial \psi}{\partial x} \right) dx = \int_{-\infty}^{\infty} \left(-i\hbar \frac{\partial \psi}{\partial x} \right)^* \psi \, dx$$

or
$$\int_{\tau} \psi^* \hat{p}_x \psi \, d\tau = \int_{\tau} (\hat{p}_x \psi)^* \psi \, d\tau \qquad \qquad \dots \text{(iv)}$$

Comparing equation (iv) with equation (i), we find that momentum operator is hermitian.

Let λ be the eigen value of the momentum operator $\hat{p}_x$. Then

$$\hat{p}_x \psi = \lambda \psi$$

$\therefore$
$$-i\hbar \frac{\partial \psi}{\partial x} = \lambda \psi$$

or
$$-i\hbar \frac{d\psi}{dx} = \lambda \psi$$

$\therefore$
$$\frac{d\psi}{\psi} = i\frac{\lambda}{\hbar} dx$$

If we integrate this equation, we get

$$\psi = C \, e^{(i\lambda/\hbar)x}$$

where C is a constant.

Thus, above equation gives eigen function of $\hat{p}_x$.

5.2 Basic Operators in Quantum Mechanics

- Basic operators in quantum mechanics are position, momentum, Hamiltonian, angular momentum operators. Here after the caps (^) indicating that the symbols represent the operators are avoided for simplicity.

- The **momentum operators** corresponding to x, y and z components of $\hat{p}$ are

$$p_x = -i\hbar \frac{\partial}{\partial x}$$

$$p_y = -i\hbar \frac{\partial}{\partial y}$$

and
$$p_z = -i\hbar \frac{\partial}{\partial z}$$

- Let us consider the action of commutator $[x, p_x]$ on the arbitrary wave function $\psi(x, y, z)$.

$$[x, p_x] \psi = \left[x, -i\hbar \frac{\partial}{\partial x} \right] \psi$$

$$= -i\hbar \left[x, \frac{\partial}{\partial x} \right] \psi$$

$$= -i\hbar \left(x\frac{\partial}{\partial x} - \frac{\partial}{\partial x}x \right)\psi$$

$$= -i\hbar \left(x\frac{\partial\psi}{\partial x} - \frac{\partial}{\partial x}(x\psi) \right)$$

$$= -i\hbar \left(x\frac{\partial\psi}{\partial x} - x\frac{\partial\psi}{\partial x} - \psi \right)$$

$$= i\hbar\,\psi$$

∴　　　　　　　　　　　　$[x, p_x] = i\hbar$　　　　　　　　　　...(5.2)

- Similarly　$[y, p_y] = i\hbar$　　　and　$[z, p_z] = i\hbar$

- It is to be noted that the commutator of a position co-ordinate (say x) and the corresponding momentum operator (p_x) is non-vanishing and has value $i\hbar$.

  Let us consider commutator

$$[x, p_y]\psi = \left[x, -i\hbar\frac{\partial}{\partial y} \right]\psi$$

$$= -i\hbar\left[x, \frac{\partial}{\partial y} \right]\psi$$

$$= -i\hbar\left(x\frac{\partial}{\partial y} - \frac{\partial}{\partial y}x \right)\psi$$

$$= -i\hbar\left(x\frac{\partial\psi}{\partial y} - \frac{\partial}{\partial x}(x\psi) \right)$$

$$= -i\hbar\left(x\frac{\partial\psi}{\partial y} - x\frac{\partial\psi}{\partial y} \right)$$

$$= 0$$

∴　　　　　　　　　　　　$[x, p_y] = 0$

Similarly　　　　　　　　$[y, p_x] = 0; [z, p_y] = 0$

　　　　　　　　　　　　$[y, p_z] = 0; [z, p_x] = 0$

　　　　　　　　　　　　$[x, p_z] = 0$

- Thus, the commutator of position co-ordinate and momentum component which does not correspond to it is always zero.

- The vanishing and non-vanishing commutators involving (x, y, z) and (p_x, p_y, p_z) can be put together in the form of a single relation using x_1, x_2, x_3 for x, y, z respectively and p_1, p_2, p_3 for p_x, p_y, p_z respectively. This relation is

$$[x_i, p_j] = i\hbar\,\delta_{ij}\,, i, j = 1, 2, 3, ...$$

  where Kronecker delta function (δ_{ij}) satisfies the following properties :

$$\delta_{ij} = 1 \quad \text{if } i = j$$

$$\delta_{ij} = 0 \quad \text{if } i \neq j$$

- It may be simply mentioned here that the commutator relation $[x, p_x] = i\hbar$ is in a way alternative form of the uncertainty principle viz. $\Delta x\,\Delta p_x \geq \hbar/2$.

- *The commutator of two operators corresponding to physical quantities which cannot be measured simultaneously with arbitrary accuracy are non-vanishing.* We know that x and p_x cannot be measured simultaneously with arbitrary accuracy.

- If the commutator of the operators corresponding to two physical quantities vanishes, then these quantities can be measured with arbitrary accuracy. For example, measurement of x does not affect the measurement of p_y. Therefore, x and p_y can be measured simultaneously with arbitrary accuracy. Consequently, $[x, p_y] = 0$.

The Schrödinger's wave equation is

$$\left[-\frac{\hbar^2}{2m}\nabla^2 + V(x)\right]\psi = E\psi$$

where $\left[-\dfrac{\hbar^2}{2m}\nabla^2 + V(x)\right]$ is the operator corresponding to total energy of a system. This is called **Hamiltonian operator** $\hat{H}$.

Thus,

$$\hat{H} = \left[-\frac{\hbar^2}{2m}\nabla^2 + V(x)\right] \qquad \dots (5.3)$$

Classically, Hamiltonian represents total energy

$$E = \left[\frac{\hat{p}{}^2}{2m} + V(x)\right]$$

$$\therefore \qquad \hat{H} = \left[\frac{\hat{p}{}^2}{2m} + V(x)\right] \qquad \dots (5.4)$$

Comparing equations (5.3) and (5.4), we get

$$\hat{p} = \frac{\hbar}{i}\nabla$$

5.3 Simultaneous Eigen Functions : Commutators

- If $\hat{A}$ and $\hat{B}$ are two operators, and ψ is a function satisfying the following equations :

$$\hat{A}\,\psi = a\psi \qquad \dots (5.5)$$

and

$$\hat{B}\,\psi = b\psi \qquad \dots (5.6)$$

then ψ is called simultaneous eigen function of operators $\hat{A}$ and $\hat{B}$ belonging to the eigen values a and b respectively.

Equations (5.5) and (5.6) imply that

$$\hat{B}\,\hat{A}\,\psi = \hat{B}\,(a\psi) = a\,\hat{B}\,\psi = ab\psi$$

and

$$\hat{A}\,\hat{B}\,\psi = \hat{A}\,(b\psi) = b\,\hat{A}\,\psi = ba\psi$$

as a and b are scalars, we have $ab = ba$.

Hence by subtraction of above two equations, we get

$$(\hat{A}\,\hat{B} - \hat{B}\,\hat{A})\psi = 0 \qquad \dots (5.7)$$

- This equation shows that ψ is also an eigen function of the operator $\hat{A}\hat{B} - \hat{B}\hat{A}$ belonging to the eigen value zero. The condition (5.7) is necessary that ψ be a simultaneous eigen function of $\hat{A}$ and $\hat{B}$. The operator in equation (5.7) is called **commutator of $\hat{A}$ and $\hat{B}$**, for simplicity it is written as

$$[\hat{A}, \hat{B}] = \hat{A}\hat{B} - \hat{B}\hat{A}$$

$[\hat{A}, \hat{B}]$ is called as commutator bracket.

If $[\hat{A}, \hat{B}] = 0$, then the two operators $\hat{A}$ and $\hat{B}$ are said to commute.

- The commutator $[\hat{A}, \hat{B}]$ satisfies the following rules :

(1) $[\hat{A}, \hat{B}] = - [\hat{B}, \hat{A}]$

(2) $[\hat{A}, \hat{B}\hat{C}] = [\hat{A}, \hat{B}]\hat{C} + \hat{B}[\hat{A}, \hat{C}]$

(3) $[\hat{A}, \hat{B} + \hat{C}] = [\hat{A}, \hat{B}] + [\hat{A}, \hat{C}]$

(4) $[\hat{A}\hat{B}, \hat{C}] = [\hat{A}, \hat{C}]\hat{B} + \hat{A}[\hat{B}, \hat{C}]$

(5) $[\hat{A}, [\hat{B}, \hat{C}]] + [\hat{B}, [\hat{C}, \hat{A}]] + [\hat{C}, [\hat{A}, \hat{B}]] = 0$

(6) $[x\hat{A}, \hat{B}] = x[\hat{A}, \hat{B}]$ and $[\hat{A}, y\hat{B}] = y[\hat{A}, \hat{B}]$, where x and y are scalars.

5.4 Commutator Algebra

- The operator $(\hat{A}\hat{B} - \hat{B}\hat{A})$ is called commutator of operators $\hat{A}$ and $\hat{B}$. For example, commutator of $\dfrac{d}{dx}$ and x may be found in the following way :

$$\left[\frac{d}{dx}x - x\frac{d}{dx}\right] f(x) = f(x) \qquad \ldots (5.8)$$

$$\left\{ \because \text{ from property} \left(\frac{d}{dx}x\right) f(x) = \frac{d}{dx}[x\,f(x)] = f(x) + x\frac{df(x)}{dx} \right\}$$

- Since f(x) is arbitrary the equation (5.8) implies that operator $\left(\dfrac{d}{dx}x - x\dfrac{d}{dx}\right)$ is equivalent to multiplication by unity. Therefore, the commutator is equal to unity.

$$\left(\frac{d}{dx}x - x\frac{d}{dx}\right) = 1$$

- Similarly, from equation (5.6) commutation of position operator $\hat{x}$ and momentum operator $\hat{p} = -i\hbar\dfrac{\partial}{\partial x}$ is

$$[\hat{x}, \hat{p}] = i\hbar$$

The commutator $[\hat{A}, \hat{B}]$ satisfies the rules stated in Section 5.2.

Let us prove some rules of commutator algebra.

(1) $[\hat{A}, \hat{B}] = - [\hat{B}, \hat{A}]$

Proof :
$$[\hat{A}, \hat{B}] = \hat{A}\hat{B} - \hat{B}\hat{A}$$
$$= - (\hat{B}\hat{A} - \hat{A}\hat{B})$$
$$= - [\hat{B}, \hat{A}]$$

(2) $[\hat{A}, \hat{B} + \hat{C}] = [\hat{A}, \hat{B}] + [\hat{A}, \hat{C}]$

Proof : We have
$$[\hat{A}, \hat{B} + \hat{C}] = \hat{A}(\hat{B} + \hat{C}) - (\hat{B} + \hat{C})\hat{A}$$
$$= \hat{A}\hat{B} + \hat{A}\hat{C} - \hat{B}\hat{A} - \hat{C}\hat{A}$$
$$= \hat{A}\hat{B} - \hat{B}\hat{A} + \hat{A}\hat{C} - \hat{C}\hat{A}$$
$$= [\hat{A}, \hat{B}] + [\hat{A}, \hat{C}]$$
$$\therefore \quad [\hat{A}, \hat{B} + \hat{C}] = [\hat{A}, \hat{B}] + [\hat{A}, \hat{C}]$$

Thus, commutators obey the law of distribution with respect to. addition.

(3) $[\hat{A}, \hat{B}\hat{C}] = [\hat{A}, \hat{B}]\hat{C} + \hat{B}[\hat{A}, \hat{C}]$

Proof : We have
$$[\hat{A}, \hat{B}\hat{C}] = \hat{A}(\hat{B}\hat{C}) - (\hat{B}\hat{C})\hat{A}$$
$$= \hat{A}\hat{B}\hat{C} - \hat{B}\hat{C}\hat{A}$$

Subtracting and adding $\hat{B}\hat{A}\hat{C}$ on RHS of above equation, we get
$$[\hat{A}, \hat{B}\hat{C}] = \hat{A}\hat{B}\hat{C} - \hat{B}\hat{A}\hat{C} + \hat{B}\hat{A}\hat{C} - \hat{B}\hat{C}\hat{A}$$
$$= (\hat{A}\hat{B} - \hat{B}\hat{A})\hat{C} + \hat{B}(\hat{A}\hat{C} - \hat{C}\hat{A})$$
$$= [\hat{A}, \hat{B}]\hat{C} + \hat{B}[\hat{A}, \hat{C}]$$
$$\therefore \quad [\hat{A}, \hat{B}\hat{C}] = [\hat{A}, \hat{B}]\hat{C} + \hat{B}[\hat{A}, \hat{C}]$$

(4) $[\hat{A}, [\hat{B}, \hat{C}]] + [\hat{B}, [\hat{C}, \hat{A}]] + [\hat{C}, [\hat{A}, \hat{B}]] = 0$

Proof : We have
$$[\hat{A}, [\hat{B}, \hat{C}]] = [\hat{A}, \hat{B}\hat{C} - \hat{C}\hat{B}]$$
$$= \hat{A}(\hat{B}\hat{C} - \hat{C}\hat{B}) - (\hat{B}\hat{C} - \hat{C}\hat{B})\hat{A}$$
$$= \hat{A}\hat{B}\hat{C} - \hat{A}\hat{C}\hat{B} - \hat{B}\hat{C}\hat{A} + \hat{C}\hat{B}\hat{A}$$

Similarly
$$[\hat{B}, [\hat{C}, \hat{A}]] = \hat{B}\hat{C}\hat{A} - \hat{B}\hat{A}\hat{C} - \hat{C}\hat{A}\hat{B} + \hat{A}\hat{C}\hat{B}$$

and
$$[\hat{C}, [\hat{A}, \hat{B}]] = \hat{C}\hat{A}\hat{B} - \hat{C}\hat{B}\hat{A} - \hat{A}\hat{B}\hat{C} + \hat{B}\hat{A}\hat{C}$$

$\therefore \quad [\hat{A}, [\hat{B}, \hat{C}]] + [\hat{B}, [\hat{C}, \hat{A}]] + [\hat{C}, [\hat{A}, \hat{B}]]$

$$= \hat{A}\hat{B}\hat{C} - \hat{A}\hat{C}\hat{B} - \hat{B}\hat{C}\hat{A} + \hat{C}\hat{B}\hat{A}$$

$$+ \hat{B}\hat{C}\hat{A} - \hat{B}\hat{A}\hat{C} - \hat{C}\hat{A}\hat{B} + \hat{A}\hat{C}\hat{B}$$

$$+ \hat{C}\hat{A}\hat{B} - \hat{C}\hat{B}\hat{A} - \hat{A}\hat{B}\hat{C} + \hat{B}\hat{A}\hat{C}$$

$\therefore \quad [\hat{A}, [\hat{B}, \hat{C}]] + [\hat{B}, [\hat{C}, \hat{A}]] + [\hat{C}, [\hat{A}, \hat{B}]] = 0$

(5) $[\hat{A}, \hat{B}^{-1}] = \hat{B}^{-1}[\hat{B}, \hat{A}]\hat{B}^{-1}$

Proof : Consider the right hand side

$$\hat{B}^{-1}[\hat{B}, \hat{A}]\hat{B}^{-1} = \hat{B}^{-1}(\hat{B}\hat{A} - \hat{A}\hat{B})\hat{B}^{-1}$$

$$= \hat{B}^{-1}(\hat{B}\hat{A}\hat{B}^{-1} - \hat{A}\hat{B}\hat{B}^{-1})$$

$$= \hat{B}^{-1}\hat{B}\hat{A}\hat{B}^{-1} - \hat{B}^{-1}\hat{A}\hat{B}\hat{B}^{-1}$$

$$= \hat{A}\hat{B}^{-1} - \hat{B}^{-1}\hat{A} \qquad (\because \hat{B}^{-1}\hat{B} = \hat{B}\hat{B}^{-1} = 1)$$

$$= [\hat{A}, \hat{B}^{-1}]$$

$\therefore \qquad [\hat{A}, \hat{B}^{-1}] = \hat{B}^{-1}[\hat{B}, \hat{A}]\hat{B}^{-1}$

5.5 Commutator Brackets using Position, Momentum and Angular Momentum

- In classical mechanics, the angular momentum of a particle relative to the origin of a certain co-ordinate system is a vector quantity given by

$$\vec{L} = \vec{r} \times \vec{p}$$

where $\vec{r}$ is the position vector and $\vec{p}$ is the linear momentum vector.

We have $\vec{r} = \hat{i}x + \hat{j}y + \hat{k}z$ and $\vec{p} = \hat{i}p_x + \hat{j}p_y + \hat{k}p_z$

$\therefore \qquad \vec{L} = (\hat{i}x + \hat{j}y + \hat{k}z) \times (\hat{i}p_x + \hat{j}p_y + \hat{k}p_z)$

or $\qquad \vec{L} = \begin{vmatrix} \hat{i} & \hat{j} & \hat{k} \\ x & y & z \\ p_x & p_y & p_z \end{vmatrix}$

$$= \hat{i}(yp_z - zp_y) - \hat{j}(xp_z - zp_x) + \hat{k}(xp_y - yp_x)$$

$\because \qquad \vec{L} = \hat{i}L_x + \hat{j}L_y + \hat{k}L_z$

$\therefore \qquad L_x = (yp_z - zp_y) \qquad \qquad \qquad \dots (5.9)$

$\qquad \qquad L_y = -(xp_z - zp_x) = (zp_x - xp_z) \qquad \dots (5.10)$

$\qquad \qquad L_z = (xp_y - yp_x) \qquad \qquad \qquad \dots (5.11)$

- In order to study dynamical quantity *angular momentum* in quantum mechanics, we will construct the associated operators. This is done by using the components of momentum, operators are $p_x = -i\hbar \dfrac{\partial}{\partial x}$, $p_y = -i\hbar \dfrac{\partial}{\partial y}$ and $p_z = -i\hbar \dfrac{\partial}{\partial z}$. With these operators, angular momentum components in equations can be written in operator form as

$$L_x = i\hbar \left(z \frac{\partial}{\partial y} - y \frac{\partial}{\partial z} \right) \qquad \qquad ...(5.12)$$

$$L_y = i\hbar \left(x \frac{\partial}{\partial z} - z \frac{\partial}{\partial x} \right) \qquad \qquad ...(5.13)$$

and
$$L_z = i\hbar \left(y \frac{\partial}{\partial x} - x \frac{\partial}{\partial y} \right) \qquad \qquad ...(5.14)$$

Commutation rules for the components of orbital angular momentum with position :

- Consider commutation rule for L_x and x.

$$[L_x, x]\, \psi = \left[i\hbar \left(z \frac{\partial}{\partial y} - y \frac{\partial}{\partial z} \right), x \right] \psi$$

$$= i\hbar \left[\left(z \frac{\partial}{\partial y} - y \frac{\partial}{\partial z} \right), x \right] \psi$$

$$= i\hbar \left(\left(z \frac{\partial}{\partial y} - y \frac{\partial}{\partial z} \right) x - x \left(z \frac{\partial}{\partial y} - y \frac{\partial}{\partial z} \right) \right) \psi$$

$$= i\hbar \left(z \frac{\partial x\, \psi}{\partial y} - y \frac{\partial x\psi}{\partial z} - x z \frac{\partial \psi}{\partial y} + yx \frac{\partial \psi}{\partial z} \right)$$

$$= i\hbar \left(zx \frac{\partial \psi}{\partial y} - yx \frac{\partial \psi}{\partial z} - x z \frac{\partial \psi}{\partial y} + yx \frac{\partial \psi}{\partial z} \right)$$

$$= 0$$

$$\therefore \qquad \qquad [L_x, x] = 0$$

Similarly, $[L_y, y] = 0$ and $[L_z, z] = 0$

Consider commutation rule for L_x and y.

$$[L_x, y]\psi = \left[i\hbar \left(z \frac{\partial}{\partial y} - y \frac{\partial}{\partial z} \right), y \right] \psi$$

$$= i\hbar \left[\left(z \frac{\partial}{\partial y} - y \frac{\partial}{\partial z} \right), y \right] \psi$$

$$= i\hbar \left(\left(z \frac{\partial}{\partial y} - y \frac{\partial}{\partial z} \right) y - y \left(z \frac{\partial}{\partial y} - y \frac{\partial}{\partial z} \right) \right) \psi$$

$$= i\hbar \left(z \frac{\partial(y\, \psi)}{\partial y} - y \frac{\partial(y\, \psi)}{\partial z} - y z \frac{\partial \psi}{\partial y} + y^2 \frac{\partial \psi}{\partial z} \right)$$

$$= i\hbar \left(zy \frac{\partial \psi}{\partial y} + z\psi - y^2 \frac{\partial \psi}{\partial z} - x z \frac{\partial \psi}{\partial y} + y^2 \frac{\partial \psi}{\partial z} \right)$$

$$= i\hbar\, z\, \psi$$

$$\therefore \qquad \qquad [L_x, y] = i\hbar z \qquad \qquad ...(5.15)$$

Similarly, we can prove that

$$[L_y, z] = i\hbar x, \qquad [L_z, x] = i\hbar y,$$
$$[L_x, z] = -i\hbar y, \qquad [L_z, y] = -i\hbar x$$

Commutation rules for the various components of orbital angular momentum :

Consider the commutation relation between L_x and L_y.

$$[L_x, L_y] = L_x L_y - L_y L_x$$

Let us consider the first term on RHS.

$$L_x L_y = i\hbar\left(z\frac{\partial}{\partial y} - y\frac{\partial}{\partial z}\right) i\hbar\left(x\frac{\partial}{\partial z} - z\frac{\partial}{\partial x}\right)$$

$$= -\hbar^2\left(z\frac{\partial}{\partial y} - y\frac{\partial}{\partial z}\right)\left(x\frac{\partial}{\partial z} - z\frac{\partial}{\partial x}\right)$$

$$= -\hbar^2\left(z\frac{\partial}{\partial y}\left(x\frac{\partial}{\partial z} - z\frac{\partial}{\partial x}\right) - y\frac{\partial}{\partial z}\left(x\frac{\partial}{\partial z} - z\frac{\partial}{\partial x}\right)\right)$$

$$= -\hbar^2\left(z\frac{\partial}{\partial y}\left(x\frac{\partial}{\partial z}\right) - z\frac{\partial}{\partial y}\left(z\frac{\partial}{\partial x}\right) - y\frac{\partial}{\partial z}\left(x\frac{\partial}{\partial z}\right) + y\frac{\partial}{\partial z}\left(z\frac{\partial}{\partial x}\right)\right)$$

$$= -\hbar^2\left(y\frac{\partial}{\partial x} + yz\frac{\partial^2}{\partial z\partial x} - yx\frac{\partial^2}{\partial z^2} - z^2\frac{\partial^2}{\partial y\partial x} + zx\frac{\partial^2}{\partial y\partial z}\right)$$

Similarly,

$$L_y L_x = i\hbar\left(x\frac{\partial}{\partial z} - z\frac{\partial}{\partial x}\right) i\hbar\left(z\frac{\partial}{\partial y} - y\frac{\partial}{\partial z}\right)$$

$$= -\hbar^2\left(x\frac{\partial}{\partial z} - z\frac{\partial}{\partial x}\right)\left(z\frac{\partial}{\partial y} - y\frac{\partial}{\partial z}\right)$$

$$= -\hbar^2\left(x\frac{\partial}{\partial z}\left(z\frac{\partial}{\partial y} - y\frac{\partial}{\partial z}\right) - z\frac{\partial}{\partial x}\left(z\frac{\partial}{\partial y} - y\frac{\partial}{\partial z}\right)\right)$$

$$= -\hbar^2\left(x\frac{\partial}{\partial z}\left(z\frac{\partial}{\partial y}\right) - x\frac{\partial}{\partial z}\left(y\frac{\partial}{\partial z}\right) - z\frac{\partial}{\partial x}\left(z\frac{\partial}{\partial y}\right) + z\frac{\partial}{\partial x}\left(y\frac{\partial}{\partial z}\right)\right)$$

$$= -\hbar^2\left(x\frac{\partial}{\partial y} + zy\frac{\partial^2}{\partial x\partial z} - xy\frac{\partial^2}{\partial z^2} - z^2\frac{\partial^2}{\partial x\partial y} + xz\frac{\partial^2}{\partial z\partial y}\right)$$

$$\therefore \quad L_x L_y - L_y L_x = -\hbar^2\left(y\frac{\partial}{\partial x} + yz\frac{\partial^2}{\partial z\partial x} - yx\frac{\partial^2}{\partial z^2} - z^2\frac{\partial^2}{\partial y\partial x} + zx\frac{\partial^2}{\partial y\partial z}\right)$$

$$+ \hbar^2\left(x\frac{\partial}{\partial y} + zy\frac{\partial^2}{\partial x\partial z} - xy\frac{\partial^2}{\partial z^2} - z^2\frac{\partial^2}{\partial x\partial y} + xz\frac{\partial^2}{\partial z\partial y}\right)$$

$$\therefore \quad L_x L_y - L_y L_x = -\hbar^2\left(y\frac{\partial}{\partial x} - x\frac{\partial}{\partial y}\right) = i\hbar \times i\hbar\left(y\frac{\partial}{\partial x} - x\frac{\partial}{\partial y}\right) = i\hbar L_z$$

Thus,　　　　　　$[L_x, L_y] = i\hbar L_z$ 　　　　　　　　... (5.16)

By cyclic permutations, we can obtain

$$[L_y, L_z] = i\hbar L_x$$
$$[L_z, L_x] = i\hbar L_y$$

and

$$[L_z, L_y] = -i\hbar L_x$$
$$[L_x, L_z] = -i\hbar L_y$$

Commutation relation of L^2 with components L_x, L_y and L_z :

We have $$L^2 = L_x^2 + L_y^2 + L_z^2$$

Let us consider $[L^2, L_x]$

$$[L^2, L_x] = [L_x^2 + L_y^2 + L_z^2, L_x]$$
$$= [L_x^2, L_x] + [L_y^2, L_x] + [L_z^2, L_x]$$
$$= [L_x L_x, L_x]$$

Since we have $$[\hat{A} \hat{B}, \hat{C}] = [\hat{A}, \hat{C}]\hat{B} + \hat{A}[\hat{B}, \hat{C}]$$

Therefore,

$$[L^2, L_x] = L_x [L_x, L_x] + [L_x, L_x]L_x + [L_x, L_x]L_x + L_y[L_y, L_x] + [L_y, L_x] L_y + L_z [L_z, L_x] + [L_z, L_x]L_z$$
$$= L_x \times 0 + 0 \times L_x + L_y(-i\hbar L_z) + (-i\hbar L_z)L_y + L_z (i\hbar L_y) + (i\hbar L_y)L_z$$
$$= 0$$

Similarly,

$$[L^2, L_y] = 0$$

and $$[L^2, L_z] = 0$$

Thus, L^2 commutes with any of three components of angular momentum operators.

Ladder operators

Ladder operators are defined as

$$L_+ = L_x + iL_y$$

and $$L_- = L_x - iL_y$$

1. Let us consider commutation of L_z with L_+.

$$[L_z, L_+] = [L_z, L_x + iL_y]$$
$$= [L_z, L_x] + [L_z, iL_y]$$
$$= [L_z, L_x] + i[L_z, L_y]$$
$$= i\hbar L_y + i(-i\hbar L_x)$$
$$= i\hbar L_y + \hbar L_x$$
$$= \hbar (L_x + iL_y)$$

$\therefore$ $$[L_z, L_+] = \hbar L_+ \qquad \qquad ...(5.17)$$

2. Let us consider commutation of L_z with L_-.

$$[L_z, L_-] = [L_z, L_x - iL_y]$$
$$= [L_z, L_x] - [L_z, iL_y]$$
$$= [L_z, L_x] - i[L_z, L_y]$$
$$= i\hbar L_y - i(-i\hbar L_x)$$
$$= i\hbar L_y - \hbar L_x$$
$$= -\hbar (L_x - iL_y)$$

$\therefore$ $$[L_z, L_-] = -\hbar L_- \qquad \qquad ...(5.18)$$

3.　Let us consider commutation of L_+ with L_-.

$$[L_+, L_-] = [L_x + iL_y, L_x - iL_y]$$
$$= [L_x, L_x] - i[L_x, L_y] + i[L_y, L_x] - i^2[L_y, L_y]$$
$$= [L_x, L_x] - i[L_x, L_y] + i[L_y, L_x] + [L_y, L_y]$$
$$= 0 - i(i\hbar L_z) + i(-i\hbar L_z) + 0$$

$\therefore$　　　$$[L_+, L_-] = 2\hbar L_z \qquad \qquad ...(5.19)$$

Angular momentum operators in spherical polar co-ordinates :

- Angular momentum operators in Cartesian co-ordinates are given by equations (5.12), (5.13) and (5.14).

- We can convert these in spherical polar co-ordinates by using transformation relations,

$$x = r\sin\theta\cos\phi$$
$$y = r\sin\theta\sin\phi$$
$$z = r\cos\theta$$

- With these transformation equations, we have

$$L_x = i\hbar\left(\sin\phi\frac{\partial}{\partial\theta} + \cot\theta\sin\phi\frac{\partial}{\partial\phi}\right)$$

$$L_y = i\hbar\left(-\cos\phi\frac{\partial}{\partial\theta} + \cot\theta\sin\phi\frac{\partial}{\partial\phi}\right)$$

and　　　$$L_z = -i\hbar\frac{\partial}{\partial\phi}$$

Eigen function and Eigen value of L_z :

We now try to find the eigen value of L_z. Let

$$L_z\psi = \lambda\psi$$

where $\psi = \psi(r, \theta, \phi)$ and λ is the eigen value.

Let　　　$$\psi(r, \theta, \phi) = F(r, \theta)\,G(\phi)$$

We have　　　$$L_z = -i\hbar\frac{\partial}{\partial\phi}$$

$\therefore$　　　$$-i\hbar\frac{\partial\psi}{\partial\phi} = \lambda\psi$$

$$-i\hbar\frac{\partial F G}{\partial\phi} = \lambda FG$$

$\therefore$　　　$$-i\hbar\frac{dG}{d\phi} = \lambda G$$

or　　　$$\frac{dG}{G} = \frac{i\lambda}{\hbar}\,d\phi$$

On integration, we get

$$G = e^{i\lambda\phi/\hbar}$$

$\therefore$　　　$$\psi = F(r, \theta)\,e^{i\lambda\phi/\hbar}$$

Now ψ must be a single valued function of x, y, z. In this case, increase in ϕ by 2π should not change the function, so that

$$F(r, \theta)\, e^{i\lambda\phi/\hbar} = F(r, \theta)\, e^{i\lambda(\phi + 2\pi)/\hbar}$$

$\therefore$
$$e^{i\lambda 2\pi/\hbar} = 1$$

or
$$\cos\left(\frac{2\pi\lambda}{\hbar}\right) + i\sin\left(\frac{2\pi\lambda}{\hbar}\right) = 1$$

This gives

$$\cos\left(\frac{2\pi\lambda}{\hbar}\right) = 1 \text{ and } \sin\left(\frac{2\pi\lambda}{\hbar}\right) = 0$$

$\therefore$
$$\frac{2\pi\lambda}{\hbar} = 2m\pi, \qquad\qquad \text{where } m \text{ is an integer}$$

$\therefore$
$$\lambda = m\hbar \qquad\qquad \text{where } m = 0, 1, 2, \ldots\ldots$$

Thus eigen value of L_z operator is $m\hbar$.

5.6 Raising and Lowering Angular Momentum Operator

- Let ψ_m be an eigen function of operator L_z with eigen value $m\hbar$. Let us consider the operator $L_+ = L_x + iL_y$, such that L_z is operating on $(L_x + iL_y)\psi_m$.

$$L_z(L_x + iL_y)\psi_m = (L_zL_x + iL_zL_y)\psi_m$$
$$= L_zL_x\psi_m + iL_zL_y\psi_m \qquad\qquad \ldots (5.20)$$

We have
$$L_zL_x - L_xL_z = i\hbar L_y \text{ and } L_zL_y - L_yL_z = -i\hbar L_x$$

or
$$L_zL_x = L_xL_z + i\hbar L_y \text{ and } L_zL_y = L_yL_z - i\hbar L_x$$

Using these in equation (5.18), we get

$$L_z(L_x + iL_y)\psi_m = (L_xL_z + i\hbar L_y)\psi_m + i(L_yL_z - i\hbar L_x)\psi_m$$
$$= (L_x L_z + iL_yL_z)\psi_m + \hbar(L_x + iL_y)\psi_m$$
$$= (L_x + iL_y)L_z\,\psi_m + \hbar(L_x + iL_y)\psi_m$$
$$= (L_x + iL_y)\,(L_z\,\psi_m + \hbar\psi_m)$$
$$= (L_x + iL_y)\,(m\hbar\,\psi_m + \hbar\psi_m)$$
$$= (L_x + iL_y)\,(m + 1)\hbar\,\psi_m$$

$\therefore$
$$L_z(L_x + iL_y)\psi_m = (m + 1)\hbar\,(L_x + iL_y)\psi_m \qquad\qquad \ldots(5.21)$$

- Thus, when $(L_x + iL_y)$ operates on eigen function ψ_m, the eigen value of L_z operator increases by $\hbar$. In this sense, L_+ is called **raising operator**.

- Similarly we can show that

$$L_z(L_x - iL_y)\psi_m = (m - 1)\hbar\,(L_x - iL_y)\psi_m$$

- Eigen value of L_z decreases by $\hbar$, when $(L_x - iL_y)$ operates on eigen function ψ_m. L_- is called **lowering operator**.

5.7 Concept of Parity, Parity Operator and its Eigen Values

- Parity involves transformation that changes the algebraic sign of coordinate system. Parity is important idea in QM because the wave functions which represent particles can behave in different ways upon transformation of coordinate system which describe them under parity transformation.

  If we have function $f(x)$ such that

  $$f(x) = f(-x)$$

  i.e. if there is no change in the sign of the function when the direction of the variable is reversed, the function has a **even parity**.

  If

  $$f(x) = -f(-x)$$

  i.e. if there is change in the sign of the function when the direction of the variable is reversed, the function has **odd parity.**

  For example,

  (1) $f(x) = x^3$ $\therefore f(-x) = -x^3$

  the function has odd parity.

  (2) $f(x) = x^2 + 2$ $\therefore f(-x) = x^2 + 2$

  the function has even parity.

  The function $\sin x$ has odd parity while the function $\cos x$ has even parity.

  If we have function,

  $$f_1(x) = A \sin x$$

  and $$f_2(x) = B \cos x.$$

  What is the parity of functions $f_1(x)$ and $f_2(x)$?

  $\sin x$ has odd parity and $\cos x$ has even parity, therefore, the function $f_1(x)$ has odd parity and $f_2(x)$ has even parity.

  For function of variable x, the **parity operator P** is defined as

  $$P\psi(x) = \psi(-x) \text{ where } \textbf{P is parity operator.} \qquad \dots (5.22)$$

  i.e. when the wave function $\psi(x)$ is operated by parity operator, it gets reflected in its coordinates.

Eigen values of parity operator

Eigen value of **P** operator is given as follows. In general, let $\psi(x)$ be an eigen function, such that

$$P \psi(x) = \lambda \psi(x) \qquad \dots (5.23)$$

where λ is eigen value of operator **P,**

Operating above equation by **P**

$$P^2 \psi(x) = P \lambda \psi(x) = \lambda(P\psi(x))$$
$$= \lambda^2 \psi(x)$$

Also because $\qquad$ $\mathbf{P}\,\psi\,(x) = \psi\,(-x)$ we have

$$\mathbf{P}\,[(\mathbf{P}\,\psi\,(x))] = \mathbf{P}\,\psi\,(-x) = \psi\,(x) \qquad\qquad \text{... (5.24)}$$

Hence $\qquad\qquad$ $\mathbf{P}^2\,\psi\,(x) = \psi\,(x)$

$$\lambda^2 = 1$$

Or $\qquad\qquad\qquad\qquad$ $\lambda = \pm\,1 \qquad\qquad\qquad\qquad \text{... (5.25)}$

If eigen value $\lambda = +1$, the function $\psi\,(x)$ has *even parity*.

If eigen value $\lambda = -1$, the function $\psi\,(x)$ has *odd parity*.

• Concept of parity has importance in quantum mechanics. All eigen functions that are bound state solutions of Schrödinger's steady state equations for a potential $V(r)$ have definite parities *i.e.* either the eigen functions have *odd parity* or *even parity*. The reason is that the probability density $\psi\psi^*$ will then have same value at the point $(-x, -y, -z)$ as that of point (x, y, z), which is the requirement of the fact that the potential has the same value at that point.

• Let us now consider Schrödinger's time independent equation

$$-\frac{\hbar^2}{2m}\frac{d^2\psi\,(x)}{dx^2} + V\,(x)\,\psi\,(x) = E\,\psi\,(x)$$

• If we change x to $-x$, the equation becomes

$$-\frac{\hbar^2}{2m}\frac{d^2\psi\,(-x)}{dx^2} + V\,(-x)\,\psi\,(-x) = E\,\psi\,(-x)$$

• If $V\,(x)$ is symmetric about $x = 0$, then $V\,(-x) = V\,(x)$. Thus, from above two equations we have two eigen functions $\psi\,(x)$ and $\psi\,(-x)$ that give the same energy eigen value.

Parity concept in three-dimensional case :

Let us consider wave functions which, in general, depend upon three variables x, y and z. Let us change

$\qquad\qquad$ $x \to -x,$

$\qquad\qquad$ $y \to -y$

and $\qquad\qquad$ $z \to -z,$

i.e. $\qquad\qquad$ $\vec{r} \to -\vec{r}$

This transformation is called space inversion. It is shown in Fig. 5.1

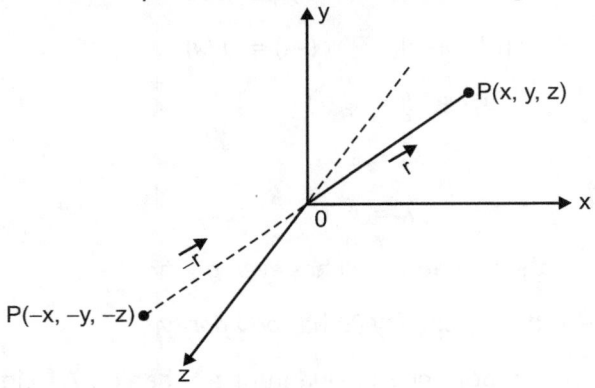

Fig. 5.1

If $\psi(x, y, z) = \psi(-x, -y, -z)$ i.e. $\psi(\vec{r}) = \psi(-\vec{r})$, the function has even parity.

If $\psi(x, y, z) = -\psi(-x, -y, -z)$ i.e. $\psi(\vec{r}) = -\psi(-\vec{r})$, the function has odd parity.

Parity in spherical polar co-ordinates:

- Quite often we have to use spherical polar co-ordinates (r, θ, ϕ). So let us see how to determine the parity of wave function $\psi(r, \theta, \phi)$. The transformation $\vec{r} \to -\vec{r}$ corresponds to going from P to P' as shown in Fig. 5.2. Fig. 5.2 shows that when the signs of rectangular co-ordinates (of point P) are changed in the parity operation, the co-ordinates of new point P' are obtained by transformations

$$r \longrightarrow r, \theta \longrightarrow \pi - \theta \text{ and } \phi \longrightarrow \pi + \phi$$

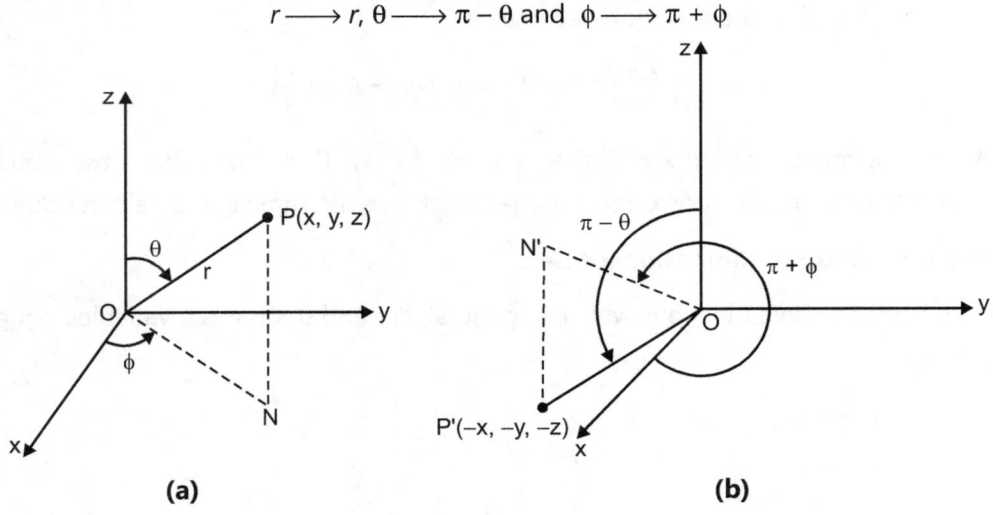

(a)   **(b)**

Fig. 5.2

If $\psi(r, \theta, \phi) = \psi(r, \pi - \theta, \pi + \phi)$, the wave function has even parity.

If $\psi(r, \theta, \phi) = -\psi(r, \pi - \theta, \pi + \phi)$, the wave function has odd parity.

Problem 5.3 : *Determine the parity for the following functions*

$$e^{-\alpha r}, \cos\theta \, e^{-\alpha r} \quad \text{and} \quad \cos\theta \, e^{-\alpha r} e^{i\phi}$$

Solution :

(1) $\psi(r) = e^{-\alpha r}$

The parity of function (even or odd) is decided by transformations $r \to r$, $\theta \to \pi$, $\phi \to \pi + \phi$. Obviously the function has even parity.

(2) $\psi(r, \theta, \phi) = \cos\theta \, e^{-\alpha r}$

$\therefore \qquad\qquad \psi(r, \pi - \theta, \pi + \phi) = \cos(\pi - \theta) \, e^{-\alpha r}$

$$= -\cos\theta \, e^{-\alpha r} \qquad\qquad (\because \cos(\pi - \theta) = -\cos\theta)$$

$\therefore \qquad\qquad \psi(r, \theta, \phi) = -\psi(r, \pi - \theta, \pi + \phi)$

Therefore, the function has odd parity.

(3) $\psi(r, \theta, \phi) = \cos\theta \, e^{-\alpha r} e^{i\phi}$

$\therefore \qquad\qquad \psi(r, \pi - \theta, \pi + \phi) = \cos(\pi - \theta) \, e^{-\alpha r} e^{i(\pi + \phi)}$

$$= \cos(\pi - \theta) \, e^{-\alpha r} e^{i\phi} \, e^{i\pi}$$

$$[\because \cos(\pi - \theta) = -\cos\theta \text{ and } e^{i\pi} = -1]$$

$\therefore \qquad\qquad \psi(r, \theta, \phi) = \psi(r, \pi - \theta, \pi + \phi)$

Therefore, the function has even parity.

Problem 5.4 : *If x and p are the coordinate and momentum operators, by mathematical induction, show that $[x, p^n] = i\hbar n \, p^{n-1}$*

Solution : The principle of mathematical induction states that if a relation is true for n = 1, 2 and supposing that the relation is also true for n = k, then if we are able to prove that it is true for n = k + 1, then in general it is true for any positive integer.

For n = 1, $\qquad\qquad\qquad\qquad [x, p] = i\hbar$

For n = 2, $\qquad\qquad\qquad\qquad [x, p^2] = [x, pp] = p[x, p] + [x, p] \, p$

$$= pi\hbar + i\hbar p$$

$$= 2i\hbar p$$

Let the relation be true for n = k, *i.e.*

$$[x, p^k] = i\hbar k p^{k-1}$$

Now, we will show that it is true for n = k + 1

$$[x, p^{k+1}] = [x, p \, p^k]$$

$$= p[x, p^k] + [x, p] \, p^k$$

$$= p \, i\hbar \, k \, p^{k-1} + i\hbar \, p^k$$

$$= (k+1) i\hbar p^{k+1}$$

Because the result is true for n = k + 1, hence in general it will be true for any positive integer.

$\therefore \qquad\qquad\qquad\qquad [x, p^n] = i\hbar n \, p^{n-1}$

Problem 5.5 : *By mathematical induction, show that*

$$[x^n, p] = i\hbar n x^{n-1}$$

Solution : The principle of mathematical induction states that if a relation is true for $n = 1, 2$ and supposing that the relation is also true for $n = k$, then if we are able to prove that it is true for $n = k + 1$, then in general it is true for any positive integer.

For $n = 1$,　　　　　　　　　　$[x, p] = i\hbar$

For $n = 2$,　　　　　　　　　　$[x^2, p] = [x\,x, p] = x[x, p] + [x, p]\,x$

$$= xi\hbar + i\hbar x$$

$$= 2i\hbar x$$

Let the relation be true for $n = k$, *i.e.*

$$[x^k, p] = i\hbar k x^{k-1}$$

Now, we will show that it is true for $n = k + 1$

$$[x^{k+1}, p] = [x\,x^k, p]$$

$$= x[x^k, p] + [x, p]\,x^k$$

$$= x\,i\hbar\,k\,x^{k-1} + i\hbar x^k$$

$$= (k + 1)i\hbar x^{k+1}$$

Because the result is true for $n = k + 1$, hence in general it will be true for any positive integer.

$$\therefore \qquad\qquad [x^n, p] = i\hbar n x^{n-1}$$

Problem 5.6 : *Show that the time dependence of the expectation value of a dynamical variable can be expressed as*

$$\frac{d<A>}{dt} = \left< \frac{\partial A}{\partial t} \right> + \frac{i}{\hbar} < [H, \hat{A}] >$$

where H is Hamiltonian operator and $\hat{A}$ is the operator corresponding to A.

Solution : Expectation value of A is given as

$$<A> = \int \psi^*(x, t)\, \hat{A}\, \psi(x, t)\, dx$$

then

$$\frac{d<A>}{dt} = \frac{\partial}{\partial t} \int \psi^*(x, t)\, \hat{A}\, \psi(x, t)\, dx$$

$$= \int \left[\frac{\partial \psi^*}{\partial t} \hat{A}\, \psi + \psi^* \frac{\partial \hat{A}}{\partial t} \psi + \psi^* \hat{A} \frac{\partial \psi}{\partial t} \right] dx$$

$$= \int \psi^* \frac{\partial \hat{A}}{\partial t} \psi dx + \int \left[\frac{\partial \psi^*}{\partial t} \hat{A}\, \psi + \psi^* \hat{A} \frac{\partial \psi}{\partial t} \right] dx \qquad \text{...(i)}$$

Schrödinger's time dependent equation is given as

$$i\hbar \frac{\partial \psi}{\partial t} = -\frac{\hbar^2}{2m}\frac{\partial^2 \psi}{\partial x^2} + V\psi$$

or

$$i\hbar \frac{\partial \psi}{\partial t} = H\psi$$

∴

$$\frac{\partial \psi}{\partial t} = \frac{1}{i\hbar} H\psi = -\frac{i}{\hbar} H\psi$$

Complex conjugate of above equation is

$$\frac{\partial \psi^*}{\partial t} = \left(\frac{1}{i\hbar} H\psi\right)^* = -\frac{1}{i\hbar}\psi^*H = \frac{i}{\hbar}\psi^*H$$

Using $\frac{\partial \psi}{\partial t}$ and $\frac{\partial \psi^*}{\partial t}$ in equation (i), we get

$$\frac{d<A>}{dt} = \int \psi^* \frac{\partial \hat{A}}{\partial t} \psi dx + \int \left[\frac{i}{\hbar}\psi^*H\hat{A}\psi + \psi^*\hat{A}(-i/\hbar)H\psi\right]dx$$

$$= \int \psi^*\frac{\partial \hat{A}}{\partial t}\psi dx + \frac{i}{\hbar}\int \left[\psi^*H\hat{A}\psi - \psi^*\hat{A}H\psi\right]dx$$

$$= <\frac{\partial A}{\partial t}> + \frac{i}{\hbar}\int \psi^*\left[H\hat{A} - \hat{A}H\right]\psi dx$$

$$= <\frac{\partial A}{\partial t}> + \frac{i}{\hbar}\int \psi^*[H, \hat{A}]\psi dx$$

∴

$$\frac{d<A>}{dt} = <\frac{\partial A}{\partial t}> + \frac{i}{\hbar}<[H, \hat{A}]>$$

Problem 5.7 : If $H = \frac{p^2}{2m} + \frac{1}{2}mw^2x^2$ show that

(i) $xH - Hx = +\frac{i\hbar}{m}p$

(ii) $pH - Hp = -i\hbar mw^2x.$

Solution : (i) $\quad xH - Hx = [x, H] = \left[x, \frac{p^2}{2m} + \frac{1}{2}mw^2x^2\right]$

$$= \frac{1}{2m}[x, p^2] + \frac{1}{2}mw^2[x, x^2]$$

$$= \frac{1}{2m}\cdot 2i\hbar p + 0$$

$$= \frac{i\hbar}{m}p$$

(ii) $[pH - Hp] = [p, H] = \left[p, \dfrac{p^2}{2m} \right] + \left[p, \dfrac{1}{2} mw^2 x^2 \right]$

$= \dfrac{1}{2} [p, p^2] + \dfrac{1}{2} mw^2 [p, x^2]$

$= 0 + \dfrac{1}{2} mw^2 (-2i\hbar x)$

$= -i\hbar mw^2 x$

Problem 5.8 : If $H = \dfrac{p^2}{2m} + V(x)$ then show that

$$[x, [x, H]] = -\dfrac{\hbar^2}{m}$$

Solution : We have, $[x, H] = \left[x, \dfrac{p^2}{2m} \right] + [x, V(x)]$

$= \dfrac{1}{2m} [x, p^2] + 0$

$= \dfrac{1}{2m} \cdot 2i\hbar p$

$= \dfrac{i\hbar}{m} p$

$\therefore$ $[x, [x, H]] = \left[x, \dfrac{i\hbar p}{m} \right]$

$= \dfrac{i\hbar}{m} [x, p]$

$= \dfrac{i\hbar}{m} \cdot i\hbar$

$= -\dfrac{\hbar^2}{m} = $ R.H.S.

Summary

1. Hermitian operator satisfies the condition

$$\int_\tau \psi^* \hat{A} \psi d\tau = \int_\tau (\hat{A}\psi)^* \psi d\tau$$

2. Eigen values of the Hermitian operator are real.

3. $[\hat{A}, \hat{B}] = \hat{A}\hat{B} - \hat{B}\hat{A}$ is a commutator bracket.

4. The momentum operator, position operator and energy operators are basic operators in Q.M.

   $[x, p_x] = i\hbar = [y, p_y] = [z, p_z]$

   $[x, p_y] = 0 = [y, p_x] = [y, p_z] = [z, p_y] = [z = p_x] = 0$

5.   Angular momentum $L = \bar{r} \times \bar{p}$

$$L_x = yp_z - zp_y$$
$$L_y = zp_x - xp_z$$
$$L_z = xp_y - yp_x$$

6. $[L_x, x] = 0 = [L_y, y] = [L_z, z]$

    $[L_x, y] = i\hbar z$

    $[L_x, L_y] = i\hbar \, L_z$

7.   Ladder operator is defined as

$$L_+ = L_x + i \, L_y \rightarrow \text{raising operator}$$
$$L_- = L_x - i \, L_y \rightarrow \text{lowering operator.}$$

8.   If $f(x) = f(-x)$, the function has even parity. If $f(x) = -f(-x)$, the function has odd parity. Function $\cos x$ has even parity and function $f(x)$ has odd parity.

Exercises

(A) Short Answer Type Questions :

1. Define operator.
2. Define Hermitian operator.
3. Define commutator.
4. Define angular momentum.
5. Define raising and lowering operator.
6. Define parity and parity operator.

(B) Long Answer Type Questions :

1. Show that eigen values of hermitian operator are real.

2. Show that momentum operator $-i\hbar \dfrac{\partial}{\partial x}$ is hermitian.

3. Show that $[x, p_x] = i\hbar$

4. Prove that $[x, p^n] = i \hbar \, n \, p^{n-1}$

5. Prove that $[x^n, p] = i \hbar \, n \, x^{n-1}$

6. Using cartesian components of operators L_x, L_y and L_z, prove that

    $[L_x, L_y] = i\hbar L_z$

   and $[L^2, L_x] = 0$

7. Prove that $[L_z, y] = -i\hbar \, x$

8. Show that $[A, B^{-1}] = B^{-1}[B, A]B^{-1}$

9. Prove that $[\hat{A}, [\hat{B}, \hat{C}]] + [\hat{B}, [\hat{C}, \hat{A}]] + [\hat{C}, [\hat{A}, \hat{B}]] = 0$.

10. Show that eigen value of operator L_z is integral multiple of $\hbar$.

11. Write a note on raising and lowering operators.

12. Show that the ladder operator L_+ increases the eigen value of operator L_z by $\hbar$.

13. Explain the concept of parity. Show that eigen values of parity operators are +1 and −1.

❑❑❑

www.ingramcontent.com/pod-product-compliance
Lightning Source LLC
Chambersburg PA
CBHW081522050726
47503CB00017B/2879

* 9 7 8 9 3 8 6 3 5 3 1 9 1 *